The Next Victim

W0010545

The Next Victim

Cutter Slagle

Doce Blant Publishing

www.DoceBlantPublishing.com

Published by
Doce Blant Publishing, Dana Point, CA 92629
www.doceblantpublishing.com

Cover design by Steve Smith
Interior Design by The Deliberate Page

ISBN: 978-0-9967622-5-0

CIP information on file at the Library of Congress.
Printed in the United States of America
www.doceblantpublishing.com

For Mom and Dad —

Thank you for putting my dreams above your own.

Fiction is the truth inside the lie.

— Stephen King

ONE

"IT'S HAPPENING AGAIN."

The words tumbled out of Elle Anderson's mouth in a haunting whisper. It's actually happening again, she thought, spreading the first page of the local newspaper out in front of her. She could feel the dampness of the freshly printed ink smearing across her fingertips and then suddenly felt light headed, as if she might get sick from the glass of orange juice she had consumed only moments ago that now sat thickly in her stomach.

"Honey, what's the matter?"

Elle turned toward her father and stared blankly at him. He was sitting there in his crisp blue shirt and perfectly knotted tie with his sandy colored hair slicked back; he seemed to only be half listening as he absently chewed on a piece of wheat toast and glanced over the sports section. His lack of interest only further upset her.

"The front page of the paper. Did you see it?"

John finally looked at her and then reached for his coffee mug. "What? Oh, no, I haven't seen it. What's happened? Something bad?"

"*This* is what's happened," Elle said. She shoved the paper across the peach kitchen countertop, allowing him to get a personal view. "The first ever murder in Gray's Lane, Ohio! This has to mean…"

His heavy sigh quickly cut her off. "Crime is common, sweetie. And murder, well, murder happens in other places than New York."

Living in New York City her entire life, she was well aware that crime was common. Rape, hit and runs, the recent string of bank robberies that, to her knowledge, still hadn't been solved. But this was different. It felt different. Something was off and Elle wasn't going to let it end like that. She couldn't. Besides, how could her father act so casual after seeing the shocking news?

"Not in Ohio, Dad. And definitely not in Gray's Lane. Did you even read what this reporter wrote?"

She watched as he ultimately gave up on his morning vices of coffee and local weekend sport's scores. He stared at her and asked, "Who wrote that piece? Which reporter are you talking about?"

Elle craned her neck and scanned the page. "Mary Evans."

"Ah," John started and smiled. "Mary Evans. Well, that makes perfect sense now."

"Why? Who's Mary Evans?"

"She's fame hungry. She's lived here her whole life. She blows every story, every *minor* accident completely out of proportion to try and create more drama. She's attempting to make a name for herself. I'm sure it's not half as bad as she's made it out to be."

Elle shook her head; tears began to fill the corners of her brown eyes. Something wasn't right. She just knew it.

Taking a look around the spacious kitchen, Elle tried to find a focus point, something to concentrate on that would help her calm down and gain an ounce of control. But all she was privileged to see were sparkling white appliances — basic stove, side-by-side refrigerator, dishwasher, trash compactor — that provided her with nothing more than a headache.

"Dad, I…"

"I know what you're thinking," John said. "I know what's going through your mind. But what happened here, what happened to…" he scanned the page…"Kim Sullivan, has nothing to do with you or your mother. That happened a while ago."

"A month ago, Dad. It happened one month ago." Not even, Elle thought, constructing a mental timeline in her head.

Her mother had been murdered on the fifteenth of September, a date she would never forget. How could she? Her life had pretty much ended the evening she had come home to find her mom stabbed to death. And then, of course, there had been the aftermath of the tragedy which had been no picnic either: moving from her home in New York City to live with her father in simple, small-minded, Gray's Lane, Ohio.

"Regardless," John began, "this is probably just some sort of accident. You know, a robbery gone wrong. The best way to get over the past is to leave it there, in the past."

She took a deep breath, closed her eyes, and then shook her head. Her chin length, dark brown hair swayed slightly, and when she spoke, it was in a faint voice. "I know."

John stood and Elle instantly welcomed the comforting arm he wrapped around her. "I'm so sorry you had to go through all of that back in New York. No seventeen year old should ever have to…" his words trailed off.

"Thanks, Dad," Elle said. She reached for his hand and then tightly gripped it. "I guess seeing that article bold and center, well, it just brought up that night. I wasn't expecting to see something like that. Not here, anyway, and not so soon."

"I know. It's bad timing and a horrible coincidence that this local woman was murdered so close to when your mom…" he stopped midsentence for the second time. His hold on Elle released and he resumed his seat beside her.

Elle wiped at her eyes, somewhat embarrassed that she had shown weakness, even though she knew that she was more than entitled to do so. Less than a month, she reminded herself. She didn't have to be so strong. Not all of the time.

"I'm sorry. I didn't mean to do that, to go there."

"I understand," he said and nodded. "But Michelle, you're safe here."

Here it comes, she thought to herself. Whenever her father or any authority figure referred to her by her birth name, she knew that she was either in trouble or due for a serious conversation. Elle assumed that this time it would be the latter.

"What happened to your mother back home was random. It was a horrible nightmare that you are going to have to work through. And you will, over time, learn to live with it."

Elle knew that her stern dad wasn't being insensitive, but factual. Her smart, well-educated father was all about the facts, a by the book, play by the rules contestant that seldom did anything wrong. He had a well-known outlook on life that centered on responsibility.

Though it had never been said, she often suspected that that had been the sole reason as to why her mother had left her father and moved some five hundred miles away to New York when Elle had just been a couple of years old.

"How's school going?"

That question, Elle recognized at once. That safe, generic question that was her father's attempt to get her mind off of the pain of recent events and onto a lighter, friendlier subject.

"Fine," she answered.

"Fine?" he repeated.

"Yes," she said. "School is fine. Well, about as fine as high school can be."

"Yeah," John said, "but you're a senior this year, the big dog on campus. This is supposed to be the best time of your life."

Elle tilted her head and raised her eyebrows at his choice of words; the gesture seemed strong enough to make her point.

"Darn it," he said and exhaled slowly. "I didn't mean to—that came out wrong, Elle. I'm sorry."

She shook her head, excusing the apology. "It's okay. And school, well, it really is fine." Elle wasn't one hundred percent sure as to why he was asking her about school. Her father was there five days a week, eight in the morning till three in the afternoon; he should know exactly how it was going.

"Any hard classes? Or how about friends? Made any friends yet?"

"No, I haven't really gotten to know anyone yet." It would take time, Elle knew. She'd only been going to Gray's Lane High School for a little over a week. Not to mention, she hadn't made herself all that easy to approach, never once smiling or showing the tiniest bit of interest in other's conversations.

"Well, give it time," John said. "I'm positive that within a couple of weeks you'll be going to football games and dances just like everyone else."

"Sure," she offered. And then, because she knew that he was trying and doing his absolute best to make her feel at ease, Elle decided to help her father out. "I like calculus, though. I'm finding the idea that there can only be one right answer kind of refreshing."

"That's great," John said through a wide, toothy smile. "I was always big into math myself. I actually considered teaching it at one time."

"Yeah, it's..." Elle quickly lost concentration of the conversation as a sharp nudge in the back of her mind forced her to form a connection to what she had skimmed over earlier.

Kim Sullivan, she thought. Sullivan. *Sullivan*. Elle hastily put two and two together: she sat next to a Niki Sullivan in calculus. Could the two be related? They had to be, Elle guessed. In a town as small as Gray's Lane, Elle knew that two people didn't share the same last name without being associated by blood or marriage.

But how?

It didn't take but a minute for Elle to figure it out: mother and daughter. Of course. She reread the last paragraph of the article and saw in black and white that Kim Sullivan was indeed survived by an eighteen-year-old daughter: Nicole

'Niki' Sullivan. Elle immediately felt pity for the poor girl.

"Hey, you still with me?" John said, waving his right hand from side to side. "You kind of zoned out there for a second."

"What?" Elle asked, shaking off the last bit of her reverie. "Yeah, no, I'm fine. I was just trying to remember whether or not I finished my homework for today."

"Well, I hope you did," John said as he clocked his leather wristwatch, "because it's time to go." He drained the last of his coffee and then stood up. "Nothing says unprofessional like a late principal on Monday morning. Do you want to ride together?"

"No, that's okay," Elle answered. "Thanks, but I've got some errands to run after school. I should probably just drive myself."

"Sure thing, sweetie," John said. He bent down to retrieve his black briefcase that was neatly leaning up against the wooden barstool. "I'll follow you out."

"I have to run upstairs and get my bag and a couple of books. But don't worry, I'll be right behind you." Elle felt as if she might have given herself away. She had never been great at lying.

"I'll see you at school then, but don't doodle. You don't want another tardy slip." He leaned in, kissed his daughter on the cheek, and then crossed over the tile flooring, exiting through the kitchen door. His deep musk scent lingered in the room.

Elle nervously sat with her hands folded together as she tapped her foot. She waited until she heard her father's engine turn over, and then gave him a few more moments to back out of the driveway.

When she thought that she had given him enough time to get at least a mile from the house, she stood, raced to the front door where she had left her tennis shoes, and stepped into them.

Elle was out the door and headed toward her dark green Honda completely empty handed. She had no plans to attend school, deciding that she would just have to deal with the consequences at a later time.

———

So his little act of violence on Saturday evening had made the front page of the paper. He wasn't surprised. In a town as small as Gray's Lane, grisly news was bound to travel fast, that was for certain.

But it still didn't change the fact that his mission could quickly turn into a three-ring circus, and that ultimately that nosey reporter, Mary Evans, might just have to be sacrificed. After all, he wasn't in this shithole town to seek fame; he had hard, honest work to do.

The man paced around the dingy living room of his rented, two bedroom apartment, bored and unsatisfied. Maybe things should be sped up, he thought. Maybe it wouldn't be such a bad idea to veer off course just a little bit.

He flopped down onto the tattered couch, instantly sending small specs of dust into the air. He pinched the bridge of his nose, hoping that all of those distracting ideas that could eventually get him caught would evaporate from his over-worked head.

Of course he couldn't speed things up, and he definitely couldn't veer off of his well-planned course. When people did that, when they became spontaneous and acted out on whims, they got caught. And he couldn't afford to get caught. He had too much riding on this little operation. And far too much to gain.

Control was the clincher, the defining factor that separated him from the rest of the pact. Control was what would get him everything he needed and wanted, as well as help to point the finger at someone else, in a completely different direction.

Yes, control would, in the end, allow him to get away with murder.

He leaned back into the cushions of the couch, and crossed his right leg over his left. He didn't want to lapse into thinking about what was already done, what had already taken place, but sometimes couldn't help the matter. At times, it seemed as if his brain worked on its own accord, sending him places that he didn't want to visit, but at the same time, he had no power of stopping.

He knew that he could make himself go crazy by rehashing the details of Saturday night. Had he left anything behind — bits of clothing or fibers, DNA of some sort, a possible witness, anything or anyone that could send the police over to his dump of a home with guns drawn?

There was nothing to worry about, he was sure of it. After all, it was Monday morning. If the Gray's Lane Police Department had anything concrete or vital from Saturday evening — if they were worth a lick of salt — he had to assume that he would have already been sitting in a jail cell, sporting that disgusting color of orange, waiting to go in front of the judge with a court appointed attorney.

No, he hadn't left anything behind. He was that good.

But he also knew that having the perfect cover, the perfect disguise, was just another useful aid, a tool that would only help him complete the task at hand.

He was good, and he was smart.

But no matter how good or smart he was, worry and second-guessing always seemed to find him. And sometimes he needed to take a moment to rethink his prior steps, if only to reassure himself that everything was going to be fine, that he hadn't slipped up.

He stood, walked across the shag carpet, and swore that he could feel mold in between his bare toes. He headed toward the downstairs bathroom, the one that offered a claw foot tub, a toilet that often clogged, and a window that was nailed shut.

He splashed cold water onto his handsome face from the leaky sink, and let it cascade down over his toned, naked body.

It was time to begin his Monday morning. His day job came first, of course, and then, later, the act of planning who would be the next victim.

TWO

SHERIFF LARRY DOUGLAS WAS HAVING A bad day, a couple of bad days to be exact. A local woman had been found dead — murdered — in his territory. It was the first murder to have ever happened in Gray's Lane, since he had been named sheriff anyway. There were no clues, evidence, or anything of the sort that pointed to a possible suspect. And to add insult to injury, Mary Evans had had the nerve to blast the news all over the front page of the morning paper as if it were some sort of event or parade for the whole town to take part in.

Sitting behind the large, scarred oak desk, Douglas became haunted by three little words that seemed to be set on repeat in his mind: one more year.

He had started telling himself "one more year" three years ago. Douglas had wanted to retire, had planned to retire. But instead, he was now nearing the dangerous side of sixty, with a wife that didn't love him anymore, a teenage grandson that didn't appreciate him, a murder investigation that he didn't quite understand, and a new deputy that was almost fifteen minutes late.

Yes, life had quickly gone to hell in a hand basket over the past three years. And now, retirement was a just a distant, longed after regret that Douglas didn't expect to see anytime soon.

"Hell, where is he?" the sheriff muttered aloud. Though the walls that enclosed him in the ridiculous space he was supposed to consider an office were thin, he didn't expect any of the other employees of the Gray's Lane Police Department to hear him.

Sheriff Larry Douglas grunted, crossed his short arms over his bulging stomach, and leaned back into the leather chair that had formed to him over the years. He refused to have another cup of the less than appetizing coffee that no one at the station really seemed to be fond of, but still didn't bother to change. He was already on edge as it was and didn't need any more caffeine pumping through his visible veins.

Douglas was many things and impatient topped the soaring list. However, his growing annoyance wasn't just caused from being made to wait. He couldn't help but believe that his new deputy, this Ben Andrews, was being down right rude, wasting his precious time like the absent man was currently doing. Especially when the sheriff had a murder to solve.

"Douglas?"

"*Sheriff* Douglas," he corrected with emphasis on his well-earned title. Damn, the sheriff thought, shaking his head. Had everyone indulged in a spoonful of ignorance this morning?

"Yes. Sorry, sir. Benjamin Andrews is here to see you, Sheriff."

"Well, it's about time," Douglas spit out as he rose from his comfortable seat. He contemplated giving the cocky deputy that stood tall and proud outside his office door a verbal tongue lashing on the theme of respect, but eventually decided to save his breath and rage for Andrews.

"Should I send him in, then?"

Douglas stared at the twenty something man for a few moments, looking him up and down, and then finally said, "Yes, Deputy Hall, send him in."

It was all the sheriff could do to keep from screaming, "Shit for brains!" as Hall pivoted and headed for the waiting area of the station.

Douglas regularly regretted hiring the less than adequate deputy, but had long ago come to terms with the idea that in a town as small as Gray's Lane, he had to take what he could get. Including the good, the bad, and the stupid.

The sheriff stood, hands on hips, trying to display a statue of importance. The last thing he needed was some other kid, new to town, not knowing right from wrong or high from low on the payroll disrespecting him. Douglas wanted it to be made perfectly clear that he was always right and high – in a matter of speaking, of course.

"Sheriff Larry Douglas?"

At least the label had been used, the sheriff thought, standing still, taking in the stranger's appearance.

The new deputy had height most basketball coaches only dreamt of, dark hair that was an appropriate length to imply a serious attitude, and an in shape frame that only came with hard discipline in the gym and even harder discipline in the kitchen.

Douglas was impressed; Ben Andrews certainly looked the part. Maybe a little more *Abercrombie & Fitch* than the sheriff would have liked, but Douglas knew that in a running match with a suspect, the deputy would win hands-down.

"Take a seat, son," the sheriff said, pointing toward the vacant chair in front of his desk. He, too, sat, and instantly cursed his word choice.

Son? When had he gotten into that filthy habit, calling everyone younger than him son or sport? When had he become that old guy?

"Thank you, sir."

"You know, you are about twenty minutes late," Douglas said, making quite clear that he wasn't a pushover. "Not the best way to make a first impression."

"I know," Ben nodded. "I'd like to apologize for my tardiness."

"Do you have a reason or an excuse? Or do you just enjoy making people wait?"

"No, sir, not at all. I got lost on the way here. I think I may have taken a wrong turn or…"

"Gray's Lane's not that big," Douglas interrupted. "How in the hell did you manage to take a wrong turn?"

"I… I… I don't know," Ben stuttered. "I guess being new here and all, I didn't…"

"You ever consider calling? Asking for directions or maybe letting me know you're running a little behind schedule?"

"Sir, I'm sorry. I left the house at what I thought was an apt time to make it here…"

"Okay, okay," the sheriff said and raised his hand. "I understand. I'm just giving you a hard time, buddy."

Dammit! There it was again, another form of son or sport. "Now you know the station's location and you won't be late again. Correct?"

"Yes, Sheriff."

"Good." Douglas half smiled. Even if he was getting older by the second, heavier, and less tolerant, he still had the power. He was still very much in charge.

"I know that we may have started out on the wrong foot, but I am very happy to be here and part of the team, sir."

"Glad to hear it, Andrews," the sheriff said and folded his hands onto his desk. "Now, if you don't mind, I'd like to ask you something. Why Ohio? Why Gray's Lane? Of all the places in the world to transfer to, why here?"

They were questions that had been nagging at the sheriff like an annoying fly ever since he'd received that first inquiring phone call regarding Ben's possible relocation. Douglas wasn't too keen on outsiders coming into his town and lending a helping hand, never had been. He believed it showed laziness, the inability to properly get the job done. However, Ben's record had spoken for itself, and the sheriff had to admit that having the young and rising cop on his side might not be such a bad thing. Especially now, at a time when professional assistance in Gray's Lane was nothing short of a dire need.

"I don't mind," Ben answered and then shrugged. "I guess I just wanted to be some place small and quiet. Maybe even a little safer."

"Safer?" the sheriff questioned and raised an eyebrow. "What do you mean?"

The deputy sighed, crossing one leg over the other. "I'm only twenty five, sir, and I've seen a lot—too much, actually. Now, I don't want to get into specifics, but it's been a rough year for me. I've had to deal with some personal issues, and I've come here looking for a fresh start."

"A fresh start, eh?"

"Yes," Ben said. "The city life with it's non-stop crime and round the clock murders isn't for me, not anymore. I suppose that's what I meant by 'safer.' I want to be in a different environment than all that, like the environment offered by Gray's Lane."

The sheriff felt his heavy jaw fall open; he quickly tried to shut it again. He even bit down on his lower lip to ensure his mouth stayed closed, but from the frown on Ben's face, Douglas was almost one hundred percent sure that the damage was already done.

"Did I say something wrong, Sheriff?"

"No, no," Douglas coughed out, and then patted his chest. "You didn't say anything wrong, but…"

"But what, sir?"

Douglas didn't speak for a moment, choosing to stay silent and rack his brain for the right words. He even let the fact slide that the young deputy had interrupted him, another tedious pet peeve the sheriff harbored.

But how was he going to address this particular issue? That was the ultimate question. How could he break it to Ben that at this precise moment there was nothing safe about Gray's Lane, Ohio? Not with a dangerous killer on the loose.

"What's going on, Sheriff?" Ben asked. "I can tell from your expression that you're trying to hide…"

"There's nothing I'm hiding, son." He didn't bother chastising himself this time for the slip; he was too busy avoiding direct eye contact with the deputy. Instead, he glanced around his depressing office.

The walls were long overdue for a new coat of paint; the hardwood floors needed swept and scrubbed, and the couple of family pictures that he had nailed up in the past where now hanging crookedly. He'd had so many plans... so many aspirations when he'd first became the head of the department. What had happened?

"Sheriff, I don't mean any disrespect by this, but you're an awfully bad liar."

The comment brought a crooked smile to Douglas' face; Ben had pegged him. Who would have thought? If there was one talent the sheriff didn't possess, it was lying. Which, of course, had been the sole reason he'd never taken up poker.

"Fine," Douglas spoke up. "You deserve to know the truth. Now, I was going to tell you anyway, I just wasn't sure how to break it to you. Not after you shared with me your reasons for coming here and all."

"Break what to me?" Ben asked.

The sheriff took a deep breath, and then released in a speedy fashion exactly what the deputy needed to be told. "There's been a murder."

"Excuse me?"

"Saturday night," Douglas started. Then, staring Ben squarely in the eyes, he said, "A local woman was found stabbed to death Saturday night."

"A woman was found here, in Gray's Lane, stabbed to…"

Douglas wasn't at all surprised that Ben had fallen speechless. The young deputy's eyes had gone extremely wide; the sheriff even leaned in toward him to make sure the kid was still breathing.

"Are you okay?" Douglas instinctively opened the top drawer of his desk and began searching for a stashed bottle of water, already knowing that the mini fridge on the floor was out and needed to be restocked. Chewed-down pencils, old papers and faxes that had begun to yellow, fattening sweets that were famous during this time of year he kept hidden from potential moochers, but no water.

"Yeah, I'm alright. I'm just trying to get over the initial shock of what you told me. I've researched Gray's Lane, and it seems unbelievable that a murder could have actually taken place here."

"Well, you better believe it, because it's true. We were all pretty surprised; no one expected that…"

"Do you know who the killer is? Have you arrested anyone?"

That's two, the sheriff thought, keeping track of the impolite interruptions. One more, Douglas decided, and he would have to warn the deputy to watch himself.

"No," Douglas said, feeling his cheeks flush with embarrassment as he looked down at the surface of his desk. "I don't even have a suspect at the moment."

"The husband?"

"Excuse me?" Douglas asked and tilted his head upward.

"The woman that was killed, did she have a husband?"

"Oh," Douglas said, finally understanding the direction that Ben was headed in. "Yes, she did, but we've ruled him out. He has an airtight alibi." The sheriff noticed a frown gradually spreading across the deputy's face. "What's that matter?"

Ben shrugged. "It's been in my experience that nothing is ever really as airtight as it originally seems to be."

"You telling me how to do my job, son?" The sheriff asked and bent his rough knuckles to create a painful cracking sound.

"No, not at all, sir. I just meant that..."

"I know what you meant, and I'm sorry I snapped at you. But this is tough for me. Gray's Lane is a peaceful community. Well, it used to be. Everyone knows everyone, and it's hard to consider that one of our own could be responsible for this."

"Of course," Ben agreed. "I'm sorry."

"Don't apologize," the sheriff said through a weighty sigh. "It was a good question to ask, a smart question to ask."

"Not that smart," Ben said. "I mean, anyone who watches those cop shows on TV knows that the spouse is always the primary person of interest."

"Look," Douglas began. "Are you sure that you want to do this?"

"What do you mean?"

"Do you want to be in Gray's Lane? Working on a murder case? I would completely understand if you changed your mind and wanted to get out before officially getting involved."

"Like I said, Sheriff, I came here to get away from my past. Now, I didn't expect to fall right into a murder investigation, but at the same time, I can't keep running. I'll stay. I'll help. I mean, I'd like to help."

"Good," Douglas said and nodded. "I'm glad to hear it; your assistance will be much appreciated. Now," the sheriff picked up a thin manila folder from the center of his messy desk. "I need you to take a gander at this. It will be nice to get a new perspective and have a fresh pair of eyes looking at what we do have." He handed the case file to the deputy.

"Sure," Ben said and took the folder. "Hopefully I can come up with some new opinions to offer."

"Well, I hope so, son," the sheriff said in a dry grumble. "Because I know for a fact that the killer is going to strike again."

THREE

"TAKE OFF THAT RIDICULOUS HAT! YOU'RE not a frat boy."

"I like this hat. Do you have any idea how many times they've won the World Series? More than any…"

"I'm sorry, but do you see any indication on my face that I give a flying fuck?"

"You know, Mary, when people say that you're a raging bitch, they're just not giving you enough credit. Maybe if they mentioned 'heartless'…"

"What do you know?" Mary Evans asked. "You haven't been here long enough to form an accurate opinion of me. I'm just career-oriented."

"If calling it that makes you sleep better at night, then more power to you."

She rolled her dark eyes. What a waste, she thought. Was this God punishing her for her sins? Sticking her with Henry Wren, a less than desirable human being who was actually supposed to pass as a co-worker?

Well, maybe "co-worker" wasn't the right word to use, Mary considered. After all, she was the talent, the face of all local news. And Henry?

Well, he was just the camera guy, the behind-the-scenes technician that was here only to follow her around, keep his mouth shut, and do what she told him to do.

Yes, Mary finally decided: she was in charge, the boss, the head honcho. And she wasn't going to take any more lip from the pathetic, underachiever who was standing in front of her.

"I don't have time to argue with you, Henry. I've got a story to cover."

"What story?" he asked through a light chuckle. "There *is* no story here, not anymore. So some woman got butchered two nights ago. Big deal. You already reported everything there was to share in this morning's paper. You've picked the issue dry, Mary."

"You don't know what you're talking about," Mary argued. "All you need to worry about is the camera. Make sure that it's fully charged, ready to go, and directly pointed at the spot I indicate. Understand? You can leave everything else to me; I know what I'm doing."

"Well, since we're on the subject," Henry began. He crossed his arms over his chest, which made the dry leather of his coat squeak. "Why do you need a cameraman in the first place? I thought print was your expertise, not live coverage."

"I do it all, Henry. Don't forget that. Live coverage, print—it's all journalism. My God, you know nothing about this business. How did you even get this job?"

"If I had to guess, I'd say it's probably because I'm the only person in this town that would work with you. Of course, before I signed on for this job I had never met you, which would have been…"

"Stop talking," she ordered and raised her right hand. Mary quickly became distracted by her freshly painted manicure. She couldn't wait until it was time to get the cameras rolling; the long, black microphone would look perfect and proper nestled in her small, delicate hand.

Yes, Mary definitely had the right attitude and she more than looked the part.

But, unfortunately, Henry was right about something: she needed a new angle to the already tired story.

Mary took a deep breath, flipped her flat-ironed red hair off her shoulder, and stood completely still. It was time to get down to business. This story could be the break in her fifteen-year-old career that she desperately needed. Even if she had to push the boundaries just a little bit, she was going to get what she wanted. But then again, she almost always did.

"This isn't over, Henry, not by a long shot. There's going to be another murder, and when there is, I need to be there. *We* need to be there."

"Why do you assume that the killer is going to do it again? There's nothing that indicates this wasn't a one time deal."

"Oh, please," Mary said. She shot Henry a glare, and then flopped down onto the floral patterned chair that decorated one corner of her office. "Don't try and burst my bubble."

"Then, what you're saying is that you want more people to die? Just so you can have more airtime, something to keep you relevant and in the public eye?"

"Don't put words in my mouth!" she hollered. Mary closed her eyes; she could feel a headache coming on. She kicked off her black heels that flawlessly matched her pinstriped skirt and jacket, and brought her knees up to her chest. "All I'm trying to say is that I can't control what happens or who dies, but there is no reason as to why I can't benefit from it."

"You know," Henry started as he took a seat in the opposite corner of the room, "if you ever win a Pulitzer one day, I think that should be your acceptance speech."

"Fuck off!"

"Or maybe that?" he said with a shrug. "Look, all I'm trying to say is that Kim Sullivan could have been purposely killed for some personal reason."

"What do you mean?" Mary asked. She opened her eyes and stared into Henry's blue ones. Was he an asshole that knew all too well how to get under her skin? Yes. But she had to admit that he was a very attractive asshole that, had they met under different circumstances, would have most likely ended up in her bed. Or backseat of her car, she considered, almost laughing out loud, remembering that one time with that bartender.

"Kim could have been having an affair, you know? Her husband could have found out and reacted by stabbing her to death."

"No," Mary disputed and shook her head. "The husband didn't do it; he's got several witnesses that place him nowhere near the scene at the time of the murder."

"Okay," Henry said and tried again. "Then maybe it was *her* lover. She was going to end things with him, and in a jealous rage, he killed her. Oh, get this!" He sat up taller in his chair. "Maybe she was sleeping with her daughter's boyfriend. Maybe he killed her."

Mary felt a look of disgust spread widely across her face. "You've been watching too many daytime soaps," she said through gritted teeth. "Kim Sullivan wasn't having an affair, and her daughter's boyfriend had nothing to do with her murder."

"How do you know that for certain?"

"Well, for starters, he's the sheriff's grandson."

"So?" Henry asked.

"So," Mary repeated, "I highly doubt that Robbie Douglas committed a crime right under his grandfather's nose without the sheriff knowing about it. And second of all, he's a senior in high school. I don't think he's capable of…"

"Of what?" Henry interrupted. "Killing a defenseless woman? You'd be surprised at what kids can do these days. And by the way, isn't rule number one of being a good journalist to not be biased? I wouldn't rule out any suspects if I were you."

"Well, Henry, you're not me. And I am a good journalist, a damn good one. In fact, it's my good, journalistic intuition that is telling me there is going to be another murder. And soon, which rules out your theory that Kim Sullivan was specifically targeted by her husband, lover, or daughter's boyfriend."

"Fine, fine," Henry said and threw up both of his hands. "You know, you don't have to get all self-righteous on me; I'm only trying to play out every possible scenario."

"Oh, is that what you're doing?" Mary asked, the tone of her voice dripping with sarcasm. "Are you trying to help out? Be a team player?"

"Then, since you seem to know it all, who's next on the chopping block?"

"You actually expect me to predict who the killer's next victim is going to be?"

"Why not?" Henry asked.

"Because I don't think like a psychopath," she reasoned. "And furthermore, how in the hell would I know? If the killer is murdering people at random, then anyone could be next. Depending on the motive or how often he or she plans to kill, we're practically sitting around and waiting for a ticking time bomb to explode."

"She?" Henry responded.

"Why not?" Mary disputed. "Didn't you just tell me not to rule out any suspects? Therefore, the killer could easily be female. Maybe Kim Sullivan's own daughter did it."

"You think?"

"No," she said and shook her head, "I don't. I was making fun of you and your stupid assumptions."

"Hey," he protested, "don't call my assumptions stupid, not yet. Until another body is found, I could still be right. For all you know, this murder could solely be connected to the Sullivan family and no one else."

"Care to make it interesting?" Mary asked. She brought her legs down and planted her bare feet on the hardwood floor.

"How so?"

"I'm talking about a little wager."

"Like a bet?" Henry confirmed.

"Jeez, Henry! Yes, like a bet. Exactly like a bet!" She stared at him in complete shock, wondering how a person who was so dense could function on a daily basis.

"What would be the terms?"

"Let's see," Mary started. She folded her hands in her lap, trying to concentrate. "If there are no more murders in Gray's Lane, then you obviously win."

"And if someone else is found stabbed to death, then you win," Henry offered. "Of course, only after it's been proven that the work was done by the same killer. It wouldn't be fair if some new guy started hacking people up with no connection to the Sullivan case."

"In Gray's Lane?" Mary mocked. "I can't believe that there is even one murderer here. Believe you me, there's no way that a second, unrelated killer is going to show up."

"What does the winner get?"

"Fifty bucks?" she suggested.

"Fifty?" Henry asked. "I guess even though you're the hot shot in town, they're still not paying you the big bucks."

"Fine," she sighed, "make it a hundred dollars, then."

"One hundred dollars," he repeated. "You've got a deal, Mary Evans. Should we shake hands on it?"

"I'd rather not," she answered with a frown. "I have absolutely no idea where your hands have been."

"Would you like to know?" he asked with a smile.

"You're disgusting!" Mary screamed. She stood, stretched, and then walked around to the back of her desk. "And don't tell anyone about this, either. Betting on death isn't something that will get you voted most popular in this town, or any town, for that matter."

"Oh," Henry said, also standing, "you *do* care what people think of you."

"No, no that's not true," Mary argued and shook her head. "I don't give two shits as to what people in this town think of me. Love me, hate me, I couldn't care less."

"Well, I'm sure no one in Gray's Lane loves you. Let's be honest."

"My point," Mary spit out, "is that if something like this got out to the public, my career would be permanently damaged. I don't want that to happen, so let this be our little secret."

"Will do," Henry agreed. "But I really don't think there is anything to worry about: most, if not all, of the public pretty much knows how ruthless and cold-blooded you truly are, Mary. You'd just about do anything for a story, and to be in the spotlight."

"Do me a favor and stop talking as if you know everything about me, because you don't. You haven't been here, you haven't seen what I've had to do and put up with over the years. I've worked hard, and have literally had to claw my way to the top."

"Don't you mean that you've slept your way to the top?" he asked.

She chose to ignore his cheap, easy comment. "I may have stepped on a few toes along the way, but I made sacrifices that needed to be made. And currently, I have no regrets. My work is everything to me, and I've only just begun. I still have a lot of things to accomplish."

"Wow, Mary," Henry said and started to clap, "you're so inspiring. Maybe if you had that printed on a t-shirt or a coffee mug…"

"You're a prick!" she shouted. "Get out of here. I'm leaving, and I don't want you snooping around my office like some lost puppy while I'm gone."

"Where are you going?" he asked.

"That's none of your damn business, now is it?"

"I thought you said that we needed to stick together? You know, in case the killer strikes again. We, Mary – you and me. Remember?"

"Whatever," she grunted, making her way back around the desk to where she had taken off her shoes. "You can come with me, but you have to do what I say. That means if I tell you not to speak, then you keep your damn mouth shut. Understand?"

"Belittling me like you just did, well, it's a wonder that you're still not married."

"I'm not married because I choose not to be," she informed him. "And try not to piss me off more than what you already have today. It is only Monday." Her heels made a sharp sound as she headed for her office door.

"Where are we going, anyway?"

"To the police station; I have some follow up questions for the sheriff."

"You actually think he is going to see you?" Henry asked and began to laugh. "There's no way that he's going to answer anybody's questions."

"I'm not just anybody," she said and exited the room. "But for some reason if he chooses not to see me, then I'm sure someone there will speak to me."

Mary Evans wasn't worried, not in the least. She was dedicated, determined, and he decided long ago that she would do anything to get what she needed for a story. *Anything!*

FOUR

ELLE TURNED RIGHT ONTO BROWN STREET and immediately slowed the car; she was looking for the address the Information operator had given her. Three houses down, on the left side of the cul-de-sac, she found her destination. She pulled into the driveway and killed the engine. Easy, she thought. The Sullivan home was only about fifteen minutes from her own. But now, she knew, came the difficult part.

She leisurely stepped from her car, trying to build up enough courage for what she was about to do. Elle hit the auto lock button on the key ring and began walking toward the brick home.

Fall was definitely in full swing, she noted, as she stepped through piles of fallen leaves on the concrete path. They made a quick crunching sound as Elle made contact with them. A heavy, smoky scent filled the atmosphere; a neighbor had obviously started a burn pile. And as she stepped up to the front entrance of the house, she couldn't help but notice the four round pumpkins that were placed side-by-side to the left of the white door. Someone had taken the time to prepare for the upcoming holiday.

"It's too late to back out now," she whispered, and then raised her small fist and tapped twice on the door.

Elle waited. Part of her wanted to run and get back into the car as her legs started to shake with nerves. She wasn't exactly sure why she had so suddenly decided to do this, jump the gun and put herself into the midst of things. This, she admitted to herself, was definitely out of her comfort zone.

"Yes? Can I help you?"

Elle hadn't heard the door open. She looked up toward the deep voice; the voice's owner, Robbie, she knew, definitely had a familiar face. She had seen him around school, maybe even had a class with him. Robbie Douglas, that was it. He was a senior, Elle thought. But what was he doing at the Sullivan home?

"Robbie, who's at the door?"

"I'm not sure, she..."

"Sorry," Elle managed to get out. She told herself to relax a bit and gain a grip on the task she had set out to do. "I'm Elle Anderson; I go to Gray's Lane High."

"Yeah," Robbie nodded. "I thought I'd seen you somewhere before."

He wasn't that tall, Elle noted. He also didn't have that common jock build, but she was almost sure that he played a sport of some sort. She'd often seen him wearing a letterman's jacket. Not today, though. No, today he wore dark jeans and a basic white t-shirt. Very attractive, Elle considered, especially with the dark shaggy hair and plastic framed glasses that somewhat concealed his green eyes.

But what was he doing here?

"Were you looking for someone or…"

"Sorry," Elle repeated. "I was looking for Niki. Is she…"

"I'm Niki."

Elle watched as the girl stepped out from cover and up to the opened door. She was very pretty, Elle thought. Despite the red puffiness that surrounded the girl's face, Niki's beauty was something that still stood out. The shoulder length blond hair that bordered her thin face seemed to almost glow. Niki's blue eyes still seemed to shine, even through the milky tears that glazed over them. She had obviously dressed for comfort, standing as tall as Robbie, in loose sweats and a faded school t-shirt.

Elle was quick to compare herself to her classmate. Her own hair, dark and naturally curly, was now pulled back from her face with a large clip. Not fat by any standards, she also realized that she wasn't as slender as Niki. Elle's skin was considerably paler, but mostly hidden with tight jeans and a black button down sweater. She'd been told more than once that she was cute, maybe attractive. But next to Niki, Elle couldn't help but feel just average, even plain.

"Was there something you needed?" Niki asked.

"No, not really," Elle spoke up. She took a step back and looked at the ground. Was this a mistake? She wasn't quite sure how to precede, how to display her reasoning for coming here.

"I don't understand," Niki said with a frown. "What are you doing…"

"I go to school with you," Elle jumped in. She crossed her arms over her chest and sighed. "We have…"

"Calculus together," Niki finished, "I know. But I still don't understand…"

"This is awkward," Elle quietly said to herself more than she did to Niki or Robbie. She bit her lower lip, and tried to decide what her next move might be.

"You're not here because of class?" Robbie asked. "Because that should all be taken care of."

"No," Elle said and shook her head. "I'm not here because of class. I read about your mother this morning, you know, in the paper, and…"

A high-pitched wail immediately cut Elle off. She looked to Niki, who had covered her face with a trembling hand.

"I'm so sorry," Elle apologized and took a step forward, toward Niki. "I didn't mean to upset you or anything, I just—I just wanted to offer my condolences. I know what it's like to have a parent, well…" she let her words trail off.

"This isn't really a good time," Robbie said and placed an arm around Niki. He pulled her into him.

Of course, Elle thought, he was her boyfriend. That was why Robbie Douglas had skipped school and was at the Sullivan home. It all made sense now.

"Right, sure," Elle said and nodded. "I completely understand." She looked from Niki to Robbie, who seemed to stare at her with a dull, angry glare. Elle tried to offer a warm smile, but the gesture didn't completely form. She swiftly turned around and started for her car in the driveway.

Stupid, she told herself. Utterly, down right stupid! She wasn't entirely certain what had motivated her to do it in the first place, to seek out Niki and confess her similar tragedy. What did she actually expect to come from it? And now, as Elle dug into her pocket for the keys to the Honda, she couldn't help but wonder what school was going to be like tomorrow when news got out about her actions.

"Michelle, right? Michelle, wait up."

She'd just gotten her car unlocked and was in the process of opening the driver's side door, but suddenly stopped at the sound of her name. She twisted back to see Niki moving rapidly toward her.

"Please, it's—it's Elle. Call me Elle."

"Okay," Niki said, "Elle, then. Don't go just yet."

"Look," Elle started as Niki stopped in front of her, "I wasn't trying to... I..."

"I know," Niki offered. She paused for a moment, which created an eerie silence, and then: "You'll have to forgive Robbie, he's just a little bit on edge. We all are since... since... I appreciate what you said though, and your coming here. You didn't have to do that."

Elle wasn't quite sure how to respond. She still held the car door open with one hand, and gripped her car keys with the other. She tried not to look at Niki, but there was a tight force pulling her in and making her stare wide-eyed at the girl. And then, finally, Elle understood. It was simple, really.

Elle identified with Niki. She *was* Niki.

"You don't have to leave. Why don't you come in, hang out for a little bit?"

"No," Elle said, finding her voice, "that's not necessary. I should go."

It all made sense to her now, why she had shown up at a stranger's doorstep, willing to share her own painful history with Niki. Elle had subconsciously wanted to help Niki, of course. But at the same time, Elle hastily realized, she needed to help herself, too. She needed someone to lean on, someone who empathized with her and her situation.

Someone like Niki.

After all, she reminded herself, her very own mother had been murdered in New York less than a month ago. Maybe it wasn't such a bad idea coming here, Elle considered. Maybe, just maybe, she was supposed to be here. Perhaps she and Niki were meant to meet, get to know each other, become friends. Because then, Elle knew, they would at least have each other to confide in.

"Really," Niki said, "come in. Robbie's not too bad once you get to know him," she half grinned. "Besides, you're new to Gray's Lane and we haven't officially been introduced. I'd like to talk to you."

Elle moved her keys over in her hand, which created a clinging sound as metal hit metal. She contemplated Niki's words – let them slip around inside her head. It didn't take her long to come to a conclusion: she knew what she wanted to do.

"Sure, I'll come in," Elle said and then pushed the car door shut behind her. "I'd like to talk, too." She shoved her keys back into her pocket, and then shook her hands down at her side as she tried to rid herself of the new anxieties that now filled her. This is what she had set out to do in the first place.

"Great," Niki said and stretched out her hand. "It's nice to formally meet you."

"You, too," Elle responded, and then took Niki's hand with her own and lightly shook it. "And again, I'm very sorry for your loss."

"Thank you," Niki whispered with a bit of a quiver in her voice. "If you want to, you can follow me into the house." She turned and began leading the way back up the drive.

Elle started behind Niki; she made a mental note to stop apologizing, to stop alluding to the girl's mother. Elle knew that when the time was right, or when the moment presented itself, Niki would have to make the first move.

Elle was guided into the two-story house through the front door. Immediately, a thick metallic stench hit her nostrils. Blood. She attempted to ignore the remote smell, but knew right away that Niki's mother had definitely been murdered here.

Next, she was directed past the cozy front living room that held a small loveseat, chair, and ottoman all upholstered in matching earth tones. Then, they walked down a narrow hallway that was painted maroon and held framed paintings depicting different scenes of nature, and into the back of the home that seemed to be the hang-out spot.

A wraparound gray couch filled most of the space. Straight across from the couch and hanging on the wall was a large TV. Underneath the TV sat a mahogany cabinet that was opened and revealed neat rows of DVDs with a few VHSs thrown into the mix. Robbie sat on the far end of the coach. He was leaning back with his bare feet reclined into the air.

The entire home was clearly in order, the downstairs, anyway. But Elle had still been able to make out the faint trace of white powder, the kind used to dust for fingerprints. It littered the entire first floor, but was the only thing that seemed out of the ordinary. That must have meant, Elle contemplated, that Kim had died upstairs. In her bedroom, maybe?

"Robbie, this is Elle," Niki said. She took a seat next to him. "Elle, this is Robbie."

"Right," Elle said and nodded. She sat down on the edge of the couch at the opposite side and crossed her legs.

"I didn't mean to be rude earlier," Robbie said, never once taking his gaze from what appeared to be the sports channel. "It's just that it's been a rough couple of days."

"Don't worry about it," Elle offered. She turned her focus from Robbie to Niki. And then she noticed the half empty box of tissues sitting to the girl's left. A necessity at a time like this, Elle thought.

She still often found herself breaking out in random sobs. Sometimes due to a specific memory popping into her head, or other times the water works would come from simply retrieving a distant scent of her mother's favorite lilac perfume. The grieving period was still very much upon her.

"Can I get you a drink?" Niki asked as she leaned over and rested her head on Robbie's shoulder. "Water, ice tea, coffee…"

"No, I'm fine," Elle answered and waved her hand at the offer. "I really shouldn't stay too long."

"Are you going to school?" Robbie still didn't look at her.

"Oh, no, probably not now." Elle searched the room for a clock, realizing that she had forgotten to put her watch on this morning. It had to be after nine.

"I hope I'm not being too forward," Niki started, "but before, earlier, you were saying something about how you know what it's like to…"

"… lose a parent," Elle finished for her. "Yes, I do," she said and tightly folded her hands in her lap. "My mother died about a month ago. She was killed in New York, and that's when I moved here to live with my dad."

"Principal Anderson?" Robbie asked.

"Yeah," Elle swallowed. "Principal Anderson—John—is my dad." She took a deep breath. Both Niki and Robbie had the right to ask her questions, and she'd thought that she was prepared and more than ready to answer them. But maybe not.

"I'm sorry about your mom," Niki said in a soft tone. "How did she, I mean, if you don't mind me asking, how did she…"

"Murdered," Elle answered, cutting her off.

"Murdered?" Robbie repeated. He finally made eye contact with her.

"Yes," Elle confirmed. She felt the burning sensation of tears beginning to form at the corners of both her eyes, but refused to let them escape.

This was inevitable, she thought to herself. She had sought Niki out, not the other way around. She had willingly spoken of her own experience, and the fact that, she too, had lost a parent. And talking about the details, Elle knew, well, that was a given.

But it's okay to talk about it, she told herself. It wouldn't be natural or healthy to keep the tragedy bottled up inside. After all, Niki would understand more than anyone else what she had gone through. What she was *still* going through. Not to mention, Elle was beginning to like Niki, and could definitely see a friendship speedily forming.

"I don't know what to say," Niki said. She brought her hand up to her face and let it cover her mouth.

Though Niki's complexion had turned shockingly white, Elle was still able to make out a genuine look of compassion on the girl.

"The killer," Elle said, but then quickly became silent as she looked down at the hardwood floor. It was too late, though; she knew that she had to finish what she'd already started.

"The killer still hasn't been found."

———

"What the hell were you thinking?"

He was definitely mad, that was made abundantly clear by his choice of words. Though 'hell' was hardy offensive and pretty commonly used, Elle still flinched as the profanity flew out of her father's mouth, dripping in anger.

She may not have known her father that well, or been that close to him, not like she had been with her mother. But the time she had spent with him, specifically in the past month, had given her some helpful insight as to who her father really was and what he was like. And one thing about John Anderson, Elle had come to know, was that he never cursed.

Until now.

"Dad, please, I really think that you're over-reacting." Elle sat at the same bar stool she had occupied earlier this morning. She set down her fork beside the square plate that held an untouched piece of dry chicken breast, and crossed her arms over her chest. Her appetite had vanished as soon as her father had started in on her.

"You don't get to tell me how to act," John said. "You cut school today, and you lied to me. Did you honestly think that I wouldn't find out? I am the principal, don't forget. I tend to notice when my daughter is missing in action."

"It was one day!" Elle finally burst out. She turned toward her father. Eyes wide, she couldn't believe that he was making such a big deal out of something so small, so juvenile.

"Yes," John agreed, "until next time, right? And then it will have just been two days, or maybe only three. Michelle, you just moved here; you haven't even been going to Gray's Lane High a whole month. You've been tardy, and now absent. Is this really how you want to begin…"

"I'm adjusting!" she interrupted. "It's going to take time for me…"

"Well, what you need is some structure, honey. You need to be focused and have a schedule. Schoolwork should be something that helps you keep your mind off of…"

"Mom? New York? What happened to her there?"

"I didn't say that," he sighed. "Of course you're not going to be able to forget everything you've been through so soon. I just think that if you got involved with a sport or after school activity that you might…"

She shook her head, cutting him off. He didn't get it. He just didn't get it. But then, how could he? Elle thought. His whole world hadn't been turned upside down; his life hadn't been shattered at the age of seventeen. He couldn't possibly understand.

But she also had to admit: this wasn't his fault. Her father was trying.

"I'm sorry I skipped school today," she whispered and then changed her focus to the sweating glass of ice water next to her plate. She couldn't look her father in the eye, not while she was apologizing. "And I'm sorry for what I said about…"

"It's fine," he said firmly in between bites of brown rice. He reached for his own water, took a long gulp, and then faced her. "But, I would like to know what you did today. What was so important that it couldn't wait until after three?"

She knew that this question would come, had even been anticipating it. She did know her father well enough to know that he would definitely ask her this question. There was no way that she could get away from the issue with a simple 'I'm sorry' and promise to never do it again. Naturally, she thought, he wanted an explanation.

"I didn't doing anything bad," she started, hoping that the innocence imbedded in her tone was coming through loud and clear.

"Okay," he said slowly. "What does that mean, exactly?"

"I went to visit a friend. I went to visit Niki Sullivan."

"I didn't realize you two were friends," John said with a frown. "In fact, you said this morning that you hadn't yet made any friends and…"

"I know what I said, Dad." She paused for a moment and tried to figure out her next move. Would her father think that she was crazy if she told him the truth? Would he be upset or frustrated that she had personally sought Niki out just because of this morning's paper? Elle knew that she was about to find out; lying was not going to be an option here.

"Well, then, I guess I don't understand…"

"I went there today to offer her my condolences. I figured that she wouldn't be in class, and I wanted to personally let her know that I was sorry for what happened."

"And?" he asked.

"And what?"

"That's not all, is it?"

"No," she managed to get out. Of course, he wanted the whole story. "I told her about my past, that I understood exactly what she was going through."

"Dammit, Michelle!"

Two choice words in the last fifteen minutes, he was definitely upset. But why? Did it really matter if she shared her history with someone? And not just someone, Elle thought, but a classmate that could potentially be a good friend. Why was her father so keen on keeping what had taken place in New York private?

"Why does it matter that I told her?" Elle asked. "I might be able to help her; we might be able to help each other. I would have thought that you'd be happy I'm trying to make a new friend."

"I am," John began and then pinched the bridge of his nose with his left hand. "Believe me, nothing would please me more than you making a new friend."

"But?" she asked the inevitable question.

"But," he repeated, "I don't think bonding over, I mean—I just thought that you would want

51

a fresh start. Gray's Lane is an opportunity to have a clean slate…"

"That's easier said than done!"

"Well, if you would stop rehashing the past and actually try to…"

"Forget?" There was that word again, the infamous "F" word. If only it were that simple, she thought. If only. "Dad, no matter how much time passes or what club I join or who I meet and become friends with, I'm never going to forget what happened back home. It's always going to be a part of me. Forever."

"Elle, this is your home now. Here, with me. I'm not trying to sound insensitive, but the sooner you accept that…"

"What?" she asked and rose to her feet. "The sooner I will get over the fact that I no longer have a mother?"

"I wasn't implying that; you're putting words into…"

She wasn't listening, not anymore, not tonight. Elle knew the tears were coming, and in the form of a flood. She needed to get away, be alone. Perhaps then she could calm down and find some peace. Maybe even relax.

"Honey, where are you going?"

"I'm sorry, but I just need to be alone for a little bit," she said with her back to her father. "Thanks for dinner."

"But you didn't even…"

She walked away. Elle left her dad sitting alone at the counter; she passed through the dimly lit dining room and down the long hallway, turned, and started up the beige-carpeted stairs. Her bedroom was the first one on the left, and as soon as she entered it, she quickly closed and locked the door.

Complete solitude.

Elle didn't bother undressing. She fell onto the large bed, and embraced the softness of the dark purple comforter.

Lying on her side in the darkness, she angled her head toward the right where her wooden nightstand stood short and wide. Though she couldn't actually see the contents that were on top of it, she knew what the piece of furniture contained: the last picture she and her mother had ever taken together. The five-by-seven photo was kept securely in place by a silver frame. It had traveled with Elle all the way from New York.

She closed her eyes and tried to concentrate on happier times.

FIVE

CANDY CORN. REALLY? BEN THOUGHT. That was the killer's signature? That was why Sheriff Douglas was banking on there being another murder? All because Kim Sullivan's body had been scattered with tiny orange, yellow, and white sugary treats post mortem?

He sat at the wooden table that was barely big enough for two, crossed one leg over the other, and popped the tab to his third beer can of the evening. He wasn't a drinker, a lightweight, really. And Ben knew that if he kept up at this pace, he would be completely buzzed in less than an hour. Maybe even drunk.

But it had been one of those days. A day from hell, actually, and alcohol seemed to be the only option that could put him at ease.

Besides, Ben considered, he was off duty until morning and didn't plan on driving anywhere the rest of the evening. Therefore, he believed he was entitled to a few adult beverages that were ultimately helping him to unwind a little bit.

He began flipping through the slim file that the sheriff had asked him to take home and study.

So far, Ben's attempts at finding anything valuable in the report had proven to be useless. Nothing stood out, nothing quite made sense, and there was definitely no evidence as to who was exactly behind Saturday night's act of terror.

Or, more importantly, there was no way of knowing who would be the next victim.

Ben shook his head in frustration, took a long swallow of his beer, and then decided it was time to get down to business. Even though he knew that he could now recite the listed information verbatim, he concluded that one more look wouldn't hurt. In fact, he thought, one more look just might grant him with the golden ticket.

Kimberly Ann Sullivan had been stabbed multiple times. Though the murder weapon hadn't been found, Ben guessed by the size and shape of the woman's wounds that a large fixed-blade hunting knife of some type had been used. Then again, he had to admit that he wasn't a hunter himself and really knew nothing about knives. Hell, a basic kitchen knife could have been the killer's weapon of choice. The only thing Ben was absolutely sure of was that Kim's cuts hadn't been made by anything serrated.

Kim had been found early Saturday evening by her husband. According to Jeff Sullivan's statement, he'd left around four that afternoon with a long list or errands to keep him busy.

First, the dry cleaners, then the video store, followed by the grocery store, and then, finally, he had stopped off to pick up a pizza for dinner. When he had returned home he'd found his wife lying on their bedroom floor covered in blood — dead. There was no question whatsoever that Kim had been murdered in her own bedroom and not just placed there afterwards. One glance at the grisly crime scene photos more than proved that.

Ben leaned back and ran his fingers through his thick hair. This case was bad, ugly even, but he knew that it could have been a lot worse. For instance, he considered, the teenage daughter could have been home at the time. Luckily, she'd been out to dinner and then on her way to the movies with a couple of friends when the murder had taken place.

Ben shuddered to think what would have happened had Nicole been home. He'd probably be staring at photos of a double homicide instead of just one.

And then, of course, there was the whole problem of where the body had been located. Why the bedroom? Ben thought. He quickly wrote the question down on the top page of a yellow legal pad.

Kim had been fully clothed, no rips or tears of any kind except for the ones where she'd been stabbed had been made to what she'd been wearing at the time of her death. So she clearly hadn't been sexually assaulted; Ben recognized that they weren't dealing with *that* kind of problem. Then, again, why the bedroom?

Ben began making more notes, using a freshly sharpened pencil to write down any and all thoughts that burst into his mind. He figured that he could always mark stuff out later if it proved to be unimportant.

Had the killer wanted to attack Kim in the most intimate place available — the woman's own bedroom? Did he overpower her, drag her up the stairs, and trap her in the room before stabbing her to death?

Ben crossed out the questions with a thick dark line. The bedroom wasn't an important factor, it couldn't be. Had it been, then a lot more would have been done to Kimberly Sullivan, more gruesome, disturbing things. Ben had seen too many cases like it before. He was all too familiar with the kind of predators that had other motives than just killing, and what those predators did once inside a woman's private quarters.

Ben started again. Kim had been in her bedroom, doing who knows what during the moments prior to her death, when the killer had surprised her. He must have been quiet, even calm, Ben considered, for the woman not to realize that she was no longer alone in the house. The killer had to have known what he was doing, been composed, almost invisible, to roam the house undetected.

Ben thought of something and rapidly made another memo: the killer had to have been watching the Sullivan home. And, more specifically, he had to have been watching Kim Sullivan herself. Before entering the house, the killer had to have known that Kim was not only alone, but also that her husband wouldn't be returning for quite some time.

The guy they were dealing with was smart, cunning, and hadn't made the smallest mistake of leaving so much as a thumbprint behind. He knew what he was doing, Ben figured. And there was no way that he would have entered the home with the slightest chance of being interrupted. Yes, the killer knew the Sullivans' routines.

But there was another issue of concern, a question of grave importance, Ben knew; a question that would definitely have to be answered in order to find the person responsible for the murder.

Why Kimberly Sullivan?

Though it had been implied to the media and everyone else outside of the Gray's Lane Police Department that a robbery gone awry had taken place, Sheriff Douglas had personally informed Ben that nothing could be further from the truth. Nothing had been taken or destroyed. There had been no mess, other than in the bedroom; no evidence alluding to the fact that the killer had been specifically searching for something. And Ben thought that he knew the reason behind this.

The killer had been on a mission, showing up at the Sullivan home with an agenda, one sole purpose: murder. He hadn't just wanted to kill Kim, he had *planned* it. But again, Ben thought, struggling like a mad dog without his bone to keep his irritation at bay — why? Why was Kimberly Sullivan chosen as the specific target?

The embarrassingly inevitable would have to take place: digging into the victim's life. Her past, her present, and any future plans. Though it would be an invasive process for the family, Ben knew that it would be vital for the investigation.

He wrote the suggestion down in all capital letters. First thing tomorrow morning, he would meet with the sheriff and discuss the idea of turning over every stone in Kim's life. Who her friends were, where she ate, shopped, her education, and any past employment. She'd been a stay-at-home mom since the birth of her daughter.

The department needed to know if the woman had ever been involved with anything illegal, or had any known enemies. Even the slightest detail of a parking ticket had to be revealed; every single skeleton in her closet had to be brushed over with a fine tooth comb. Definitely intrusive, Ben calculated, but necessary.

Finding out who Kimberly Sullivan had really been would be the only chance at revealing the killer's identity. And hopefully, Ben silently prayed, this could all happen before someone else had to die.

Sheriff Douglas had already stated that he believed they were dealing with a potential serial killer, all because of the candy corn. Hesitant at first, Ben had finally given in and believed in the same alarming conclusion. After speculating, Ben had been informed that the candy hadn't come from the Sullivan house — i.e. the killer had brought it with him.

Ben hated to admit it, but the fact most likely remained that the killer had used the candy to sign his victim, to take credit for the act. And because the killer had done that, Ben knew that there was no getting around the actuality that the killer was planning on striking again. But when, where, and who was all left unknown.

Ben gradually released a heavy yawn and then stood, allowing his legs to stretch out a bit. Studying the case file had sobered him up quicker than a pot of strong coffee. And as a result, he now had a pounding headache that seemed to be picking up speed by the second.

He had been tempted back at Sheriff Douglas' office this morning to step down — to say the least. He'd literally been so close to taking the man's offer, that Ben could now still feel the heat of that situation that had occurred earlier today.

But Ben had never once considered himself a quitter, and he refused to do so now. He would stay in Gray's Lane and just have to make the best of it. Besides, he knew that it was long past time to get over his own troubled history and move on with his life.

After all, he thought to himself, was there any place in existence these days that was considered "safe?"

Ben didn't think so. Especially now.

He began pacing back and forth in the small space that was a sorry excuse for a dining room. With his long strides, he only got about three steps before reaching one end of the area and having to turn back around and head toward the other wall.

Though loosely tied, he kept his black boots on to prevent the chance of piercing his bare feet with any mysterious item that might be hiding in the less-than-clean dark carpet. Not exactly the Ritz, or anything like he had been used to back home, but the place would just have to due until he came up with a more permanent arrangement.

Damn, he thought, back home. The words echoed loudly in his already cramped mind. The last thing he wanted to be addressing were recollections of back home. That had been the whole reason for coming to Gray's Lane, Ohio, a distraction and a chance at a fresh start. But instead, he was now working a new murder case and only being further reminded of past tragedies.

That night Ben shook his head and tried to rid himself of the memories, but they wouldn't break away from him. They clung tightly to his insides, almost as if they'd been glued there. It was like his eyelids had been stapled open and he was now being repeatedly forced to watch the events of his past play out like some unsettling horror movie, without the ability to look away or even so much as blink and miss the really nasty parts.

Yes, he reflected, memories of his past. No matter how hard he tried, there was simply no avoiding them.

Ben was beginning to feel light headed, like someone had snuck up behind him and swiftly hit him in the lower back with a wooden baseball bat. Tears burned the corners of his eyes, and his legs turned to Jell-O; he knew that he could crumple to the ground at any moment.

Suddenly, the doorbell rang. The musical chime sounded throughout the entire house. With blurry vision and hazy, sluggish movements, Ben found himself starting toward the front door.

After what seemed like several weary minutes, he finally reached it, caught his breath, and pressed his face to the cool metal entrance. With one squinty eye, he searched through the tiny peephole, trying to place his unwanted company. But night had already fallen, and without a porch light, the darkness was too overwhelming to make out a face.

Ben's temper was beginning to boil, and he knew that anger would soon be cascading through every inch of his body. He wasn't in the mood for this. Not now, and *definitely* not tonight.

Ben's hand seemed to shoot out on its own accord, grasp the circular handle, and without much force, pull the door open. Light from the inside foyer splashed out and illuminated the guest.

He felt confusion flood his face as he stared out at the stranger. "Yes?" he asked. He could clearly hear the annoyance that poured from his own voice. "Can I help you?"

"I think we can help each other," the visitor answered, and then stepped into the house and shut and locked the door.

SIX

"DAD, ARE YOU ALRIGHT?"

He was sure his daughter had said something, maybe even had asked him a question. He'd seen her lips move, knew she'd been talking, but exactly what words she had spoken, Jeff Sullivan didn't know. He was struggling desperately not to lose it now, not here. Jeff was holding desperately onto sanity, clawing at it like a wild hawk, refusing to let it go. There will be no scene made today, he told himself. Not on the morning his wife was to be buried; he wouldn't allow it.

But guilt was eating at him. Like a hungry beast that hadn't been fed in weeks, it tore at his insides and ripped through his chest, causing a razor-sharp pain to erupt throughout his entire body.

His last words to Kim had been: "I hope you die a slow, painful death." How was that even possible? She'd been his wife, his partner, and now she was gone — forever.

"Dad, did you hear me? Are you okay?"

"What?" he asked and turned to face his daughter. "Oh, yes, sorry. I'm fine."

But of course, he wasn't fine. He was a far cry away from *fine*. Not only was his wife dead—murdered and mutilated—but if Sheriff Douglas happened to discover the truth, his dirty little secret so to speak, then Jeff would be more than just a grieving widow. He knew that he would be considered the number one suspect in his wife's death.

Yes, Jeff Sullivan had a secret to keep. And he would try his damnedest to keep it—no matter what that entailed.

"It's hard to believe that we are here, you know?" Niki said to her father. "Doing this, saying goodbye to Mom." She reached for his hand.

"It is, sweetie." Jeff took his daughter's tiny hand in his own. His hand glistening in sweat; his daughter's cold, trembling. Jeff couldn't help but believe that if she knew the reality of things, Niki wouldn't be holding his hand right now. In fact, she would probably be making a scene, the kind that he was so adamant in avoiding.

Jeff's back was beginning to ache due to the stiffness offered by the pew. Though squeaky clean and smelling of fresh lemon, one thing the seat didn't provide was comfort. And his neck was starting to twinge, too, matching his other pains, as he constantly craned around from the front of the church to see who had come out on this Tuesday morning to either give support or pay final respects.

The small, claustrophobic room was more than half filled with distant relatives, friends, and local acquaintances, who were obviously attending the service for more curiosity purposes rather than sympathetic ones.

Jeff knew exactly who to blame for this: Mary Evans.

He had read her article in Monday's edition of *Gray's Lane Examiner*. Actually, he'd read it twice. Jeff recalled it now, word for word, and how the trashy, sorry excuse for a reporter had glorified his spouse's murder. Mary hadn't made it news; she'd made it entertainment. A second-rate tabloid writer at best, he'd never had a problem with the woman.

Until now, that was.

Now, he could hardly stomach her, and personally held her accountable for the spectacle that Kim's funeral had become.

But something else was nagging Jeff. A nasty thought had snuck into his head and taken up residence. And that little thought was continuing to grow and torment the hell out of him.

Murder. His wife had been murdered. Though no one else in the community may have been one hundred percent sure, Jeff personally knew that he, himself, had not been responsible for his wife's death. He hadn't been the one to grip the knife and repeatedly stab her.

So who had killed Kim? And why? And was that person attending the funeral now?

The idea made sense to Jeff. He wasn't aware of anything missing from his home; robbery clearly hadn't been a motive. So what had been the killer's motive? Had Kim had a stalker, an unwanted love interest that he hadn't known about?

Or maybe, Jeff thought, running his free hand through his thin, graying hair, he really was the one to blame for his wife's early demise. Though he hadn't been the one wielding the knife, perhaps it had been his actions that had created this great tragedy.

Could jealousy truly be the motive here? He pondered the question to himself. But then how did the candy corn fit in? What in the hell was that all about?

He rolled his shoulders back and tried to rid himself of all the thoughts and questions he didn't currently have answers for. He wasn't a cop, far from it. And while it would be difficult to not be personally involved, Jeff knew that he would just have to sit back and let Sheriff Douglas do all of the work. And until more light was shined onto the situation, Jeff vowed to not let himself get tangled up in the tight feeling that was guilt.

After all, he attempted to comfort himself, his wife's death could have been completely random. Though highly unlikely, and a first for Gray's Lane, Jeff considered the impossible: there could very well be an active serial killer hiding in his once-safe hometown.

Therefore, he would keep his mouth shut and his personal endeavors private until he was absolutely sure that his own actions hadn't set Kim's slaying into motion.

"Mom would have loved the lilies; they're perfect. So beautiful."

Jeff nodded, indicating to his daughter that he agreed with the observation. But in all actuality, he didn't. He found the flowers to be gaudy, blinding even. And their heavy, musk scent was not only overpowering, but nearly nauseating. But they had been Kim's favorite, and therefore, most appropriate for the day's event.

"I miss her already," Niki whispered. "I keep thinking that she's going to come home, walk through the door, like she's been visiting an old friend or something. Like—like none of this has really happened."

Jeff let go of his daughter's hand, and instead placed his arm around her petite shoulder. She was shivering uncontrollably, and when he heard her break out into a heavy sob, he felt his own heart bust and shatter into millions of pieces.

A new concern, he thought, and now his main one: getting Niki through this.

He wondered to himself if it was even possible. Niki was just seventeen; she needed a mother, a woman to confide in. How on earth could he provide her with that?

Jeff took some responsibility, knew that he had barely been one parent to her over the years. And now what? He was supposed to be two? He wasn't sure that he had it in him, didn't know if he could actually pull it off. But he acknowledged that he would ultimately have to try, for his only child's sake. There were just no other options.

"What are we going to do?" Niki asked. "How are we…"

"Shhh," he said, attempting to soothe her. Then, pulled her in closer.

Jeff tightened his hold on his daughter and tried to soothe her with warmth. He wasn't sure the gesture was working, and frantically wrenched his head from side-to-side, looking for Robbie.

Where is he? Jeff's mind silently screamed. Niki and Robbie had been dating for almost a year now; there was no reason why Robbie shouldn't be at the church, in attendance, giving Niki the relief she deserved and needed — the relief that Jeff couldn't give his own daughter.

"Is Robbie coming?" Jeff asked. He hoped to distract Niki, even if it was just for the slightest moment. "The pastor will be starting soon."

"I don't know," she answered in between sobs. "He didn't answer his cell this morning. But I thought, I mean, I *expected* that he would be here."

"Well, I'm sure he's on his way. He's probably just running a little late." Jeff closed his eyes and then bit down on his lower lip. He regretted speaking out, making the observation of her MIA boyfriend, and now wished that he had let it go. In an attempt to soothe his daughter, Jeff knew that he had accomplished the opposite. He'd made Niki feel worse by bringing Robbie's absence to light.

"Should I try calling him again? Maybe he didn't get my messages."

"No, I don't think…" Jeff stopped. He tried to find the right words. Were there any? "He's probably on his way. Give him a few more minutes." He checked his watch again; the services would be starting any moment now. Jeff made a commitment to himself. If Robbie was a complete no show, he would make the teenager deeply sorry.

"Okay," Niki agreed, "a few more moments."

Jeff suddenly realized that he didn't have it in him to wait. Ignoring his own advice, he slowly stood.

"What are you doing, Dad?"

"Don't worry; I'll be right back." Jeff left his daughter sitting alone, eased himself out of the pew, and began walking down the center aisle toward the back entrance of the church.

He did his best to avoid stares and whispered comments, and kept focus on the main doors that were propped open.

He nervously ran his hand through his hair again; he could feel himself growing older. He quickly jammed both hands into the pockets of his black dress pants and edged out into the hallway. The space was deserted, which made him happy. He had a phone call to make, a very *private* phone call.

Jeff pulled out the cell phone from his pocket and desperately tried to remember the number. There was a four, he knew, and definitely a nine, but that's all of the numbers that would come to mind.

He looked up, willing the mobile number to come to him, and suddenly realized it as no longer needed. The person he wanted to talk to had finally entered the building.

"Mr. Sullivan, again, I'm so sorry for your loss."

"Where in the hell have you been, Robbie?" Jeff demanded. He took a deep breath, reminding himself where he was and of all the people that were within earshot.

"Sorry, sir. I wasn't sure what time to exactly be here, and my cell phone wasn't…"

"Bullshit!" Jeff exploded, but then rapidly bit down on his lower lip. He had to keep his cool. When he started again, it was in a low whisper. "Don't play games with me, Robbie. Don't you dare…"

"I'm not. Seriously," he said and threw up his hands. "I swear it."

"You could have at least dressed for the occasion," Jeff said as he took in the boy's appearance. The worst was the wrinkled jeans, followed by the blue dress shirt that wasn't even tucked in and loosely hanging gray tie, which was topped off with sneakers and uncombed hair. Jeff hadn't expected Robbie to be in a suit, not like himself, but thought that the teenager would have presented himself with just a little more decorum.

But, then again, Jeff contemplated; at least he had shown up. Finally.

"I know," Robbie agreed. "I was running late and just wanted to get here for Niki. This was all I could find that was clean and…"

"It doesn't matter now," Jeff said, interrupting him. "Go find Niki. She's inside and has been waiting for you."

"Right," Robbie said and made a quick move toward the entrance of the chapel.

"Hold on a second," Jeff stuck out his right arm. He placed it on Robbie's chest, which made the boy come to an instant halt.

"What is it?"

"Well, I… ah…" Jeff struggled. He knew that his next question would be awkward, somewhat painful, even. But it had to be asked.

"Yes?" Robbie prompted.

"It's just, well, you haven't said anything to Niki, right? I mean about…"

"I told you that I wouldn't, sir."

"I know, I know," Jeff said. "But I wanted to make sure that it stayed that way."

"Look," Robbie said and leaned in. "It's our little secret. I'm not going to tell anybody what I saw. Especially Niki. I think she's already suffered enough, and I don't want her getting more hurt."

It was as if Jeff had gotten punched right in the jaw. The blow hadn't actually happened, but he could still feel the burn. He was too embarrassed to even look Robbie in the face and quickly turned away from him.

"Thank you," he finally mumbled and looked to the ground. "I owe you one."

"Yes, you do," Robbie said. "A big one." He turned and walked through the open doorway.

Anger and fear forcefully combined and began coursing through Jeff. He felt his body flush, and then grow increasingly warmer with rage. He had made a mistake, and that mistake might eventually cost him.

He took a deep breath, let his emotions cool, and then walked back into the chapel, where he found his daughter being comforted by Robbie.

As he resumed his seat, Jeff forced a slight smile. Robbie Douglas was a liability, he knew. A liability that just might have to be permanently handled.

SEVEN

ELLE DIDN'T GET OFF TO A GOOD START THE next morning. Greeted by a pounding headache with thoughts of her mother still overwhelming her, she ultimately knew that playing hooky wasn't going to be an option. Therefore, she'd powered on in her weakened state and began her monotonous routine.

First, she hopped in the shower. The slick water that usually provided a certain comfort wasn't doing its job this morning. Instead of feeling relaxed, refreshed, or even rejuvenated, Elle was consumed with only more exhaustion and more confusion.

She still didn't understand her father. Did he honestly believe the best way to get over the past was to cover it up? To bury it? To forget that it had even taken place or been a huge part of her life?

Elle wasn't completely sure that she would ever get over her mother's murder. But one thing was for certain: she knew that it would definitely take longer than a month's time, *if* it was going to happen at all.

Perhaps when the killer was actually found, or when the reasoning behind her mother's untimely death was revealed, then she could better navigate through this whole grieving process. But not a moment's sooner.

Her themes for dressing were plain and comfort: dark jeans, gray t-shirt paired with a blue flannel, and white tennis shoes. After being washed and dried, her hair was combed back and put into a ponytail. Elle didn't bother with a watch, bracelets, or makeup; she wasn't in the mood to impress anyone, least of all a boy at school.

The only piece of jewelry Elle did wear was a sterling silver necklace that looped around a large Amethyst stone. She rarely took the chain off; it had been the last thing her mother had ever given her. The jewelry had been a surprise; a gift given out of the blue for no particular reason. Elle often wondered how her mother had been able to afford something so expensive. Elle wondered how her mother had been able to afford a lot of things. The woman had always managed to somehow make everything work out.

Elle made sure her black backpack was properly packed before slinging it over her right shoulder. She then tiptoed down the stairs and tried to be as quiet as possible. The last thing she wanted to do was run into her father and have another "talk." Not today. Not this morning.

She was more than relieved to see the kitchen vacant when she rounded the corner; John wasn't anywhere in sight. Feeling as if a crippling weight had been removed from her chest, she took a few moments to breathe.

The yellow post-it note on the counter explained her father's absence: he was getting an early start at work this morning. Elle crumpled up the note, threw it in the garbage can underneath the sink, grabbed a banana from the glass fruit dish, and then started for the front of the house.

The drive to school had been the same as always—fast, easy, uneventful. And now, sitting in calculus class, Elle couldn't help but stare at the empty desk that was usually occupied by Niki.

Today was the day, Elle knew. Today was the day that Niki's mother would be put to rest. And though Elle wanted to be there, to show support for Niki and their newfound friendship, Elle knew that it wasn't possible. Especially considering the stunt she had pulled yesterday.

So Elle did the next best thing: she paid her respects from afar, and sent out strong thoughts of empathy for the Sullivan family. After all, she knew *exactly*, probably more so than anyone else living in Gray's Lane, the magnitude of hurt and suffering that had been inflicted by recent events.

Elle was finding it particularly difficult to stay focused on the teacher. He was standing there, propped up in front of the whiteboard, glasses barely hanging onto the edge of his sweaty nose, reading aloud from the secondhand textbook. The properties and solutions he was talking about were far too out of reach for today. So as an alternative, her train of thought traveled the rickety, narrow path that was murder — otherwise known as Gray's Lane's new, most popular topic.

Murder! Elle's mind screamed. The word tried unsuccessfully to escape her. She could taste it in her mouth; it was sour, like warm vinegar. And though she kept silent, thoughts and questions began flooding her mind.

Kim Sullivan had been stabbed; Elle found herself shivering uncontrollably at the fact. The metal of her dull green chair suddenly felt like a solid brick of ice, which seemed to bleed through her clothing, touch bare skin, and create an even colder atmosphere.

She took a deep breath and told herself to get her wild emotions under control. After all, she wasn't alone, and the last thing she wanted to do was draw attention to herself. If she was going to play commentator, then she knew that she had to it with a certain degree of couth.

A local woman was dead at the hands of an unknown person. Of course, this wasn't new information; anyone within a thirty-mile radius of town knew about the murder. But the idea still sent chills down the center of Elle's spine every time she considered the fact.

Though she'd only been living in Gray's Lane for about a month now, Elle had still been able to come to the conclusion that violence and acts of terror just didn't take place in such a peaceful community. The town had perfectly clean sidewalks and friendly business owners that always offered warm conversation. Strangers were even personable and ever too eager to smile and wave at every stoplight or checkout counter.

Something didn't fit; something didn't make sense, because violence *had* taken place in Gray's Lane, Ohio, and an act of terror *had* occurred.

Why? she pondered. Why had this woman been killed? Who had killed her? And would he or she kill again?

This was familiar territory for Elle — too familiar. Sweat abruptly appeared at the base of her neck, and she could feel it ever so slightly cascading down her back in a prickly sort of way. She was no longer cold, but hot — extremely hot. Her body was on fire.

She closed her eyes, pinched the bridge of her nose, and tried to find a soothing place inside herself, a place that would provide comfort, ease, maybe even peace.

But a place like that didn't exist, not at the moment, anyway. Elle's mind was off swimming in deep, dark waters that were out of her control. Niki's mother's murder was no longer at the center of her attention, Elle's own mother's death now held that spot.

She'd been stabbed to death, too, Elle thought. That night was securely stained in her mind. It was almost as if someone had used a permanent marker to draw out a detailed description of what had taken place on September fifteenth, and then placed that description directly in her line of vision.

Elle remembered that claustrophobic feeling that had abruptly engulfed her as soon as she'd entered the house that evening. She hadn't used her key to gain access; the front door had already been unlocked. That had been the first clue that something was most likely wrong.

The second clue had been the darkness that greeted her. Then, lastly, there'd been a certain stillness that she just couldn't place. But a loud, gunshot-like warning had promptly exploded in her head — she knew something was up.

Nothing had appeared to have been taken or ransacked as she'd made her way through the living room. But still, a harboring sense of fear had prevented Elle from reaching out and flicking on a light switch. Instead, she'd chosen to let the moonlight guide her way.

It had been that very same moonlight that had touched down onto the thin line of scarlet, alerting her of the stain embedded in the carpet. Elle had guessed it at once to be blood. And though quite hesitant at first, she'd ultimately decided to follow the trail.

Down the bare and narrow hallway and straight into the kitchen, she distinctly remembered grabbing the wall for support, before abruptly changing her hold and deciding to grip her aching throat, as if to hold back a piercing scream.

Though it had been made abundantly clear that an unwanted guest had been in the house, it wasn't obvious if that guest had yet left. She'd been terrified, but she was also smart. Elle had refused to give her presence away.

Her mother's body had been sprawled out on the black and white checkered-tile flooring of the kitchen. She had been on her back, eyes open and gazing upward at the slowly spinning ceiling fan, as if hypnotized into a trance.

Her mother had been soaked, *drenched,* completely covered in blood. But the blood and heavy gore hadn't been the only things to stand out. Elle distinctly recalled the bright and colorful orange, yellow, and white pieces of —

"You okay?"

She was being pulled away. A tight, forceful claw was ripping her away from her dark memory, taking her out of the past, and placing her in the present, the now. But who? And why?

"Hello?" It was the same broad and unfamiliar voice from before. "It's Elle, right? Elle, are you okay?"

"Yes, I'm Elle," she heard her own weak voice answer. But she still didn't feel whole. Her mind and body were in two separate places, being controlled and operated by two separate entities.

"You don't look so good. Maybe I should get you some water or…"

"No, I'm fine." And finally, she was set free and able to become aware of her surroundings.

Elle was no longer in La La Land. She was no longer in New York with her butchered mother. She was in Ohio. She was in calculus class with what appeared to be just one other student.

He must have noticed her look of puzzlement, because he suddenly said: "Class was dismissed a couple of minutes ago. I didn't want to leave you here alone, daydreaming or sleeping or whatever it was that you were doing."

"Thank you," Elle said. He stood, turned away from him, and began gathering her things. "I guess I zoned out."

"Understandable," he said. "Mr. Stover's not really known for his stimulating lesson plans." And then he awkwardly laughed at his own little joke. "So, Elle Anderson, you're new here, right?"

"Yes," she answered and then nodded. She wasn't sure why he had asked the question when he obviously already knew the answer. She wonder if this was small talk—a beginning lead into another area of conversation?

"And Principal Anderson is…"

"My father," she finished for him.

"Cool," he offered. "Well, I'm Kyle Burke. I'm pretty sure that we also have the same lunch period."

Elle finally turned to face the friendly classmate. She tried to nonchalantly look him up and down and take in his entire appearance.

He was cute, that was definitely clear. He had dark hair, but it was short, trimmed, neat. He'd used gel or some other sort of product to slick it hair back ever so slightly, creating a somewhat wet look. And although he was wearing a navy hooded sweatshirt and baggy jeans, Elle was still able to make out his muscular form. Perhaps a jock, she thought.

But what stood out most of all about Kyle Burke were his eyes: dark, yet warm and somehow inviting.

It was then that Elle quickly realized she was blatantly staring, possibly even on the verge of getting lost again. She swiftly looked away and changed her focus.

"It's nice to meet you," she said, and then filled the weighty silence with a half smile.

"And you as well," he replied with a grin. A perfect, white smile was revealed, causing Elle to no longer consider him as cute, but hot—*really* hot.

"Thanks again for waking me up. If it hadn't been for you, I'd probably still be sitting off in space somewhere." Elle tried to laugh, to match his gesture from before, but feared that the action had come off too weak, maybe even fake.

"No problem."

The silence was quickly back, but it was much more dreadful this time. It was as if the air around them had been filled with an indefinite amount of pressure. Elle willed herself to say something, anything. She even went as far as opening her mouth, but nothing would come out.

"Well, if you need anything," Kyle started, "finding your way around school or even town, just let me know."

She didn't blink. Her eyes never once left him as she watched him exit the classroom and then make a hard right.

Elle brought her books and notepads up to her chest, and began following his lead. She started down the long corridor and headed toward the cafeteria.

A small twitch of regret pressed inside of her, causing her to wonder if she should have said something else, something more. Had Kyle been flirting with her? Trying to get her to talk so that he could get to know her better? Or had he simply just been playing nice guy to the new girl?

Elle's head began pounding again, only more fiercely this time. As if she didn't have enough to think about, her mind now seemed to work on overtime to try and decipher Kyle's motive.

But in the end, she knew, it didn't much matter. After all, her relationship with her boyfriend from New York had just recently ended. And that hadn't gone too smoothly. 'Messy' was an appropriate word that frantically came to mind.

So, Elle concluded as she stepped into the crowded eating area, immediately spotting Kyle, a friendship was all that she was interested in at the moment.

———

Time was standing still, or at least seemed to be. Living in Gray's Lane, Ohio was about as exciting as watching paint dry. No, he instantly reconsidered. Watching paint dry *was* more exciting, and the smell was much better, too.

He was desperately trying to get used to his surroundings and blend in, but felt the task was getting harder and harder to do all the time. He wasn't on vacation. He wasn't here visiting an old friend. He had a job to do. And dammit, he wanted to do it, finish it, and then move on and go home.

Time was a crucial factor, though. Everything had to be done at a certain time. Well, that was only *if* he wanted to get away with murder. And he did, he *really* did. After all, killing hadn't been on his agenda, not at first, anyway. But he'd made a mistake; he messed up, and as a result, he'd been backed into a corner. And now, well, now he had a mess to clean up.

He'd killed Kimberley Sullivan Saturday night because it had been part of the plan. And what a wonderful plan it was all turning out to be. If everything went in his favor, by tomorrow morning the Sullivan woman would be old news, and the town would be talking about a new murder, another dead woman, the next victim.

This is good, he thought to himself as he bent down to tie the laces of his dark boots. The quicker he got the killings out of the way, the quicker he could start searching for what he needed, what he wanted, his sole reason for coming to this *quaint,* little town.

As he walked into the kitchen, the weathered floorboards squeaked under his weight. He wanted alcohol. He craved something strong and with a numbing effect.

He ended up settling on a diet soda. The light, fizzy beverage was still refreshing, and he liked that it kept his mind clear, clean, and focused. Maybe after he accomplished his evening task, then he would celebrate with something stronger, and hopefully find that smooth, relaxing stage that was only fueled by an adult beverage.

He drained the can, crumpled it with his right fist, and then threw it down onto the scratched counter. He looked down at his wristwatch; he was going to be late. He could *not* be late. Not again.

He raced into the living room and hastily began searching for his keys. He started digging through the couch cushions, knowing that they had to be somewhere in the clutter.

He bit down hard on his lower lip and cursed himself. He immediately regretted the fact that he hadn't placed the keys in a more obvious, convenient location. Like on the cheap coffee table, he considered. Or even in a jacket pocket.

Finally, after discarding several bits and pieces of random garbage—an empty potato chip bag, numerous dirty and stained paper plates, silverware, and an array of chewed up toothpicks—he was able to find what he'd been looking for, *underneath* the couch.

He grasped the plastic key chain. Holding on tight to his treasure, he started for the door. He couldn't help but smile, though. And as he made sure that his home was securely locked and loaded to avoid any and all unwanted intruders, he headed toward his vehicle. His smile was quickly replaced with a full, healthy laugh.

It's funny, he thought to himself. He had no problem whatsoever planning and getting away with murder, not to mention, a whole other long list of recent criminal activity. But when it came to keeping an orderly house and track of objects that were as important as car keys, he was at a total loss. Kind of ironic, he contemplated.

He shoved the lone key into the ignition and turned the engine over. After a few raw, gasping chokes, the vehicle came to life and started up.

He slowly backed out of the gravel driveway, craning his neck to the right to watch for oncoming traffic. The warm smile was promptly back on his face. After tonight, he knew that he would be one giant step closer to getting what he wanted.

EIGHT

"WHAT EXACTLY DO YOU THINK YOU MIGHT find, son?" With just a tad bit of resistance, Douglas had finally given up and thrown in the towel on his issues with the youngsters that seemed to be surrounding his life.

Deputy Andrews, Deputy Hall, his grandson — they were all, notably, at a more active and prime age. And if he wanted to refer to each of them as son, sport, or even kid, well dammit, that was his prerogative.

It was time to stop struggling with this whole concern of age. After all, there was really nothing he could do about it anyway. He was fighting a losing battle.

So, he thought, as he crossed his arms over his mountain of a stomach and leaned back into his black chair, it was high time to concentrate on a battle that he *could* win. A battle that he *had* to win.

"I don't really see the point of digging into Kim Sullivan's life. She's already dead. What good will it do us?"

"Well, sir," Ben began. "For starters, we might be able to find out why she was murdered; why the killer chose her."

"And?"

"I'm sorry?" Ben asked.

"You said, 'for starters.' What are your other reasons for causing a grieving family more grief?"

"Sheriff Douglas, the killer might not have chosen Kim Sullivan at random. What if there was a specific point for killing her? If we look into her life, into her past, we might be able to find out what that point was, which could then lead us to finding the next victim. You know, before it's too late? Or even better yet, we could find the killer."

Douglas let the words of his newest deputy sink in. The sheriff was hoping desperately that at any moment he would wake up screaming from this nauseating nightmare.

Had his life actually come to this? Was this really happening here and now? Was there truly a crazed killer on the loose that was either killing at random or by plan? *Was* there a motive? A reasoning behind this madness?

At the moment, Douglas wasn't sure which scenario would be worse.

Suddenly, he felt his hands begin to shake; he knew that he had to busy them in some way. He had to hide the tingling tremors to avoid any high raised eyebrows or angry- looking frowns from the deputy. The last thing the sheriff wanted to imply was that he was incompetent, and unable to complete the task at hand.

Or worse, that he was scared shitless.

He quickly reached out for the ceramic coffee mug on his desk that was about as old as he was. He abruptly stopped himself though, knowing that he didn't have the willpower to choke down anymore of the heavy brew.

He started sorting through the top drawer in his desk. Candy would be good, but he knew that if he chose to unwrap the foiled pieces of dark chocolate that he might have to share. And he sure as hell wasn't going to do that.

Douglas settled on an old highlighter. Though the marker didn't shine anymore, the large cap still snapped off and then clicked back on. The piercing noise quickly filled the small office, but the motion of the exercise caused his hands to ease into relaxation.

"Sir, Sheriff Douglas, you never answered me. What do you think about…"

"I'm still thinking about it," Douglas interrupted. The shaking seemed to have stopped, so he released the highlighter and let it fall onto the surface in front of him. The marker immediately started rolling and picking up speed, like it had a destination; it escaped his desk and hit the hardwood floor with a soft *ping*. The sheriff didn't bother retrieving it.

He contemplated, *what are my thoughts?* He had never been a part of anything like this before, an actual murder investigation. And now what? He was supposed to be in charge of one?

Sheriff Douglas knew that he was in a classic no-win situation, and the simple fact was more than obvious: someone was going to get pissed off. Either Jeff Sullivan for the intrusive search into his deceased wife's life, or Ben Andrews because he didn't answer the well-trained, clever deputy's request.

Decisions, decisions, the sheriff thought. What a great time it was to be the leader of the pack.

But ultimately, Sheriff Douglas knew what was the right thing to do. Or he knew what *he* wanted to do, at least.

"Kim Sullivan is already dead," he repeated. "There's nothing we can do now for her or her family, except solve her murder."

"I agree," Ben said.

"But we're not going to solve her murder by digging through her dirty laundry. That's assuming that she even has or *had* any," the sheriff continued. "Now, kid, I know that you're new here and haven't really familiarized yourself with the community or people in it, but know this: residents of Gray's Lane don't do bad things, and therefore, aren't involved in bad things."

"Sir, no offense, but that statement seems a little…"

Douglas put up both of his hands palms out; he wasn't interested in the deputy's protest. He even managed to overlook the sudden appearance of Ben's sullen eyes and deep frown.

"No," he went on. "I'm going to go out on a limb and say that Kim Sullivan was chosen at random. Going through her past and personals will only be a huge waste of time and an invasion of privacy."

Not to mention, the sheriff thought, what would the residents of Gray's Lane actually think if he started going through people's lives with a fine-toothed comb? He had a murder to solve, yes, but wasn't it at all possible to keep his reputation intact while solving it? He'd worked so damn hard to get where he was in his career. The last thing he wanted to do was get booed out of the department. *His* department.

"Think about it, Deputy Andrews," the sheriff started again. "You were at the funeral this morning. Did you happen to notice anything suspicious? Anything solid that might make you believe the killer had a personal vendetta against Kimberly Sullivan?"

"Well, no," Ben admitted. "Nothing or no one appeared to be out of the ordinary. And because of the candy corn, I still believe that we are dealing with a potential serial killer. But what if this person has a certain type, or a grudge against specific women? By looking into the first victim, and right now *only* victim, we might…"

"You've used the words 'might' and 'if' an awfully lot today, Andrews." The sheriff folded his hands together and placed them on top of his desk. He looked down and made a quick mental note: it was time to get organized. Past time, even. Maybe he would be respected more, *appreciated* more, if he presented himself and his office in a more coherent, articulate manner.

Different sizes and shapes of papers flooded his working area, papers that dated back from who knew when. Pens that had long ago run out of ink, a variety of faded business cards, and random phone messages that had more than likely gone unreturned all added to the clutter.

And that smell, the sheriff thought, taking a nonchalant whiff of the stuffy atmosphere that surrounded him. Something had to be done about the stench of soggy socks and burnt tomato soup.

Yes, Sheriff Douglas determined, something had to be done about his working environment. Especially considering that he might now actually brave retirement, he wanted to go out with a *bang!*

"Now, who we need to be focusing on is the killer. We need to put all of our effort and attention on the one responsible for the murder. That is the only way to stop another one from taking place."

"But we don't have any leads," Ben argued. "There are no suspects, not even evidence that could possibly point to a potential suspect. There's Jeff Sullivan, but…"

"I've already told you," Douglas shouted, bringing his voice to a pitch that was usually reserved for traffic violators and punks that liked to start bar fights, "Jeff Sullivan is one hundred percent innocent of the crime. His alibi *thoroughly* checked out; he didn't murder his wife."

"He could have hired someone to do it."

"Excuse me?"

"Now, this is just a theory," Ben started, "but what if for some unknown reason Jeff wanted his wife dead? Money problems, an affair, not enough home-cooked meals — I don't know the specifics. But today, he seemed on edge at the funeral, and even walked out of the church when…"

"His wife was just murdered!" Douglas exploded. "He laid her to rest today; he had to say goodbye. Of course he was on edge!"

"But…"

"No," the sheriff said and waved his hands for a stern emphasis. "No! There is no indication to believe anything you just said. And I'm not going to let you go digging into Jeff's background either so that you can fuel this so-called *theory* of yours."

"It could be possible that…"

"Then how does the candy corn fit in? Huh? This is the work of a potential serial killer, not an angry, jealous spouse. Kim Sullivan was chosen at random. Find a new angle!" And then, simply for good measure, the sheriff decided to add: "This is Gray's Lane, Ohio; we don't have murderers for hire here."

"Well, there are no other angles to work, sir. Not until the killer strikes again and another woman is found stabbed to death."

"You bite your tongue, son!" The sheriff's temperature hit the danger zone and he rapidly rose from his chair. He felt his thick hands clench into fists, and for a split second thought about diving over the barrier that separated him from the deputy.

He took a deep breath. Douglas knew that he had to get a grip, get himself under control. But for a slight moment, he'd seen the hot, fiery color of red. And now, as a result, his entire body was fuming.

Just who in the hell did this Benjamin Andrews think he was?

"I didn't mean any disrespect, Sheriff. I was only trying to convey that without another victim, it's virtually impossible to…"

"Shut up! Just shut the hell up!"

"Sir?"

"You come into this town not knowing anyone, wanting to accuse and probe and pass judgment. You may be able to detach yourself from the residents here, but I can't. These people are my family, my friends, and I'll be damned if…"

"Sheriff Douglas?"

"What?" he roared. His cheeks stung uncontrollably. And it was no longer just his hands that were shaking this time, but his entire body. His head rattled around as if he were a Hawaiian girl on a dashboard.

"Is this a bad time?"

It took Douglas a moment to realize that it hadn't been Ben that had interrupted him, but someone at the door: Deputy Hall. Hall stood slumped over, looking both confused and guilty, as if he had just wet himself.

"What is it?" the sheriff asked, lowering his voice and his body back down into his leather seat.

"Someone is here to see you. They said it's pretty urgent."

"Who is it?" the sheriff asked. He could feel his interest beginning to peak.

"Mary Evans," Deputy Hall answered. "Should I send her in?"

"What?" Douglas was back on his feet again. He felt his jaw drop dangerously open; he crossed his arms over his heaving chest. "She's here? That no good, nose in the air, trouble-seeking woman is actually in *my* building? Again?"

"Yes," Hall answered. "She's standing right outside your office, over in the lobby."

Douglas turned and saw Andrews follow suite. What a surprise, the sheriff thought, the woman hadn't even been in the building for a whole five minutes and was already making a spectacle.

"*That's* Mary Evans?" Ben asked. "She's a reporter?"

"Yes," Douglas answered. He never once took his eyes off of her, or the inappropriately tight brown pantsuit she was wearing. "And she's the worst kind. Mary was poking around here yesterday; you must have missed her. I sent a deputy to get rid of her, but I see that today I will have to do the job myself."

"Do you want me to…"

"No, Hall, *I'll* take care of it." Douglas edged around the corner of his desk. He barely avoided bumping into the piece of furniture. He stopped to the left of Ben and put a hand on the deputy's shoulder. "Now that you've seen her and know exactly who she is, I'm advising that you to stay away from Mary Evans. She is nothing but a problem, a thorn in the department's side that will only get in the way of our murder investigation."

"Will do, sir."

"Good," the sheriff nodded. "Now, if you'll excuse me, I need to go throw that bitch out on her ass."

NINE

"WHO DOES THAT BASTARD THINK HE IS? Escorting me out of the building like that? Like I'm some common criminal or something. I have rights, dammit! I'm a respected journalist!"

"Okay, Mary. If you say so."

"And you!" She quickly turned on her heel, extended her long index finger, and pointed it directly at him. "You have no right to say anything! You're still wearing that stupid hat, after I specifically…"

"Well, you're still a raging bitch on wheels," Henry said through a smile. "I guess we're even."

"You should have had my back," Mary continued. She was on a roll now, gaining speed, and refusing to slow down. Though she would have much more enjoyed giving that ridiculous Sheriff Douglas a piece of her mind, unfortunately, he had the power to throw her into a dark jail cell. So she'd had to look elsewhere, find someone else to unwind on. And that someone was Henry Wren.

"Look, Mary," Henry began. "I'm not sure…"

"That's right," she agreed with a nod. Her long hair was styled in a messy bun and sat on top of her head; she could feel it slowly bobbing back and forth. "You're not sure of anything! If you would have joined me down at the police station today, then…"

"Then what?" Henry prompted. "I could have distracted Sheriff Douglas while you secretly ransacked his office? Fat chance, Mary."

"You were supposed to be…"

"Here!" he interrupted her. "I was supposed to be here, and I have been here. I've been waiting for you for the past forty-five minutes while you were off playing some second-rate version of Barbara Walters."

The comment stopped her in her tracks. It even stung a little bit.

Mary quit pacing the distance of her office and fell into her favorite chair that occupied the far corner. She let out a deep sigh; her face melted down into both of her hands. Her mind started racing.

Henry Wren was right. Of course, Mary would never admit the fact in a hundred years. A hundred and one, even. In fact, she decided as she lowered her hands and frustratingly shoved them into the pockets of her pantsuit, her wide eyes falling on the framed poster of New York City that hung on the otherwise naked wall behind her desk: she'd much rather prefer to eat the picture of busy Time Square than admit that she'd been wrong.

But she had been wrong. She remembered quite clearly now that she had made plans to meet Henry in her office this morning. Going to the Gray's Lane Police Department had just been a whim, an afterthought.

"What's wrong, Mary?" Henry asked. "Don't tell me you actually have a heart? Did I *really* hurt your feelings?"

"Please," she frowned. She glared over at him as if he had just lapsed into French. "Mary Evans doesn't have feelings. Feelings are for the weak. I'm just frustrated, okay?" Not a complete lie; she most certainly *was* on edge. But more importantly, she was in dire need of a subject change. Henry Wren couldn't discover that he'd been right; she'd rather die.

"Why are you so frustrated?" he asked.

In no way, shape, or form did Mary appreciate his patronizing tone. In fact, it made her want to stand up, fly to the other side of the room at lightening speed, and smack him across his unshaven face. She had a longing urge to rip the navy hat off of his head, tear it to shreds, and burn what remained. Mary wanted to kick him, bite him, stick her sharp and thick claws into the skin of his back until he bled and admitted that she was the boss and superior to him.

But at least he'd fallen for her clever ruse; they were finally on to talking about something else.

"Nothing's happening with this story," she confessed. She crossed one toned leg over the other and placed her hands in her lap.

Maybe a long run on the treadmill at the local gym would help to ease her irritation — or perhaps a roll in the hay with some random guy that she wouldn't have to worry about calling the next day. A "fuck and duck," she often called the task. And out of the two workouts, Mary knew all to well how she preferred to work up a sweat.

"What do you mean?"

She rolled her eyes. Was he really so dense to ask such a question? How had she gotten stuck with such an idiot? That's right, she quickly reminded herself, Henry had been the only one to apply for the job.

Mary made a side note to start taking time to work on her attitude and the way she presented herself. Then, maybe she'd attract better people. But sometimes, she knew, it was just too damn difficult to mask the bitch that was within her.

Mary stood, suddenly tired of sitting. Her hands were back on her hips, and she was pacing again. As her tan stilettos glided across the smooth hardwood floor, she never once took her gaze off of Henry.

He was sitting, of course, in a relaxed, comfortable position. He clearly didn't have one care in the world, slumped down in his chair with his muscular legs spread ever so slightly apart.

Mary had to remind herself that he was completely off limits. Therefore, instead of thinking about just how strong his legs actually were, she had to find something about Henry Wren that drove her completely insane. Problem solved.

Mary casually took in his choice of clothing. Not that he would ever be in front of the camera and needed to wear a three piece suit, but she couldn't help but believe that Henry still could have dressed a little more appropriately. With his wrinkled jeans and a sweatshirt that was stained and torn in a few spots, he appeared to be more of a bum than a man with a job.

"Are you going to answer my question or play the staring game all day?"

"I didn't answer your question because it was stupid, Henry." She stopped moving once again, and leaned up against the edge of her wooden desk. Mary had to find a new focus point, because even with all of Henry's flaws and minor disadvantages, he still possessed one big advantage: he was hot. Great body, unpolished face, and that dark attitude that made her want to savagely rip out every strand of hair on her own head.

Mary suddenly found herself looking down at the ground; she was craving a cigarette. She could smell, even *feel* the smoldering sweetness of nicotine somewhere far off in the air.

But she effortlessly managed to fight the urge and win the battle. After all, there was absolutely nothing sexy about a woman with yellow teeth and matching fingertips. No thank you, she thought. Especially not when part of her job, the most *important* part of her job, was to always be ready and looking good for the camera.

"I can't report anything if there's nothing new to report," she said, finally acknowledging Henry's question. "I need…"

"Someone else to be found murdered?"

"Yes," she said, too quickly. On instinct, she threw her right hand over her mouth and waited a minute. "I didn't mean that, not in such a cold-hearted way, anyway."

"Sure you did," Henry argued and crossed his arms over his chest. "You most certainly did mean what you said, because all you care about is yourself. Not anyone else in this lame, behind-the-times town; it's all about you. You, you, *you!*"

"Just knock it off, Henry!" she ordered. "You're holier than thou demeanor is getting pretty old."

"Maybe you're the killer," Henry continued. "Maybe you killed Kim Sullivan."

"Excuse me?" Mary felt her eyebrows shoot up from the blast of Henry's statement. She started to lean back, but then hastily recalling that nothing was behind her, held herself up to stop the fall. "You think I'm a murderer?" She clutched at her chest as if she had just been accused of something as preposterous as wearing white after Labor Day.

"Why not?" Henry pushed on. "You've definitely got the rage to be one."

"Rage?" Mary repeated. "So now I'm a psychopath?"

"Yes, you've got the means to stab another woman to death. And most certainly the motive."

Mary felt herself frown, and immediately tried to lose the gesture; she feared frown lines. But she was still so confused.

"What possible motive could I have had for killing Kimberly Sullivan?"

"Not Sullivan specifically," he corrected, "but anyone. Think about it: you're the only person in Gray's Lane that could possibly prosper by a crime like this. By committing murder, you are literally creating news. Huge news! You're keeping yourself relevant with the biggest story this town has ever seen."

"That doesn't make any sense," she said and shook her head.

"Why not?" Henry asked and then shrugged.

"Okay, okay," she said and balled her hands into fists. She attempted to get on his page. "I'm cruel and selfish and determined. I would do anything to make a name for myself. But do you honestly believe that includes taking an innocent life? Am I really *that* person? Am I that evil?"

"Fuckin' A you are," Henry said without any hesitation.

"No, no," she said. She jumped down from her desk and started for the other side of it. Her body was now stiff, and she was predicting an upcoming headache; she needed the comfort of her leather chair. "Like I said, that doesn't make any sense."

"But you haven't told me why it doesn't," he persisted like a bad flu virus.

"Because Kim was murdered on Saturday; it's now Tuesday. If I were the killer, I would have already murdered someone else to create more drama and add another story."

"Wow!" Henry said. He provided a slow smirk that seemed to painfully screech, "I told you so."

"Wipe that look off your face!" Mary ordered. "I'm capable of a lot of things, but murder isn't one of them, okay? There is no way in hell that I could have snuck into the Sullivan home, stabbed Kim to death, and then scattered her body with pieces of candy corn. Surprisingly, I don't have the stomach to do something like that."

"What did you just say?"

"I don't have the stomach to do something like that," she repeated. "Jesus, Henry. Get your dick our of your ear!"

"No, no," he said, clearly choosing to ignore her cheap insult. "The part about the candy corn. What was that again?"

She felt her entire body and face suddenly go numb. For a split second, her mind went blank;

she had to remind herself where she was and what had just happened.

"Mary, silence isn't going to help distract me," Henry said. He rose, walked to her desk, and placed both firm firsts onto it. "Talk," he ordered. "So far, there has been no mention of candy corn. Anywhere. Not even from you. What does candy corn have to do with the case? How did you find out about it? And dammit, why haven't you reported it in the newspaper yet?"

"Stop with all of your questions, Henry," she ordered. "I'm not on trial."

"Maybe you should be."

Mary wasn't sure what to say to that. She flung herself into her chair and closed her eyes. Suddenly, it was a struggle to hold her head steady. She leaned back, hoping he would just go away—Henry, that was. Mary wanted Henry Wren to disappear.

Her mind began turning, wondering, trying to greedily clutch at something, anything that might change the subject yet again and provoke Henry to focus his attention elsewhere. But she ultimately knew that she wasn't going to get that lucky. Not twice in one day, anyway.

"I can and will sit here all day," Henry said in a low, monotone voice, breaking the sticky silence. "Just tell me how…"

"Stop!" Mary screamed. She quickly brought up both of her hands and cupped them over her ears as if she was a little girl attempting to ignore the school bully. She couldn't stand to listen to him anymore; she assumed that it was as painful as listening to a cat being strangled. Maybe even worse, she considered.

There was going to be no easy way out of this; she was going to have to come to terms with that. Mary knew that she would have to reveal to Henry what she had come to discover, and then swear the man to secrecy. Or, better yet, *threaten* him to secrecy — whichever would be more affective.

"I'll tell you what I know," she said, ultimately deciding to give in to him. She lowered her hands, tightly placed them in her lap, and stared across at Henry. She gave him a long, "I hate you" type glare.

"And who you got it from?" he asked.

"Get real," she said through a throaty laugh. "The last thing I'm going to do is reveal my source. Especially to you."

He sighed. "But I want to know it all. I want to know where this information came from and how you got it. We're a team."

"Eat shit and die," she muttered, never once blinking. "You only want to be a 'team' because I now know more than you. We're still in the middle of a bet, remember? No one has won yet."

"Touché," Henry said. "So, are you going to share this tidbit? Or are you selfishly going to keep the information all to yourself?"

"I'll spill my guts," she answered. "Well, partly. I'll share some of what I know with you, but only because I accidentally slipped earlier. You got lucky, Wren."

"Yes, I did," he agreed. "This morning, before work." He winked. "Now, what is it that you know?"

"You're a pig!"

"And you're a whore. I thought we were revealing *new* information."

"Fine, fine," Mary said. She threw up her hands; the gesture was supposed to offer some sort of truce. "The killer stabbed Kim Sullivan to death and then scattered her body with candy corn."

"So you said."

"That's pretty much it," she said coldly. "It's believed that the candy pieces are the killer's calling card, his signature. And since he signed the body, he's most likely going to kill again."

"Lame."

"Excuse me?" Mary asked.

"That is lame," Henry repeated, "and a sorry excuse to believe that another body is going to turn up. The killer decorates his victims with Halloween candy? Give me a break."

"Well, it's all I have right now," she confessed in a somewhat weaker tone. Though Mary wanted to defend the new information she had, now that she'd heard herself speak it aloud, she wasn't one hundred percent sure if it was worth the trouble.

"Then why haven't you reported it?"

"Because I'm waiting," she answered.

"Waiting for what?"

"Another murder," she said casually. "I need to make sure the candy theory pans out before I go live with it. Therefore, I need the killer to strike again. You want me to say it, Henry? Fine, I'll say it: I need another body to turn up."

"And what are your personal beliefs?" he asked. "Do you think this all makes sense? Do you honestly think there will be more murders? All because of candy corn?"

Mary waited a beat, and then finally answered. "I hope so. Not only will I have a new angle to the story, but you'll owe me a hundred bucks!"

TEN

WHY WAS SHERIFF DOUGLAS FIGHTING HIM on this? Did the man actually have a valid point? Was Kimberly Sullivan chosen at random by the killer? Was that the type of situation the Gray's Lane Police Department was dealing with?

Ben found himself in the same position he'd been in the other night: sitting alone, drinking yet another cheap, canned beer, and contemplating the case. The deputy knew that most murders were usually resolved within the first forty-eight hours of having been committed, if they were ever resolved at all. Therefore, he was already working at a disadvantage; he hadn't been given the facts of this crime until after the initial forty-eight hours. And now, they were closing in on seventy-two.

So now what? Ben considered. What would need to happen in order for the murderer to be caught? A lucky break? The reveal of some sort of clue or missed evidence? Another body to turn up?

If the sheriff's theory panned out, if a potential serial killer was currently active in Gray's Lane, Ben knew that it was only a short matter of time before another body *did* turn up. But who, when, and where were all questions that Deputy Andrews didn't presently have answers to.

Ben leaned back into the rough surface of the corduroy-like material that covered the chair, and slowly stretched out his bare feet. He couldn't remember the last time he had actually drank two nights in a row. Maybe college? But truthfully, he re-evaluated, probably not even then. He instantly feared an aggressive alcohol problem approaching him — or worse, a future beer belly.

But there was really nothing else to do in this town, no other way to unwind. So Ben justified his actions. And for the first time, he'd realized that if he consumed enough beer, then his body would finally settle into a sort of tranquil ease. And, if he were lucky, his mind would sometimes even take a vacation, too, allowing him to forget the past. Even for just a little bit of time.

Ben closed his eyes; he couldn't think about the case anymore. Not tonight. Actually, there was nothing else to even remotely think about tonight. He had dwelled over the Sullivan murder long enough. And, as a result, he'd exhausted all of the available information.

So what if the woman had been stabbed four times? How could that little fact help catch the killer? So what if the angle of the wounds had proven that the killer was right handed? Were Ben and the Sheriff going to go door-to-door in the neighborhood and question everyone that was right-hand dominant? He didn't think so.

In reality, Ben knew what needed to happen in order for there to be a break in the investigation. And though he had already considered the idea, he absolutely refused to say it out loud — again. It would be impractical for a police deputy in a new town to have such thoughts.

Bottom line: there was nothing else that could be done at the moment, and Ben needed to stop obsessing.

He set the half empty beer can on the end table to his right; the beverage had lost its coolness and was no longer appealing. He stretched his long arms over his head and released a thin yawn. Ben laced his thin fingers together to form a tight wall, and then placed them at the back of his skull. He inhaled deeply. He wanted to find a happy place. But the atmosphere around him was filled with a thick sour stench of booze, and a heavy bile began rising in his throat. For a moment, Ben thought he might be sick.

But after a few seconds, the feeling subsided.

Ben released a shallow breath. A soft moment of peace washed over him, and he tried to lavish in it for as long as possible. He knew that the opportunity didn't present itself too often. And when it did, it never lasted.

This time was no different. A thought quickly burst into Ben's aching head and stung, almost as if he'd been pricked with a sharp thorn. He found himself leaning upright, no longer reclining, as several questions began flooding his *already* cramped mind.

For the first time, Ben abruptly wondered about Sheriff Douglas and what the man did when he left the station? Did he have a family? Friends? A poker club?

But the head honcho wasn't the only one that Ben became concerned with; he also couldn't help but think about Deputy Hall—a man who, Ben had decided quite quickly, seemed like a weasel—and the rest of the Gray's Lane Police Department.

Were the other men and women in uniform able to shut out the crime once they left the office for the day? Or did Kimberly Sullivan's murder affect them like it did him? Was it an everlasting shadow that hovered and haunted, refusing to disappear.

Surely, Ben assumed, he wasn't the only one that was constantly tormented by the woman's grisly death. After all, if he'd heard the comment once, he'd heard it a hundred times: this was Gray's Lane's first murder—ever! Therefore, Ben knew that Sheriff Douglas, Deputy Hall, and everyone else who carried a badge had to also have stress levels that were dangerously close to reaching their peak.

Actually, Ben contemplated, others in the department were probably worse off than him.

Gray's Lane wasn't his hometown; he'd only been a resident for a few days.

"Why am I infatuated with this case *so* damn much?" Ben asked aloud.

Though he was positive that he already knew the answer to his question, he tried not focus on it. In fact, he attempted to flat out avoid it.

He searched deeply for something else, *any-thing* else, to center on. But his efforts, like most other times, were ultimately useless. Ben just couldn't steer clear of the main issue at hand: his mother.

He closed his eyes, and as if on cue, an image of a woman quickly overcame him. Ben saw his mom as if the woman was sitting right next to him. She'd always been so beautiful—petite, dark hair, warm and comforting smile.

In reality, it had been years since he'd actually seen his mom. But at the moment, she appeared to look the same as he'd always remembered. And in his mind, she was even wearing the exact outfit she'd been wearing the last day he'd seen her: black dress pants, a crisp button-down blue shirt, and basic heels to match. Her hair had been pulled back out of her face, and she'd hardly been wearing any make up.

Everything about that last day was still so fresh in his mind, as if it were happening all over again, right now, at this precise moment. Ben didn't want to relive the past, not again. But at the same time, he was frantically drawn to it, and didn't possess enough strength to look away. Even the last bit of conversation he'd shared with his mother was stuck to him, as if the pieces had permanently been glued to him.

"We're still on for dinner, right?" she'd asked from the kitchen, propped up against the laminate countertop, finishing the last of her coffee.

"Yes, but I can't meet until after seven. Will that work?" He recalled casually answering her, only half paying attention, concentrating on his search for his hat.

"That will be great," she'd replied. "Antonio's? Or do you want to try something different?"

"Nope, Antonio's sounds good. I've been craving Italian lately."

"Will you have time to change, or will you be coming in uniform?"

He remembered sighing, showing a noticeable degree of annoyance that he now genuinely regretted. But it had always been the same with her, ever since he'd become a cop. His mother's opinion had always remained constant: she wanted him to separate his work life from his personal one. "A balancing act" was what she'd often called it. It had always been her opinion that life was way too short to be completely consumed by a job. Therefore, she'd continuously check-in to make sure that his life wasn't entirely devoted to crime.

"Yes, mom," he'd answered heatedly. "I will change before dinner. I know how much you hate seeing me in uniform."

"It's not that I *hate* seeing you in uniform, Ben," she'd protested. "I just don't want you to continuously be in that dark place, solving murders and being surrounded by bad people. I want you to be able to shut off that part of your life every once in a while."

"I can't shut off who I am, Mom. I chose to be a cop; this is my career."

"I understand that, honey, and I'm very proud of you. But it's not healthy to always have crime on the brain."

"Mom, I don't *always* have crime on the brain. I do other things; I have a life. I fish, I hunt, I spend time with friends."

"*Cop* friends," she'd corrected. "If you're happy, that's all that matters. I just don't want you to wake up one day and find that you're whole life has been dedicated to death."

"Don't worry so much, Mom; I like my life. And despite what you may think, it's not dedicated to death or crime or anything specific, really. I'm happy."

And then the conversation had ended. She'd left the house to run a long list of errands before dinner — post office, bank, dry cleaners, grocery — and he'd gone to the station until time to meet at the restaurant. But seven o'clock had quickly rolled around, and then seven thirty, and she still hadn't shown up, creating a bit of aggravation to course throughout him.

Ben had taken the time to change into jeans, a white collard shirt, and dress boots. And when his mother was officially forty-five minutes late, he had no longer found himself irritated, but severely worried. He'd decided then to do something about it.

First, he'd tried her cell one more time. He hadn't expected her to answer it, though, and she hadn't. It was common for his mother to forget the device at the house. And on the rare occasion that she did have it with her, it was usually turned off or uncharged.

Ben had left a short, frantic message saying that he was very concerned and that she was to call him back right away. Despite the stares and constant bickering from the waitress, he'd decided to wait at the restaurant and sit alone in the red leather booth until he heard back from his mom.

And almost instantly after leaving the alarmed voicemail, his phone had vibrated. He'd hastily reached for it, not bothering to look at the caller ID, answered it, and shouted, "Mom?" into the mouthpiece.

"Ben? Ben, it's Eric."

"Oh, sorry, Eric. I thought you might be my mom calling." Eric was a friend, a *cop* friend, Ben had promptly thought with a half smile. However, the gesture had soon faded; Ben had just seen Eric at the station less than an hour and a half ago. So what did the co-worker want? Why had he phoned?

"Ben, where are you?"

"Eric, what's going on? Is everything okay?"

But the other officer had never answered. Instead, he'd only repeated his question. "Ben, where are you?"

"I'm at Antonio's. I'm waiting on my mom; we're having dinner."

"Okay. Don't leave, Ben. I will be there in ten minutes."

"You're coming here?" Ben had asked, the heavy feeling of confusion almost suffocating him. "What? Why? Eric, has something happened? Is it my mother?"

"Just sit tight, Ben. I'll be there soon."

He hadn't had time to respond; Eric had ended the call, leaving Ben only more baffled. And suddenly, a sour discomfort had formed all around Ben, flooding him, making it difficult for him to breathe.

The wide table in front of him had acted like a barrier, trapping him, keeping him locked in place. He hadn't been able to move; the air around him became stifling, and he remembered sweating. All he had been able to do was sit achingly still in the abruptly quiet restaurant and wait for Eric to arrive.

The ten-minute wait had only been about seven, but to Ben it had felt like an eternity. He'd grown antsy, impatient, and had even begun the annoying procedure of drumming his smooth fingertips across the surface of the off-white tablecloth.

And when Ben had first spotted Eric come into the dining area, he had tried to stand. However, he hadn't accounted for his legs feeling like two massive bottles filled to the brim with sand. He'd wobbled, lost his footing, and fell back into the sleek cushion of the booth, causing the silverware to fall to the floor with a sharp *cling*.

"Are you alright?" Eric had rushed to the table and taken a fast seat across from Ben. "Maybe I should get you some water."

"Just tell me what's going on," Ben had ordered. "Is it my mother?"

"Please, let me get you some…"

"I don't want any damn water, Eric. Water won't make this situation any better. Just tell me what in the hell has happened. I *want* to know."

"Ben…" a long pause had been immediately followed by a heavy sigh, and Ben had instantly expected the worse. "There was an incident."

"What kind of incident? Is my mother — is she…" he hadn't been able to finish the thought. He clearly recalled the goosebumps that had rapidly invaded every inch of him, beginning at the base of his legs and gradually moving upwards.

"She was murdered."

"E-E-Excuse me?" Ben hadn't believed that he'd heard Eric correctly. *Murdered?* It didn't make any sense. A car accident? Yes. A fatal heart attack? Perhaps. But there was absolutely no way that she could have been murdered.

"She was found in her car a little over an hour ago. The first cop on the scene identified her. Her purse was missing, so it appears that robbery was the motive."

"How?"

"Ben, it doesn't matter…"

"It matters to me. How?" He knew he had repeated the word, but he'd also been aware that his voice had changed. It had gotten dimmer, jagged, and he hadn't recognized it as the question had fallen out.

"She was shot at close range — twice. She didn't suffer."

It had been as if he'd been repeatedly kicked in the stomach. The gut-wrenching pain of loss had quickly overtaken him, causing him to shake and then double over, believing that at any moment he might get sick.

"That's why I'm infatuated so damn much," Ben said aloud, finally coming out of his reverie. And just under the wire, he contemplated, realizing that he had mentally stepped away from his own, tragic past just before the warm, flowing sensation of tears had had time to assault him.

He put pressure on the footrest of the recliner, pressed backwards, and snapped the piece into place. Ben stood, balanced his weight on his tiptoes, reached his arms high over his head, and stretched upward. The motion was difficult to perform and he couldn't stay in the position for too long. His body felt extremely tense and rigid.

Ben knew exactly what he needed.

The tender parallel that had easily formed between his mother's never solved murder and the unexplained killing that had recently taken place in Gray's Lane had him craving something dangerous.

Ben reached into the deep pocket of his pants, grasped hold of the key ring, and started for the front door. He didn't mind that what he was about to do was morally, ethically, and practically illegal. Not when it felt so damn good.

ELEVEN

"ELLE, COME INTO THE KITCHEN. THERE'S someone here I want you to meet."

She hadn't even had time to close the front door. Elle sat her bag down onto the blue tile flooring that decorated the entrance of the house and called out, "I'll be right there."

She took a deep breath, crossed her arms over her chest, and began gearing up for the big introduction. A wave of heat started weaving through her body. It developed at her face, causing her to feel flushed. She raised one of her hands to caress the right side of her cheek — hot to the touch.

She knew this day was coming, had even been expecting it. But now? Tonight? At this particular moment? Elle couldn't help but believe that her father had horrible timing.

Elle considered making a run for it, going up the stairs, locking herself in her bedroom, and faking sick. She wasn't exactly dreading the encounter like a trip to the dentist. But at the same time, she wasn't looking forward to it like unwrapping gifts on Christmas morning either.

"Elle, what's taking so long? Your dinner is getting cold."

"Coming." So now she wasn't only meeting her father's girlfriend, but sharing a meal with the woman, too.

What the hell? Better to get this done and over with versus dragging it out like some long, melo-dramatic soap opera.

Elle shoved her hands down into the pockets of her jeans, and started for the kitchen. She moved as slowly as possible across the carpet, tiptoeing almost, as she walked through the overstuffed living room, rounded the corner of the hallway, and stepped into the kitchen.

Elle instantly sensed a frown forming on her confused face. Was this some sort of joke? A prank? There was absolutely no way that this was the woman her father was cur-rently dating.

"Elle, have a seat." Her father gestured to the empty bar stool at the far left of the counter. There was a matching plate and glass sitting in front of it.

"Okay," she said. She quickly tried to replace the frown with a smile, but assumed the gesture had undoubtedly come off awkward, perhaps even a little forced.

"Elle, I'd like you to meet…"

"Mrs. Jacobs," she finished for her father. "Wait, I'm sorry. I guess that's *Ms.* Jacobs."

"Please," the woman said through a dull laugh, "call me Elaine. Well, when we're not at school, anyway."

Elle had only seen the other woman hours ago, wearing the same khaki pants and bright orange ruffled sweater. Her blonde hair was still down, with a few curls framing her attractive, made-up face. The only differences that appeared now, Elle decided, were the half empty wine glass in Elaine's right hand and her bare feet crossed neatly at the ankles. Elle clearly remembered that when she'd seen Elaine earlier, the woman had been clicking down the hallway in brown heels.

"I didn't realize you knew Elaine," John said, breaking the silence.

"Sure," Elle nodded. She jumped up onto the wooden stool and crossed one leg over the other. "She's your secretary."

"Well, she's not *my* secretary," John argued and reached for his own wine glass that was filled with red wine. "She's the high school's secretary."

"Sorry," Elle said. She grabbed her fork and stabbed it into what looked like overcooked tuna noodle casserole. "I know she sits outside of your office, so…"

"It's fine," Elaine offered. "You know, a lot of people actually make the same mistake."

"Do you know Elaine's daughter, then? Emily?"

Elle slowly chewed the dried bite of food, and immediately washed it down with a long gulp of ice water. "Emily Jacobs?" she asked once her throat became clear. "That sounds familiar, but I don't think we've actually met."

"She's a cheerleader," Elaine informed.

"Oh, okay," Elle said. She looked up past her father and over to Elaine. The woman had produced a wide smile; she was obviously very proud of her daughter. "Maybe that's how I've heard of her."

"I'm sure you've seen her at school," Elaine pressed on. "She's got long blonde hair, just like mine. Hers is blonder though, and she usually wears it in braids. Emily is tan and thin. And of course, she's always in her uniform on Fridays."

Elle busied herself with the task of placing more casserole onto her dinner fork. She couldn't help but notice that Elaine was in a dangerous territory. The woman was at a cross-roads where she could either veer down the slightly bragging mother path, or the over zealous, in your face, my daughter is better than you path. And right now, Elle thought Elaine's red painted toenail was on the thin line between the two.

"I'm sure I've seen her around," Elle said. She put her fork down, not bothering to eat what was on it, and transferred her gaze to her plate. "I don't think we have any classes together, though."

"Well, she wanted to be here tonight," Elaine filled in, "but she had a last minute practice."

126

"Getting ready for a big game?" Elle asked. She tried with half power strength to sound interested, but knew that with the lack of emotion and avoidance of eye contact that her question had arrived in the form of tedious small talk.

"Yes, there's a game this Friday."

"Sorry that the casserole's a little off; I had to reheat it," John said in an attempt, Elle was almost positive, to change the subject. "I thought you would have been home sooner than seven-thirty."

"Right. Sorry." She didn't bother looking up at her father, trying to ultimately avoid his gaze, too. Elle was all too familiar with that sharp, straightforward tone. She knew he was upset, that was obvious. But she wasn't sure how to clear herself from the situation.

"So, where have you been?"

She decided to go with half truth and half embellishment. She said, "I was at the library."

"The public library?"

"Yes, the public library." Elle didn't expect her father to call and check to make sure that she was telling the truth. However, she knew that if he surprisingly did make the call, she would be in the clear; she really had been at the public library."

"Why didn't you answer your phone? I tried getting a hold of you to tell you about dinner."

"I left my phone in the car; I was working on a project."

Time for the lie, Elle decided. She made a quick mental note to leave her hands stationary on the counter in front of her. Everyone had a 'tell' when it came to bluffing the truth, she knew. Hers was biting her fingernails.

She had been at the library, and she had been assigned a project that she needed to be working on. But in reality, Elle had just wanted to avoid seeing and talking to her father. She wasn't sure she was completely over the previous evening's conversation.

But the plan had backfired, Elle discovered, and now burned like thick, hot grease—because she wasn't only stuck now having dinner with her father, but with Elaine, too.

"Next time I would appreciate a call saying you're going to be late," John ordered.

Elle began shaking her head. She could feel her ponytail slightly sway against the back of her neck. To keep silent, she bit down on the inside of her cheek and abruptly tasted the metallic tang of blood.

Elle wanted to scream. An electrifying urge charged through her, causing her legs to shake and her hands to ball up into tightly wound fists.

She wanted to argue with her father, and explain that she wasn't a child. She was in high school and could be trusted. She didn't need a babysitter, or a curfew, or anything else that was equally ridiculous.

Elle desperately wanted to dispute his rash and demeaning tone, and inform her father that she was seventeen. And for the majority of those seventeen years, she had lived in the tough city of New York, and not some easy-peasy, paint-by-numbers town like Gray's Lane.

Ultimately, she kept quiet. Assessing everything she'd already learned in her short life, at the top of the list sat the fact that there was a time and place for everything. And at the moment, she knew, during dinner and in front of company was not the time or place for a battle with her father.

"Well, I commend you for taking time outside of class to work on projects," Elaine spoke up. "Emily is always finishing things at the last minute, and as a result, constantly pulling all-nighters.

And just like that, Elle's opinion of Elaine sporadically changed. Elle almost got whiplash as she turned to stare at the other woman. Elaine had a genuine smile spread across her face that seemed to say: "I understand." Elle greatly appreciated the gesture. Not only had the woman tried to smooth out the edges of the heated conversation, but she had also come down from her proud parent soapbox and shared one of Emily's faults.

Maybe she's not so bad after all, Elle thought, beginning to reconsider her former opinion of her father's new girlfriend.

"Elaine, would you like some more wine?" John asked and shifted around to face her.

"Yes, I would," she answered, and then tossed the little bit of liquid that was left in her glass down her throat. "Thank you."

Elle watched both of them closely, from her father's structured walk into the kitchen and toward the refrigerator to retrieve the dark bottle, to Elaine as she'd gulped down the last of her wine and now hungrily waited for more. Elle couldn't quite explain it, but the two appeared to somehow be in sync. She was almost jealous.

But time was the factoring variable, Elle knew. She'd been living with her father for almost a month, and it would take time for the two of them to become accustomed to each other.

But that time was not now. Bonding time with her father would have to happen later, Elle decided. She scooted her stool back and stood away from the counter. Right now she wanted to take advantage of the opportunity and escape what had been a less than perfect evening.

"Leaving so soon?" Elaine asked as she brought her now full wine glass up to her thin lips.

"Yes," Elle answered and then nodded. "I've got some more homework to finish up for tomorrow."

"Are you sure?" John asked. A sideways frown darted across his face. "I really didn't mean to run you off."

"You didn't," Elle said, protesting what seemed to be an actual sign of worry and regret from her father. "I just want to finish my work so I can get to bed early tonight."

"Okay, sweetie. But don't study too hard."

"It was very nice meeting you, Elle."

"Same to you, Elaine." And because in all actuality the woman hadn't been *that* bad and Elle really did want her father to be happy, she abruptly added, "I enjoyed talking to you." She then pivoted, turned from the kitchen, and started back toward the way she had originally entered the room.

Elle glided through the living room, past the tan leather sofa and oak end tables that became obstacles in her coarse, down the hallway, and stopped at the front door to retrieve her school-bag. She threw the weight over her shoulder and started up the stairs.

"She seems like a really nice girl."

Elle quickly stopped when she heard Elaine's voice. She knew it was extremely childish to eavesdrop, but at the same time, Elle wasn't strong enough to pull herself away from the temptation. So, as if trying to blend in with her surroundings, she stood achingly still and listened.

"Elle is a great girl," John's deep voice rang out and echoed all the way to the stairwell. "She's tough; she's been through a lot."

"I can't even imagine. The poor girl." Elaine's feminine, quiet voice was somewhat wine-stained.

"It's only been a month since she found her mother murdered. I'm actually very proud at how she's dealing with everything so far."

"John, she didn't just find her mother murdered, the woman was butchered! I'm surprised the girl isn't in a coma, or the very least, a padded room."

Elle felt her knees buckle, and immediately reached out for the wall to her right. She held on as tightly as possible, refusing to fall and cause a commotion.

She took a deep breath, wanting to find a calming, relaxing place. But she never did. Instead, the everlasting, sour taste of her dinner filled her mouth. And the bitter scent of the wine seemed to escape the kitchen, flow throughout the house, sneak up on Elle, and invade her inner space. Her stomach began doing somersaults, and she thought she was going to be sick.

Her father was nothing short of a hypocrite. How was it okay for him to freely talk about her past, but at the same time expect her to stay completely button-lipped about the whole encounter? Hadn't he just chastised her only yesterday for doing the exact same thing by reaching out to Niki? Elle suddenly became curious as to how her father was going to justify his actions.

There was absolutely no way that she could let this go ignored. But again, now wasn't the time or place to bring up the matter. She just wanted to be alone right now, and would save addressing her father's unfairness for another time. Perhaps in the morning.

Elle finished her journey up the stairs. With each step she took forward, she became more aware of the heaviness of her bag. She still felt weak, as if she'd been kicked, or more appropriately, stabbed in the back. The burning sensation of tears had already formed, but Elle tried to hold strong and block them from cascading down her face. The task was difficult; she struggled with it.

She reached the landing of the second floor, turned, and entered her room. Elle flipped the switch on the wall; a yellow flood filled the somewhat bare area. A dresser, bed, small nightstand, and cramped closet were all the furniture pieces that occupied her space.

Elle started across the carpet for the large dresser that sat against the far white wall of the room. She opened the top drawer, pulled out a gray t-shirt and pair of black shorts, and quickly changed. She then turned and squinted to see the clock that was sitting on the nightstand next to her bed. She made out the time and instantly decided that eight-thirty wasn't too late for a phone call. A quick scroll through her contacts, and then Elle hit Send.

"Hello?" Niki answered after the second ring.

"Hey, it's Elle. Are you busy?"

"No, just watching TV. What's up?"

Elle slowly sat down on the edge of her bed. She wanted to acknowledge the day's events, but she wasn't completely sure how to go about it.

"Elle, are you still there?"

"Yes," she cleared her throat. "Niki, I wanted to tell you how sorry I am for your loss. I wanted to be there today for you, but…"

"Thank you for saying that, Elle. I really appreciate it, but don't worry. I understand why you couldn't make it."

Elle placed her hand over the speaker of her cell and let out a heavy sigh of relief. The hard part of the conversation was over.

"How are you doing? Are you okay? Is there anything you need?"

"I'm doing fine," Niki answered. "I'm just really tired. I've been crying with family all day. I guess I'm managing."

"It gets easier," Elle said.

"Does it? Seriously?"

"No," Elle admitted. "But why be negative?"

Niki reacted to the comment in a way that Elle would have never guessed possible: her friend laughed. Niki released a loud, high-pitched giggle that filled Elle's ear through the device. And in return, Elle felt a small smile spread across her own face.

"Thank you for that."

"For what? I didn't do anything."

"For making me laugh," Niki said in a somewhat muffled voice. "I haven't laughed since, well,

I can't remember when. I guess your blunt answer brought it out of me."

Though Elle knew Niki couldn't see it, she still shrugged. "You asked. In all honesty, it doesn't get easier. But as time goes on, you don't think about it as much. It's only been a month for me, but..."

"Please, we've got to change the subject. I've been depressed all day; we've got to talk about something else."

"Are you sure?" Elle asked and then bit down onto her lower lip. She didn't want to question her friend, but at the same time she wanted to make sure that Niki was really okay. After all, the girl had just buried her mother, and only two days after her death. But Elle had been told that that was how Niki's father had wanted it: quick and easy, so to speak, so the family could start grieving.

"Yes, I am," Niki said, raising her voice. "I'm sad and I'm scared, but I don't want to keep dwelling on it, not anymore. Not today. Please, tell me about your day. Anything exciting happen at school?"

Elle let herself fall back onto her comforter. She was immediately greeted by the warmth and softness of her bedding. Finally, she found herself at a complete ease, and then began delving into the events of her day.

First, she revealed her meeting with Kyle Burke.

Of course, Niki had known exactly who she was talking about, and had even seemed excited that a relationship could possibly prosper. But Elle had been quick to shut it down. Point blank, she'd informed Niki that due to her recent and awkward breakup with Brian, she currently wasn't interested in a boyfriend. Niki had sighed, proving to be a little bummed at the missed opportunity to maybe play matchmaker.

"And then," Elle continued, "to complete my day, I came home and got to meet my dad's new girlfriend."

"What?" Excitement burst from Niki's voice, replacing the recent disappointment. "Who is she? I *have* to know her."

"Umm, yeah," Elle said, "I'm sure you do know her. It's Elaine Jacobs."

"What? Are you serious?

"Yeah," Elle answered. "I was kind of surprised, too."

"Elaine Jacobs? The school secretary? Emily Jacobs' mother? *That* Elaine Jacobs?"

"That's the one," Elle informed. "Do you know Emily?"

"Yes," Niki said. A thick outbreak of disgust stained her voice. "We don't get along; Robbie dated her before he started dating me."

"Oh, I see," Elle said. She tried to picture Robbie with Emily—a jock with a cheerleader.

It made sense to her. "Well, I don't really know Elaine or Emily, but it was still very strange for me."

"I bet! But tell me more about Kyle. Don't you think he's even a little bit cute?"

Elle finished her conversation with Niki, agreed to meet her in the school parking lot the next day, and then ended the call. Then, she sat her phone on the nightstand. But before she turned off the bedside lamp, she took a moment to take a long, hard stare at the picture of her and her mother, just like she always did.

Elle blew a kiss to the silver frame, and then hit the switch to the light and let the darkness consume her. She rolled over onto her side, and firmly placed both of her hands underneath her head to cradle herself.

It really doesn't get easier, she thought to herself. Elle then closed her eyes and attempted to drift off to sleep.

————

It was time.

He quickly made sure that his black hooded sweatshirt was fully zipped, and then pushed his hands into the matching formfitting gloves. And finally, he pulled down the dark ski mask that would conceal his face.

Waiting, he looked out into the night. He knew all too well that he blended in perfectly with his surroundings. It was almost as if he were invisible.

He stood completely still and gripped the eight-inch stainless steel knife, the same one that he had used last time. He was ready.

TWELVE

EMILY WASN'T COMPLETELY SURPRISED TO discover that the front door was unlocked. Her mother had always been a little forgetful. But that still didn't prevent the girl from feeling somewhat annoyed. After all, there was a killer on the loose in the neighborhood. If her mom was going to stay out late, the least she could do was make sure the house was secured. Not that Emily in any way, shape, or form expected to be the unknown murderer's next target, but still, better safe than sorry, she contemplated. Or in this case, better safe than brutally stabbed to death.

Emily closed the heavy mahogany door behind her. She made sure that both the deadbolt and locking chain were in place, and almost instantly sensed her body melt into ease just from hearing the familiar sounds.

"Mom?" Emily called out, already knowing that she wouldn't get an answer. But then, just to make sure that she was actually alone, she hollered, "Mom, are you home?"

Nothing—just silence. But Emily didn't much care. In fact, she was almost looking forward to a little bit of solitude.

Emily set her pink duffle bag down at the foot of the hardwood stairs that were directly to her left, more than relieved to release the burden of books, binders, clothes that included brown leather boots she had worn earlier in the day, and a set of pompoms. After a three-hour practice, even the red and black streamers had gotten heavy. She bypassed going up to her bedroom, and instead walked straight into the kitchen.

Stepping onto the black linoleum floor, she immediately registered that she was hungry. A deep, guttural moan erupted from the pit of her stomach and slowly escaped her small body. Emily recalled having an apple for lunch, but nothing since then. Hoping to mute any further awkward sounds, she crossed her arms over her chest and started for the white side-by-side refrigerator. It was time for some grub.

"What did you leave me for dinner?" Emily whispered as she swung open the door on the right. "Apparently nothing," she said, answering her own question as she stared into the bleak space.

Emily felt her nose wrinkle at the sight of freshly cut carrots and the sudden overwhelming stench of spinach. Vegetables were definitely not going to fill her gaping appetite tonight.

She let the door slam shut, and then moved on to the cabinet to her right. A single package of crackers and a jar of peanut butter had Emily almost wishing that she'd been able to attend the dinner at Principal Anderson's home. Almost.

The cabinet door banged shut. And again, Emily moved to her right and tried one last time to find some sort of sustenance that she'd actually enjoy putting into her mouth. The "snack drawer" was always hit or miss, depending on her mother's weekly diet regimen and whether or not the woman felt losing weight was in order—for the entire household.

Emily slowly pulled the barrier open. Eureka! A warm glow swept over her, and the familiar feeling of a wide smile spread across her petite face; she eagerly reached for the small bag of Oreo cookies. Guilt-free, she tore into the bag and greedily dug into the chocolate.

At record speed, she was sitting on the leather couch in the front living room. The television remote tightly squeezed in her right hand, a large cup of milk on the end table to her left, and a full bag of Oreos minus three cookies stationed in her lap—this was better than date night.

She began flipping through the channels, and immediately shook her head as she came to terms with a harsh realization: the only thing worse than daytime TV was late night TV.

Emily stole a quick glance at the black watch that was strapped to her wrist. It was almost eleven. She knew that she'd already missed her favorite primetime dramas, and eventually settled on some comedy rerun. It didn't much matter, though. She wouldn't be awake much longer, and the sitcom was only being used as a tool of distraction until she was completely ready for bed.

She was busy dunking an Oreo into her cold cup of milk when a thought from earlier rudely interrupted her dinner and began rattling around inside her mind: Principal Anderson.

Though a complete bitch and virtually impossible to please, Emily now silently thanked Coach Elliot for the impromptu cheerleading practice after school. She'd reconsidered her stance on the matter, now believing that she wasn't one hundred percent ready to have a sit down dinner with the school principal and his strange daughter. Even though they had most likely had something a lot better to eat than what she was munching on now.

There was an aspect about that girl, Emily began contemplating as she polished off the rest of her milk, that just didn't seem to be right. There was just something, well, odd about the new girl in school, about Michelle Anderson.

She'd seen Michelle in the hallways, knew that the girl was from New York, and that she was the principal's daughter, but that was the extent of her information. Emily hadn't taken the time to find out more, mostly because she simply hadn't cared to know more. Michelle always seemed to be alone, sad, even scared. And with a grueling schedule already, the last thing Emily needed to do was invest in more work.

Emily shrugged and leaned further back into the sleek couch. Maybe she really was cruel, a classic "mean girl," but she had enough friends. And besides, she decided as she closed her eyes and let a sleepy sensation drift over her, high school wasn't about making friends, it was about survival. And how was she supposed to survive by befriending the new girl? The same new girl that had arrived in Gray's Lane just one month before the town had experienced its first murder.

She kicked off her tennis shoes and wiggled her aching toes now that they were free. Propping her feet up on the other end of the couch, she reached above her head and pulled down the wool blanket that was suppose to be purely decorative. Her mother had warned her many times about using the blanket to get warm.

But at the moment, Emily didn't care. She was too tired, and her mother wasn't even home. She made sure that every inch of her body was covered, because a revealing pair of gym shorts and a sweaty long sleeved shirt just weren't enough for her to feel completely snug. And only then did she finally begin drifting off to sleep as the muffled sound of Ross and Rachel proclaiming their love for one another filled the living room.

Emily soon realized that she wasn't completely at rest, though. As much as she wanted to fall into a dead sleep, her mind was still roaming and bringing up more thoughts of Principal Anderson.

Maybe her mother dating the school principal wasn't such a bad thing. Perhaps it could even have its perks, she contemplated. Like sleeping in and being late to class tomorrow without any repercussions.

Emily would have to work out the details later; she didn't have the energy to care. She didn't even possess the strength to walk up the stairs and climb into her very large, very comfortable bed.

She was just getting to that place of no return, a deep dreaming state of peace, when a noise above her suddenly broke out.

Eyes wide, Emily quickly bounced into a sitting position. The blanket fell from her body to the floor, and the chill temperature of the room immediately stung her.

The ceiling. That's where the interruption had come from; so did that mean someone was upstairs? Was someone walking around in the room directly above her?

She felt her back muscles rapidly go tense. A cold sweat gradually formed at her right temple. Emily swiped at it, realizing now that the muscles in her entire body had grown tight.

Rising from the couch, she brought herself to a full standing position. She used her bare feet to push the blanket away. The last thing Emily wanted to do was panic or over react, trip, and then fall on her face.

Besides, she quickly told herself, it was probably just her mom. Perhaps her mom had been home the entire time, sleeping, and had now just gotten up to go to the bathroom or get a drink of water.

The idea made sense. It was most likely now well after eleven; would her mother really be out this late? And on a school night? Emily knew that that was just not like Elaine.

But what if it wasn't her mother? What if it was the killer? What if the person that had murdered Kim Sullivan was now in her house, wanting to commit the same crime again? Stab *her* to death?

It was times like these Emily wished she had an older brother, or that her mother was married. Even though her father had walked out on her when she was just a baby and she'd grown up in a house in which she was only accustomed to a female presence, Emily still believed that having a male around would have provided a certain sense of safety.

She left the living room, tiptoed into the foyer, and gripped the banister with both hands. The wood was rough against the sensitive spots of her palms, causing a dull sensation of pain as she debated to go up to the second floor and investigate the noise.

Emily knew that she couldn't call the police. What could she possibly say to them? "Hello? Yes,

I heard a noise in my house. But the noise wasn't completely out of the ordinary. In fact, my mom could have been the one to make it."

No, Emily thought. She brought up her trembling hands and nervously ran them through her hair. She *definitely* couldn't call the cops, not until she knew for sure who or what had made the noise. She wouldn't risk being the laughing stock of Gray's Lane.

She contemplated calling her mom's cell, but then immediately shot down the idea. If her mom really was home and got woken up by the phone call, well, Emily knew that her mother wouldn't be pleased. Emily also knew that the woman would be equally upset if disturbed while being at the Anderson home.

No, Emily ultimately decided. The only way to place the noise would be to investigate it herself. She would just have to walk up the stairs, and checkout the scene if she really wanted to put her curious mind to rest.

But first, Emily knew, she would have to prepare herself for the journey. She would need a little bit of courage to get up the stairs, and she knew exactly how to get it: she was going to psyche herself up for the task.

"It's fine," she whispered. "No one is up there."

Legs shaking as if she'd just finished running a marathon, she stepped up onto the hardwood flooring of the first step. She reached out to her left, held onto the freshly painted wall for support, and gradually started moving. Underneath her feet, the stairs made harsh screeching sounds as she stepped up and put pressure onto each one, instantly reminding her all too well of the possibility that she may not be alone in the house.

"I'm not going to be next," she said, inching closer to the second landing. "I'm not going to be next."

She stopped halfway up the steps, really letting her words sink in this time. "I'm *not* going to be next," she repeated. And this time, Emily believed them.

She had absolutely no connection to the Sullivans. Emily hadn't known Kim, she wasn't friends with Niki. Therefore, she knew she had no reason to be concerned with the remote idea that a stranger could be waiting in her house.

Emily was officially fed up. It was high time to put this mystery to rest once and for all, so that in return, she could put herself to bed.

Combining energy and bravery, Emily charged up the stairs. She wasn't exactly sure if her mother would be greeting her or not, but she was positive of who she wouldn't be seeing: a knife-wielding maniac. And she was going to prove it. Right now.

She finally reached the landing and took a deep breath. She wanted to be confident, even almost had herself completely convinced that she was safe, but there was something about the silent, dark hallway that had her beginning to second guess herself. And suddenly, she debated turning back around and fleeing the house altogether.

Time seemed to stand achingly still, as did Emily with her hands on her hips, trying to quickly make up her mind. What was she going to do?

Eventually, she made a decision. Emily flipped the switch to her left; a dim yellow light filled the area, and she started across the cold, stiff floor. Moving as silently as possible, she headed for the middle bedroom.

The door was shut, just like it was always shut when her mother was sleeping. Emily raised her fist and light tapped on the barrier. Nothing happened.

"Mom?" she called out. "Mom, are you in there?"

No one answered her. And when Emily knocked again, she received the exact same result. So she gripped the round doorknob, twisted it, and then pushed to create an opening to the room.

Darkness overwhelmed her, but she couldn't turn on a light, not this time. Straight ahead was her mother's queen sized bed. Under the thick comforter, Emily could just barely make out a small mound. She had to assume that it was her mother, and that the woman was just sleeping soundly. But Emily also knew that in order to get any sleep herself, she'd have to check and confirm the suspicion. Emily wanted to be reassured. Mentally, she had to be.

Emily knew her way around the master bedroom, and began maneuvering through it as if daylight were shining in and creating a bright environment.

Emily was aware that the bed was in front of her. There was a wide oak dresser to her left, and a glass vanity in the corner of the room that housed an array of lipsticks, nail polishes, perfumes, and other girly products that Emily was constantly borrowing. She could even smell her mother's infamous scent — a combination of fresh flowers and mango — that was still floating around the room from most likely being splashed on earlier. A walk-in closet and petite bathroom that housed a white clawfoot tub concluded her mother's personal space.

Emily padded across the thick carpet, enjoying the sensational feeling of her bare feet sinking into the soft flooring. The smoothness of the carpet allowed her to relax — somewhat.

Emily reached the right side of the bed and stopped. "Mom?" she tried once more. "Mom, are you awake?"

Again, no answer. There wasn't even the slightest movement underneath the comforter.

Doing her best to avoid the bare nightstand, Emily gripped the edge of the bulky blanket and pulled it back, towards herself and away from the headboard.

She wasn't staring down at her mother, but was instead looking at an arrangement of pillows. Why were pillows stacked underneath the comforter? To make it look like someone was actually in the bed? But why? Who would do that?

Something didn't make sense, Emily decided. Something wasn't quite right.

She released the blanket and ran her hands through her thin hair again, but this time bridged them together and stationed them at the base of her taunt neck. A white-hot sensation overtook her body; a feeling of embarrassment and confusion intertwined, causing Emily to believe that at any moment she could be sick.

Suddenly, the same noise from earlier broke out — that disturbing, eerie, *squeaking* sound. This time, however, it hadn't come from above her, but directly behind her.

Emily slowly pivoted around and turned to face the closet. The door was slightly ajar, and even though she squinted, she still wasn't able to make out what, if anything, was currently occupying the space.

Holding her breath, she took two steps forward. Without another moment's pause, she swung the door open.

Someone charged out at her!

Emily tried to scream, but the shriek was lost, muffled, and instead came out as a tiny, whimpering yelp.

Black was all she could see. Dressed from head to toe in black, even the assailant's face was fully covered. And then she caught a glimpse of the glistening object the stranger was holding — a large butcher's knife!

Instinct took hold of her, telling her to duck. She wasn't sure if she was in control, or if her body was acting out on its own accord. Either way, she flung to the floor face first. Her attacker had missed her, instead colliding with the bed.

Emily didn't look back. She was on her feet in no time. She instantly sprinted from the room and approached the stairs. Several thoughts bombarded Emily's mind , but only one in particular managed to stick out from the group: get out of the house!

She sped down the stairs, careful not to trip and fall, and caught her breath as she reached the front door. Heart beating wildly, she feared that it might pound right out of her chest and shatter into millions of pieces.

Emily reached for the door handle and twisted it. Nothing happened. She immediately tried again, willing for the door to fly open and allow her to dart into the cool, night air. But she was met with the same frustrating result: nothing happened.

He was coming down the stairs, coming for her, she knew. Emily could hear him noisily thumping her way, eagerly trying to reach her.

She jerked the doorknob; something had to give. Why wasn't the barrier opening? Emily could feel the tears burning her cheeks as they streamed off her face. A bitter bile was rising in her throat and her stomach was bouncing around, doing sharp somersaults.

Emily pounded on the door with both clenched fists; she had to survive. She knew she was quickly running out of time.

And then, suddenly, it hit her, why the front door wouldn't open: both the deadbolt and locking chain were still securely in place.

She immediately went to work and tried to release the holds; she wasn't fast enough. A fiery pain erupted in the center of her back. She couldn't breathe; she couldn't move. She felt the knife slice deeply into her once again. Her legs turned to Jell-O; she didn't have the strength to stand.

Emily slid down to the floor. Her world went black.

THIRTEEN

SHE'D MISSED HER FATHER AGAIN THIS morning. Elle was starting to wonder if John really was busy at the school, or if he was just simply avoiding her. She knew that a heated discussion was coming and would be erupting like a bad thunderstorm in the near future. But when it would exactly all go down, well, Elle was completely clueless.

She started across the asphalt parking lot and headed toward the main brick building that was definitely starting to show its age. Elle wasn't one hundred percent sure how long Gray's Lane High School had been around, but by the looks of the decaying structure, she was banking on quite a while.

Balancing her heavy bag on her right shoulder, she raised her left hand and tried to block out the burning sunlight. Though the October breeze was cruel enough to call for a long-sleeved shirt, the morning still provided a fierce glow. Elle didn't quite understand it. Couldn't Ohio make up its mind and choose just one season?

"Elle, over here!"

Elle turned toward the sound of her name, already knowing who had yelled for her.

"Hi, Niki," she called back, and then used the hand that was already raised to wave over to her friend. She began maneuvering around the messy masses of parked cars to get closer to her.

The task proved to be somewhat difficult. Edging around the wide variety of vehicles, Elle felt as if she were standing in a mall parking lot on the day before Christmas rather than the one at school on this Wednesday morning.

"Having trouble?"

"What's going on?" Elle asked. She'd finally reached Niki, who was leaning up against the hood of a red four-door Pontiac. "I've never seen so many people here so early."

"Who knows?" Niki said and then shrugged. "Maybe there's a morning assembly or something."

That could be a possibility, Elle considered. It could have also been the reason why her father had left for school sooner than usual. Maybe he really wasn't mad at her; maybe he really wasn't trying to avoid her.

"It's a dumb question, I know, but how are you doing? Are you glad to be back?"

"Surprisingly," Niki started, "I am kind of glad to be here. I think I'm ready to get back to a routine, see my friends; I need distractions. This is where I need to be right now."

"I understand. Trying to get back to normal is important," Elle agreed.

"Don't get me wrong, Valium is definitely doing its part," Niki added. "But I think school will help, too."

Elle wasn't sure if her friend was joking or not, so she chose not to comment. That was until she saw Niki crane her neck, obviously trying to see something in the distance.

"What is it? What's going on?"

"The media is here."

"What?" Elle asked. She quickly pivoted around to meet Niki's gaze. Elle was almost positive that she looked like some unsubtle rubbernecker at the scene of a bad accident.

"Mary Evans is here, and what I'm assuming is a cameraman." Niki said. "Why in the hell is that trashy reporter at our school? Do you think she's planning to do a live broadcast?"

"What could be happening here that would grab the attention of Mary Evans?"

"I don't know," Niki answered and then shrugged again. "Maybe that assembly?"

Elle wasn't convinced. She understood that she hadn't been living in the small town all that long, but she still had trouble believing a news reporter would be covering a high school assembly. Especially a woman like Mary Evans, who wasn't so much a news reporter as she was a bad gossip columnist.

"That seems odd to me," Elle said. "There has to be another reason."

"Well, I don't care what the reason is," Niki said and immediately crossed her arms over her chest. "That woman has no right to be here. Seeing her makes me want to puke. After the way she handled my mother's story…"

"I know," Elle said. She promptly reached out to give Niki a friendly pat on the back. "Don't even look at her. Just turn your head the other way."

But Elle didn't even take her own advice. Rather than follow suit and turn her own gaze away from the highly disliked woman, she stared at Mary and took in her appearance.

Unlike Niki and herself, Mary Evans was dressed to the nines. Instead of plain jeans, boring sneakers, and basic long sleeved shirts, the woman was wearing a neatly pressed charcoal pantsuit and matching stilettos. Her bright red hair was pinned back with some sort of clip that revealed small diamond earrings. Elle was having trouble deciphering if the jewelry was real or not, and even felt herself squinting trying to get a more accurate reading.

The so-called news reporter was standing tall, proud even, and sported a very obvious smile that stretched across her pale face. Mary was pointing at her attractive cameraman, clearly giving him some sort of heated order. Wearing dark jeans and a crisp white shirt, the man seemed to be frowning and muttering to himself under his navy ball cap. Apparently, he also felt the same way about Mary Evans as everyone else did in Gray's Lane, Ohio.

Elle had read Mary's articles, had heard several people's opinions of the woman, but as hard as she'd tried, she could only imagine what Niki was experiencing due to the tabloid-esque writer's recent actions.

After all, Elle's mother's murder hadn't been splashed across the front page of the newspaper. In fact, Sherry's murder hadn't even really been news. Sure, it had made the papers, but a local, single woman getting stabbed to death in the city wasn't actually anything foreign. Elle's father had hit the nail on the head: residents in New York were used to crime. Not to mention, that string of bank robberies that had recently taken place had caused all other stories in the city to take a back seat.

Elle changed her focus and looked over at her friend. She could see both the hurt and disgust in Niki's blue eyes. She wasn't sure what to say, or how to get her friend to fully relax. Elle simply didn't understand. But when she looked down at Niki's hands and saw that they were tightly squeezed into fists, Elle knew that she was going to have to come up with something, because Niki was clearly in attack mode.

"It will be fine," Elle started, "just don't look at her," she repeated. She repositioned herself, trying to make sure that she was standing directly in front of Niki and blocking her friend's view of Mary. But Elle was well aware of her own height, and knew that it was more than likely that Niki could see the woman.

"How can I just look the other way?" Niki asked and then forcefully threw up her hands. "You read the horrible article that woman wrote about my mother, and now she's here, on campus, standing less than fifty feet away from me."

"Look at me, Niki. Look at me!" Elle ordered and then waited for Niki to stare across at her. "Going over there and confronting Mary will only make matters worse. You won't feel better, it's not even worth your time."

"Okay," Niki said. She took a deep breath. "You're right; I won't go over there. I won't even look her way."

"Thank you," Elle said. She brought her bag higher up on her shoulder so that she would have a better grip on it. She followed Niki's example and leaned up against the side of the car.

And even though the words weren't actually spoken, Elle still knew the plan: they weren't entering the building until after Mary did. They were not going to walk by the reporter, which pleased Elle. She didn't want Niki within hitting distance of the woman.

"I think I may have overreacted a bit," Niki said, finally breaking the aching silence. "That woman just gets to me. Why couldn't she have reported the story like a normal human being? Why did she have to make it sound so over the top, so — so ridiculous? Didn't she realize that Kimberley Sullivan was more than just the name of a murdered woman? More than just a victim?"

"Niki, I…"

"She was a mother, a daughter, a wife. She was a *person!* And Mary splashed her name all over the front page of the paper like… like…"

Elle watched helplessly as Niki abruptly stopped talking, slowly lowered her head, and used both hands to fully cover her face. She knew that her friend was crying, releasing a bit of her pent-up rage and sorrow. She was glad that Niki was venting some of her emotions out; she was also very pleased that the other students passing by didn't seem to notice. Everyone appeared to be too captivated by Mary Evans and her purpose for being at the school.

"Ladies."

Elle turned to her left, looked past Niki, and focused her attention on the deep voice that had suddenly approached them. It was Kyle.

"Hi, Kyle." Elle wasn't quite sure why, but as she spoke Kyle's name, she felt a tiny smile spread across her own face that seemed to mirror the one on his. There was no way to avoid this, Elle knew, she was getting into dangerous territory.

Niki must have sensed it, too, Elle decided, because her friend abruptly lifted her head, eyes somewhat dry now, smiled, and then subtly nudged Elle in her arm.

"What's with all of the excitement?" Kyle asked. Elle watched as he joined their line, taking the vacant spot beside Niki, and leaned up against the car.

"We haven't been able to figure that out yet," Niki answered.

"Must be something important if local celebrity Mary Evans dragged her ass all the way down to the school yard this morning to mingle with us commoners." His voice was dripping with a sarcasm, Elle noticed.

Mary Evans *really* was one unpopular woman.

"She's been here for a while," Elle started, "but…" she let her words trail off and looked over at Niki. Niki's eyes had grown wide and the girl was shaking her head; Elle understood immediately.

Niki was trying to communicate to her without words. Her friend's expression seemed to shriek: "Please don't say anything to him or anyone else about my meltdown."

But Elle hadn't needed a warning; she knew the code of ethics when it came to girlfriends. What she had just witnessed would be kept secret between Niki and her.

"Hey, do you know what's going on here?" Elle quickly realized that Kyle hadn't even been paying attention to Niki and her silent conversation; he had stopped another student, and was asking about all of the commotion.

"Nope." The greasy haired teenager offered the single word answer before squeezing through two closely parked trucks and then headed toward the main building.

"Who knows?" Kyle offered with a slight shrug.

Elle found her gaze gradually shifting over to Kyle. Trying not to get caught, she took in his appearance out of the corner of her eye, and soon realized that he looked almost exactly as he had the day before. Dressed casually in form-fitting jeans and a sweatshirt that promoted the Gray's Lane football team, he'd pushed the sleeves up to his elbows. Again, his trimmed hair was styled with gel. And just like yesterday, Elle struggled with turning away from his dark eyes.

"Well, I'd ask Robbie what was going on, *if* he was here," Niki said. She repositioned herself. She placed her back to the school building and looked out into the full parking lot. "I don't know where he is, but he's going to be late."

"There he is," Kyle said, pointing to his left. "He's coming over here."

Elle turned and saw Robbie rapidly moving their way. As he got closer, she noticed that he appeared to be out of breath. His long hair was messy, and his glasses seemed to be on the verge of fogging up. Where had he come from? Had he been running?

"Robbie, what in the hell is going on?" Niki asked as soon as he came within earshot of the group.

"You haven't heard?" His eyes grew wide as he stared in what was an obvious look of shock and disbelief. "Emily Jacobs and her mother were murdered last night. Both of them were stabbed to death."

FOURTEEN

THIS WAS HER DAY — THAT MUCH WAS FOR certain: a double homicide with a new angle to the story that only she was privy to!

Mary Evans knew that she had struck gold. Literally. And she'd be enjoying every minute of it, too, if it weren't for Henry Wren. Lazy, incompetent, dumb as a box of rocks, Henry Wren. He couldn't even handle the simplest of orders, and had there been anyone else available to do the job, she would have sent the cameraman packing. But unfortunately for her, he was all there was. Slim fucking pickings in Gray's Lane, Ohio.

She went to work trying to smooth out a barely visible wrinkle in her jacket. Mary wanted to look absolutely perfect today; she had to. In about an hour, the community of would be seeing her in a new light. They would all finally give her the respect that she deserved, the respect that she had been seeking for over fifteen years. After she revealed her latest tip, the newest piece of information in the *now* multiple murder case, Mary knew that she would rightfully be seen as a hardworking, worth-her-salt, leading lady journalist. And it was about damn time, too.

"Is the camera ready, Henry? We're wasting time." She held out both hands and looked down at her nails — French manicure intact, and not one of them was chipped. Smart, yet fashionably presentable. Just like career women should be in this day and age, she thought.

"What's the big hurry, Mary?" Henry asked through tightly clenched teeth. "You're the only reporter here; you're the only one with the inside story, or that's what you keep telling me, anyway. Are you seriously concerned that you might get scooped?"

"Don't be ridiculous," she ordered through a thick cackle. "There isn't anyone in a fifty — no," Mary abruptly reconsidered her wording, "make that one hundred. There isn't anyone in a hundred mile radius that could handle this story like I can. I *own* this story!"

"Well, do you mind sharing what this so-called secret tip is, then? You know, just so we're on the same page?"

"We're not on the same page, Henry." She decided not to yell at him, and even let his very obvious eye-roll go unmentioned. "I'm the talent, the star, the one in charge here. You will hear my piece when the rest of Gray's Lane does."

"Let's get real, Mary," Henry said and then smirked. "The whole town already knows all about you and your *piece*."

"Go to hell!" she backfired.

"Believe me, I think I'm already there."

"Shouldn't you be opening up your wallet? Perhaps counting out some money?"

"What do you mean?"

Mary saw the look of confusion spread across his unlined face; she felt her whole body tingle as she began thriving in Henry's Wren's discomfort.

"The bet," she said.

"Right." He nodded. "The bet. What about it?"

"You owe me one hundred dollars, remember?"

"I do remember. The terms of the bet, that is. And so far, I don't owe you jack!"

"Excuse me?" she asked. She immediately heard her own voice rise. Mary forcefully placed her hands on her hips and took a step toward Henry. "There's been another murder, two in fact, and the deal was…"

"Yes, there has been another murder," Henry said, lifting his left hand to stop her. "Two murders, as you've stated. However, it hasn't been proven that the new victims are related to Kim Sullivan."

"Are you kidding me?" she screamed. "Of course all of the victims are related. I can prove it, too!"

"Great!" Henry said. A smile bloomed across the lower half of his face. "As soon as you connect all of the dead bodies and officially announce that there is a serial killer picking off females in Gray's

Lane, I'll give you the money. But," he deepened his voice, "not one second before you do."

"Fine!" Mary agreed. She realized right away that her lower lip was sticking out, no doubt evoking the look of an upset child who was on the verge of throwing a tantrum. She quickly retracted it. "But I want cash. No way will I trust a check from you."

She turned on her heel and put her back toward the annoying cameraman. Mary took a deep breath and tried to calm herself down, ultimately giving Henry a chance to get all of the equipment up and running.

She told herself that she had to relax; it was important to be worry-free. Mary wasn't exactly sure how long it took for stress lines to sink in and show, but she knew for certain that she didn't want them anywhere on her body when she went live.

Mary watched as a group of what had to be high school virgins open the wide metal doors and enter the rustic brick building. It had been a while, more years than what she would ever admit, since she'd been in the high school. But as an overwhelming stench swiftly invaded her nostrils and caused her small body to quiver in sickness, she recalled where this particular entrance led: the cafeteria.

A heavy wave of fattening grease attacked her, forcing her body to take a giant step to her left. Mary felt herself losing balance, and a sour-tasting fear of falling down in front of witnesses suddenly smacked her.

She was quick to pick up on the problem: one of her shoes had slid off the sidewalk, hit grass, and was now beginning to sink in the moist dirt. But before any damage could be done, she was able to catch herself, shift her lone leg that was in the mud, and reposition her body so that she was now fully on the concrete.

Today must be my lucky day, Mary thought to herself. She hadn't fallen; she hadn't created an embarrassing scene. Her shoe hadn't even been stained in the process. She made a mental note to buy a lottery ticket later.

"It's clear that Gray's Lane is still serving the same obesity-laced meals they were famous for when I was a student here."

"Schools had kitchens back then?" Henry asked. His eyebrows shot up in what was a look of apparent shock. "In those days, I thought there were only single room buildings. No cafeterias."

"You know, you really missed your calling, Henry. You should have been a stand-up comedian."

"So I've been told."

"You know," she started, placing her hands back on her hips, "I was only making an observation. You don't have to be smart ass all of the time."

"Is that a fact?" Henry asked. The same look of confusion from before swam into his eyes. "But you're a bitch all of the time, so I have to have some sort of defense. Right?"

"I was trying to be nice."

"You mean for the first time in your life? Please forgive me, Mary, if I don't seem to recognize the gesture on you."

"Just get what you need out of the van so we can get started," she ordered. "Not only have you successfully put me in a bad mood, but being back at this hellhole is starting to give me the creeps."

"Why are we here, then?" Henry fired off and shook his head. "Why did you insist on doing the broadcast at the high school?"

"Not that I have to justify my actions to you, but doing the broadcast at Gray's Lane High School is a brilliant idea. One of my most brilliant ideas, actually."

"And why exactly is that?"

He didn't get it, and he probably never would. Henry Wren didn't have the brain cells to do what she did. Then again, most people didn't. Mary knew that she was one in a million. Maybe even in two million after all of the rum-dumbs of Gray's Lane were taken into consideration.

She thought about running her fingers through her silky hair to release some frustration, but then remembered that she couldn't. Her hair was styled just perfectly, and she would be on camera within minutes. Well, hopefully.

Therefore, she settled on balling her hands into fists, released the hold quickly, and then repeated the process. Mary didn't have a stress ball handy, so she made due without one. And surprisingly enough, the action still seemed to help. She felt her body temperature cool down, and finally go from boiling to tepid.

"Two women were brutally stabbed to death last night, Henry — the high school secretary and her daughter, who just happened to be enrolled at Gray's Lane High. Therefore, this is the perfect place to reveal the story to viewers."

"Are you saying the murders are school related?"

"I'm not going to say anything like that," she informed. "However, there are a few coincidences that could stand to be connected."

Mary heard him exhale loudly. Henry was obviously irritated and probably didn't believe her.

"And you're sure this live broadcast is appropriate? Whatever you have to say, whatever this *alleged* new lead is couldn't have waited for the print edition of tomorrow's paper?"

"Absolutely not," she spit out. "You honestly think I would give someone else the opportunity to discover what I have? You've gone crazy! I'm officially done sitting on this new information."

"Mary," Henry started, but then took a break to pinch the bridge of his nose. "I've already told you: there is no one else here. You're the only reporter in Gray's Lane, that's why you do both print and television duties."

"Well," she said and then offered an uncaring shrug, "there's a perfectly good reason for that."

"Which is?"

"Like a good competitor, I ran everyone else out of town."

"Let me guess," Henry said. He took a step back toward the black van, "The nice Mary has met her quota for the day. You're officially back to your well known, bitchy self?"

She chose to ignore his comment. At the moment, she didn't have the time, interest, or energy to get into yet another dispute with Henry. She'd already swallowed her fury about his jock-inspired wardrobe—jeans, t-shirt, leather jacket, ball cap—and decided she'd do the same with his latest comment.

"Are you any closer to getting the camera up and rolling? We need to do this before the principal comes out and orders me to leave."

"Or worse," Henry offered, "the police."

"Yes," Mary agreed. "It would be bad if Sheriff Douglas were to show up here and stop me. That's exactly why I want to get this done before he or anyone else with a little bit of authority gets wind of this."

"I'm ready," Henry informed. "I just need to get your microphone from the back."

"Well, hurry," she demanded in a brittle whisper. "A crowd is starting to form."

Mary hadn't been exaggerating. An array of teenagers were approaching the van and gathering around to form a loose circle.

"What's going on?" A male student with a green messenger bag and thick sunglasses asked. "Has something else bad happened?"

"Are we going to be on TV?" A bubbly cheerleader-looking type hollered over the growing group.

"Are classes cancelled?"

"Why are you here?"

The questions kept flying in from all directions at lightening speed. An amateur would have felt bombarded, but Mary knew how to play the game and get out alive: she wasn't going to answer anyone.

She was well aware of the fact that if she spoke up now, only more inquiries would come, and then she'd be stuck talking to useless teenagers that could do nothing for her career. Mary had a task to get done, a goal to accomplish, and nothing was going to stand in the way of that—not now, not ever. She'd traveled too far.

Henry was still in the van, doing God knows what, and she felt her eyes beginning to wonder. As nonchalantly as possible, Mary began looking over the hordes of diversity that currently made up Gray's Lane High School. Taking in clothing choices, hair styles, and attitudes that ranged from annoyed to bored to just plain tired, a thought crept into Mary's mind and seemed to get stuck on repeat: times sure had changed.

And then she spotted her, the girl she'd only seen pictures of and had hoped to avoid coming into contact with today. Mary didn't know her personally, but was guessing that the teenager hadn't reacted lightly to what had been printed on the front page of the paper a few days ago.

The last thing Mary wanted was a sloppy confrontation with Nicole Sullivan, especially when a live camera was going to be filming the scene rather shortly.

However, that was a chance that she had had to take, a chance that she *did* take by coming to the high school. And though she knew that her article on Kim Sullivan's murder had been cruel, brutal, and blown completely out of proportion, Mary was also mindful of the fact that there was simply no room for a conscious when it came to journalism. Or, more importantly, when it came to getting what you wanted out of life.

She studied Niki as closely as she could without getting caught. Above all else, rage seemed to be pouring out of the girl in full force. Her three friends, two males and another girl, seemed to be leaking fury as well, but the group also appeared to be curious.

Mary was quite familiar with their gazes. Though obviously upset, they still wanted to see what was going to happen next. She was *that* good!

And never one to disappoint, she was going to show them what was coming next. Right now!

"Henry, let's go!"

"One second," he called back. "Your cell phone's ringing."

"If it's someone important, then they'll leave a voicemail. We need to get rolling! Now!" She increased the sharpness of her voice, hoping some of the students standing near by would pick up on the fact that she was in charge.

"Wait, it's not a call," Henry said. He stood hunched over at the back of the van. "It's a text. You've got a text from Baby Always. Who's Baby Always?"

"Give me my fucking phone, Henry!" Mary gave the order through gritted teeth. She almost immediately felt her face flush and her entire body start to grow increasingly warm.

"Mary," Henry started, stepping away from the vehicle. "Do you have a boyfriend? A lover of some sort?" A sly smile spread evenly across his face; he was obviously enjoying this way too much.

"Henry!"

"You've been holding out on me, Mary." A steady laugh started to escape him. "Why didn't you tell me about this mystery man?"

"My personal life is none of your damn business," she said, refusing to answer his inappropriate question. "Give me my phone! Now!"

He walked over to her with his right palm out. "Don't worry, I didn't read it."

She didn't respond to the comment; she snatched the silver device out of his hand, entered her pass code, and began reading. As if on cue, her rage began to melt away. Mary was no longer fuming; her body had suddenly cooled down. A fuzzy feeling began overtaking her; she became cool and lightheaded. She was sure that she was smiling, but also believed that she was now glowing.

"I take it someone received some good news?"

Mary reread the message to make sure that she'd correctly seen the contents. Yes, she understood exactly what was going on. Then, she deleted the text, turned off her phone, and threw it back to Henry.

"What?" he asked as he caught the device.

"It's show time! Now!"

Mary began the broadcast by backtracking. She was quite clear of who was in the audience, but that didn't stop her from following the detailed outline she had handwritten this morning.

First up, she mentioned the original prey, Kimberley Sullivan. She didn't dwell on the subject, as it was still a recent act and permanently glued to everyone's mind. Instead, she simply touched upon it before jumping head first into the story of the fresh murders.

"Found brutally stabbed to death early this morning in their home," Mary spoke in a brisk, clear monotone, "were two more female victims. Elaine Jacobs and her daughter, Emily, both were targets of the same psychotic monster that struck just four days ago.

"And now, for the first time, I'm offering new information on the case that not only links all three victims, but also proves that the Gray's Lane Police Department might have an actual serial killer on their hands.

"My sources have confirmed that pieces of candy corn were found at each crime scene. Yes, you heard me correctly, Gray's Lane. The sugary Halloween candies were placed on all three of the slain women.

"The question 'why?' hasn't been answered yet, but it looks as if the killer is signing his victims. He's taking credit for his work, and wants us to know that he's responsible for these deaths. Candy corn is the killer's calling card."

Mary took a lingering breath; it was time for the closer. She allowed herself a moment to bask in the thrill of what she was unfolding to the town. She was *finally* in the limelight. People were actually listening to what she had to say, and this was only the beginning. And though she desperately wanted to savor the affair, to cling to it like a hungry moth to a bright, burning flame, she knew that it was time to move on.

This is only the beginning, she told herself once more.

"But residents of Gray's Lane, there's no reason to panic. Though a name hasn't been provided yet, it looks as if Sheriff Douglas has a suspect in custody. Let's just pray that the real killer has been caught, and that these horrific murders will officially come to end.

"Once more, this is Mary Evans, and I'm hoping that the nightmare that has recently rocked our small community is over."

FIFTEEN

"LET ME GET THIS STRAIGHT," BEN STARTED. "You think the killer, the person who is responsible for murdering three women in Gray's Lane, Ohio, actually followed you here from New York?"

"I know how it sounds, but..."

"How does it sound, Michelle?" Ben took a deep breath. To stop his frustrated hands from balling into fists and punching the wall behind him, he placed them tightly in his lap.

Without a doubt, this was definitely the last place he wanted to be. Sheriff Douglas had a suspect, a real life flesh and blood person of interest who might have truly been behind the town's brutal stabbings. Ben knew that he should have been in the sheriff's office, lending a hand, helping shake down the possible culprit. That's where he so desperately wanted to be anyway, where his pounding heart was currently stationed.

However, the deputy was stuck. He was trapped at his own desk with some crazy, out of her mind teenage girl who claimed to have proof that the killer had crossed state lines. If this was some kind of joke, Ben considered, she was going to be sorry. He was in no mood to laugh.

"You didn't answer my question, Michelle." Ben said. He asked again, "How do you think this all sounds?"

"Elle."

"Excuse me?" Ben asked. He felt himself frown.

"Elle," she repeated. "Please call me Elle. I'm more comfortable with Elle. When people, mostly authority figures, call me Michelle, I get nervous, intimidated." She reached out for the sweating glass of ice water in front of her. When she spoke again, her voice seemed weak, shallow. "Please call me Elle."

"Fine," Ben said. And deciding to grant the girl's wish, added, "Elle."

After all, he wanted to make her as comfortable as possible so that she wouldn't clam up. He needed her to share what she had to offer — in full. She wasn't a suspect, Ben reminded himself, but a potential witness. And not only that, he suddenly realized as he brought his hands up placed his fingers together in a steeple position on his tidy desk, Elle appeared to be scared, terrified even. He felt sorry for her.

"Look," she started, breaking the silence. "I know I sound insane, like some pathetic new girl in town who just wants some attention. But that's not me, okay? That's not who I am, and that's not why I'm here."

"How do I know that?" Ben asked and then shrugged. "How do I know that you're not lying, that this all isn't some twisted act? A game?"

"Hear me out," she pleaded. "Hear my story before you pass judgment. And then, if you don't believe me, or you think I'm whacked or want attention…"

"Then?"

"Well, then at least I tried."

Ben softly bit down on his lower lip as he began contemplating her proposal. He really didn't have much of a choice, he ultimately decided. After all, he was already missing the interrogation in the sheriff's office.

And who knew? Ben thought to himself. He wasn't completely positive if he was just trying to psyche himself up or if he actually believed this new idea, but maybe, just maybe Elle was telling him the truth. Perhaps she did have a valid story, and by sharing the information, there would be another productive turn in the case.

What do I have to lose? he asked himself. He then nodded, almost as if he were the only one at his desk, like he was having a conversation with himself.

Elle was already at the station; someone had to take her story. And Ben finally concluded that it might as well be him.

"Five minutes," he stated.

"That's all I'm asking of you," she said. Elle then added, "Besides, I think that's all the time I'll need."

"Fine," he nodded. "Then whenever you're ready, you can begin."

But she didn't start talking. Instead, her gaze shifted and her eyes began traveling around the station. Ben tried to follow her line of vision; he wanted to see what she was seeing.

The crowded, main room of the station definitely left more to be desired, that was for certain. But then again, Ben considered, the area was pretty standard for a small town police station: water cooler in the corner, a handful of mismatched desks and chairs scattered throughout, a whiteboard stretched along the space of one wall that appeared to not have been written on in some time. Ultimately, the building was designed for potential criminals to confess their darkest sins. And looking at Elle now, he wondered what hers were, or if she even possessed any.

Probably not, Ben guessed. The girl was only a high school student. However, he knew better than to jump to conclusions. Evil had no age limitations. And Ben found it quite suspicious that he was having difficulty interpreting how the young girl was feeling, or what she was even thinking.

Ben heard a slight tapping noise, which caused him to shift his focus from the blank tablet of paper in front him to the ground. Elle was slowly smacking her right foot against the cracked vinyl flooring. It was only then that Ben finally understood: the girl was nervous.

Going out on a limb, he was almost positive the stench of stale coffee that had combined with the foul odors of smoke and sweat did absolutely nothing to help put her at ease. And as if he had come full circle, Ben suddenly recognized that raw, tingling sensation of sorrow. He felt sorry for Elle.

"I've never really shared this with anyone," Elle finally said in what was a barely audible whisper. "I suppose my dad knows, but..."

"Shared what? Your dad knows what?" He had to strain his ears to fully hear her, and even found himself leaning across the surface that divided them. He didn't want to miss a single word.

"About my mother's murder," she answered. "The full story."

Ben slowly leaned back into his chair, giving Elle some space. He took a long, deep breath and then asked, "Why don't you start at the beginning? I want to make sure I completely understand what you're saying. Don't leave anything out, okay?"

She nodded. "This is kind of difficult for me," Elle began. "I've only been living in Gray's Lane for about a month now."

"We have something in common," Ben said. He picked up the freshly sharpened pencil, but then almost immediately placed it back on his desk. He looked into Elle's eyes and said, "I'm also new to town."

"Yeah? And where are you from originally?"

He wasn't stupid. The young deputy caught on to her tactic rather quickly: she was stalling, shifting the conversation so that the topic was about him rather than her. But for some reason, he didn't seem to mind. Ben gave in, deciding he would play the game and allow Elle to take all the time she needed.

"A few hundred miles north of here," he said. "A completely different place than Gray's Lane."

"Tell me about it," she said, and then released a half smile. "I've lived in New York the past seventeen years, so you can imagine…" Her words trailed off for a moment. And then, "What city are you from?"

Okay, Ben concluded. It was time to change focus. He didn't mind sharing some of his history, but Elle needed to give him something. It was almost as if time were standing still while they cautiously danced around the silly small talk.

"I'd like to hear what you have to say," Ben said. And then, seeing her entire face somewhat drop, he added, "If you're ready. I'm curious about the connection you've made between the murder in New York and the one here in Ohio."

"Fine," Elle said, no longer giving him eye contact. "About a month ago, my mother was murdered. I came home and found her stabbed to…"

Ben suddenly knew where this was going, and just like that, he felt his heart sink even lower for the girl. No longer annoyed or distraught about missing the interrogation in the sheriff's office, a thick feeling of empathy now consumed him.

Just like Elle, Ben knew what it was like to lose his mother at such a young age, and in such a devastating manner. And then of course, there was the suffering of watching the crime go unsolved. Like a dull razor blade being repeatedly pulled over dry, bare skin.

But benching his own feelings, Ben had been able to catch on to what was happening here. It was actually quite clear.

Just one month ago, Elle's mother had been brutally murdered. Unfortunately, she had had to witness the aftermath of the slaying, which had rightfully scarred her. And now, with the worst possible timing ever, Ben thought to himself, connecting the dots in his sleep deprived mind, a local woman had been murdered almost immediately following Elle's move to Gray's Lane.

And it hadn't just been some random incident either, Ben determined. Kim Sullivan had been a mother, a mother who had been killed the exact same way Elle's own mother had been killed — stabbed to death. Butchered.

No, Elle wasn't crazy. She was a sad teenage girl who was desperately grasping at straws. She obviously wanted, no, she *needed* answers for her mother's death, and was simply trying to find them wherever she possibly could. Ben knew this was true, because he identified with her and the situation. Probably more so than anyone else in Gray's Lane.

His mother's shooter would never be found. He was trying to accept that haunting fact every single day. It was obvious that Elle wasn't at that stage of the grieving process yet. Time could only help heel her wounds.

Ben suddenly felt his entire body go rigid. He knew that he was going to have to shut down her theory.

"Deputy?" she asked.

The soft sound of her voice brought him back. "Elle," he began. He instantly recognized a sharp prickling feeling in his gut, as if he, too, had been stabbed. "I'm not quite sure how to say this."

"Deputy?"

"Please," he raised his hand. "As hard as this is going to sound, I still think it's something you need to hear."

"Alright, Deputy Andrews."

Ben stalled for a moment. He tried to find the right words, but then quickly came to the daunting conclusion that there weren't any. He was just going to have to wing it and tread lightly.

"I know where you're coming from," he said, choosing to offer up the fact that the two of them were standing on cold, common ground. "I recently lost my mother. Murdered, too. And the killer hasn't been found. In all reality, the killer will probably *never* be found."

"I'm sorry for your loss," Elle said.

"Therefore," he continued, "I understand how you feel." It wasn't that he didn't appreciate her comment, but Ben feared that if he acknowledged it, then the conversation would go off course again. This was about *her*, not him.

"There's no doubt in my mind you know how I feel."

"Which is also why I'm sympathetic for you being here. I think that wanting to create a parallel between what happened to your mother in New York and what's been taking place here is only…"

"Create?" Elle repeated. "I'm not creating anything. The murders are connected. The person who killed my mother in New York followed me to Ohio. He stabbed…"

"Elle, please," Ben stopped her. "I know you want to believe that the murders are connected, that there's still a chance the person responsible for killing your mother can be caught, that justice will be served. And even though there may be some similarities between the two crimes, there's still nothing concrete that proves that…"

"What about the candy corn?" she asked.

"Excuse me?" Ben quickly found himself sitting straight up in his chair and leaning in towards the girl. There was no way he' heard her correctly. "Did you say 'candy corn'?"

"Yes," Elle said and then nodded.

Ben felt his eyes go wide. A sharp pain hit his right temple. He thought his head was going to explode right off of his rigid shoulders.

What the hell? The candy corn was the one piece of the investigation that had been kept under wraps; Sheriff Douglas and Ben were positive that it would eventually lead to catching the killer, the *real* killer. How did Elle know about the killer's signature?

"Elle, how do you know about the candy corn? Who told you about that?"

"I heard it this morning at school," she said. "Everyone knows about the candy corn. I also know that both Elaine and Emily Jacobs were murdered last night, and that candy corn was found on their bodies. Just like Kim Sullivan."

He pinched the bridge of his nose. The pounding in his head was only getting worse. For a moment, he saw red; he wanted to scream.

How had this gotten out? And so quickly? Sheriff Douglas and Ben had only learned about the two new victims a few hours ago. And upon arriving at the scene, that's when they'd witnessed the use of the candy corn. Sheriff Douglas had been correct, the killer had struck again — twice — and he'd signed the bodies with the Halloween candy.

There was officially a serial killer in Gray's Lane, Ohio.

But how had all of this privileged information leaked out? Ben wondered again.

And as soon as the question roared inside his mind, Ben instantly knew who was to blame. The culprit was so damn obvious. He had to confirm it.

His stomach muscles tightened. It felt as if someone was trying to claw their way into his insides. He hunched over his desk and bit the inside of his cheek to try and conceal the pain. Trouble was coming, he knew. In fact, trouble was already here.

"Elle," Ben began through a heavy breath. He gripped the rough sides of his chair, attempting to steady himself and concentrate. "Who told you about the new murders and the candy corn?"

"Robbie Douglas was the first one to tell me about Elaine and Emily being stabbed to death late last night."

"The sheriff's grandson?" Ben asked, finally releasing his hold on the chair. Color slowly began swimming back into his hands; he had feeling in his fingers once again.

"Yes," she confirmed. "Robbie told me about the new murders, but I would have found out with or without him."

"Huh?" Ben frowned. "What do you mean? Someone else knew about the murders?"

"Yes," Elle repeated. "Mary Evans did a live broadcast at school this morning."

187

"What?"

"She reported the new murders, the candy corn calling card, and that there's a suspect currently in custody." The girl waited a beat. "You didn't see it?"

Ben shrugged off her question.

This was a nightmare, plain and simple. How was this case successfully supposed to get solved when every aspect of it was being revealed to the community? Ben wondered if the sheriff knew about this, and if so, how long it would be before heads started to roll.

Ben leaned back into the chair, pushed it away from the table, and stood up. "Elle, I'm sorry, but I've got to go. Thanks for coming in, but I'm afraid I can't…"

"You didn't let me finish," she said, also rising to her feet.

He took a deep breath. Ben desperately wanted to stay calm; this wasn't Elle's fault. But anger was starting to course through every inch of his body. He needed to hit something. Or better yet, maybe a drink.

"I don't see how the killings are related," he finally stated. Perhaps it was time to just be blunt with the girl. "Yes, the method is the same, but stabbings are common." He realized then that he was losing patience, and at a dangerous rate. He couldn't stop himself. "Cut and dry, it's a bad coincidence. That's all."

"Candy corn was also found on my mother's body," Elle started. "She was stabbed to death and…" her words trailed off. The girl lowered her face into her hands and promptly broke into a sob.

Ben instantly froze. It was as if his legs had turned to stone — he couldn't move.

If Elle was telling the truth, then this changed everything. Not just a coincidence, Ben swallowed, but the same killer — the same killer who had struck at least three times and in two different states.

And if Elle really was telling the truth, then the entire case had just been spun on its head. This was a whole new ballgame, and he had to speak with Sheriff Douglas. Now!

"Elle," he managed to choke out in a somewhat stable tone, "I'm so sorry, but I really need to go. Is there someone I can call for you before I leave?"

She finally looked up. Her face was a somber shade of red, and stained with tears. "Yes," Elle said. "Can you get a hold of my father? I haven't seen him today, but he's probably at the school."

"Sure," Ben said. "What's his name?"

"John Anderson," Elle answered. "He's the principal."

Ben felt the blood rush from his head. His legs, still heavy, were going to cause him to tip over. He quickly reached out and grabbed at the back of his chair for support. This couldn't be happening.

"John Anderson is your father?" he asked.

"Yes," Elle nodded. "Why?"

Ben didn't respond, he couldn't. Not only was he not allowed to, but he also had no idea how to tell the young girl that her father was currently being questioned for the murders of three women.

SIXTEEN

SHERIFF LARRY DOUGLAS WASN'T ONE hundred percent certain that he was staring at the man who was responsible for committing multiple murders in his town. And though half of him hoped that John Anderson was behind the act, the other part of him, the part that was human and had known John for well over thirty years, found it too damn difficult to believe that an educated, well liked and highly established man could be capable of stabbing someone to death. Let alone three someones.

Just another day, Douglas ultimately decided. Just another privilege that went hand-in-hand with being the sheriff of the town.

I really should have retired, he thought, repeating the mantra to himself. Then, he could have avoided this whole mess like the plague it was proving more and more to be.   But too little, too late. There was now officially no room left for regret; the sheriff knew what he was going to have to do.

He was going to question John. The sheriff had a theory, enough circumstantial evidence to at least

191

warrant a little chat. And during that chat, one of two things was going to happen: John would either be revealed as the killer, ending the madness that had surrounded Gray's Lane for the past five days, or an innocent man's reputation would be tainted and a diabolical killer would still be on the loose.

Sheriff Douglas slowly shook his head back and forth. Again, he'd managed to find himself in a no-win situation. It seemed to be a common place for the old man.

"Come on, Larry," John pleaded. "You know me. You know I didn't do this."

"That's *Sheriff* Douglas," the sheriff corrected. He could hear the sharpness in his own voice, but the man knew he had to be cold. He had a job to do and a community to protect. This wasn't social hour.

"Fine," John said. "Sheriff Douglas, I didn't do this!"

"Don't raise your voice, John," the Sheriff ordered. "If you stay calm, then this will all go smoother. Now, are you sure you don't want a lawyer?"

"Of course I don't want a lawyer," John answered. "I've done nothing wrong. Elaine is my... was... she was my girlfriend. I loved her."

"Just hold up a minute," Douglas started, "we'll get to all of that. I'm going to want you to start at the beginning. But first things first, I had to offer you council. It's your right."

"I don't want a lawyer," John repeated. "I just want to get this over with as fast as possible. Alright?"

"I understand, but…"

"I don't think you do understand, Sheriff. I was arrested for something I didn't do, for a crime I didn't commit."

"I already told you, John. Relax! Stay cool and I'll make this as easy as I can," Douglas said. "And you weren't arrested. No one put you in handcuffs."

"Then what I am I doing here?"

"I have an obligation," Douglas answered. "I have to question you."

"Why?" John demanded. "Just because I knew Elaine? Because I was dating her when she was…"

"No," Douglas argued. "I brought you in for questioning, John, because you were found standing over the victim, covered in her blood!" The tone of his voice was like a piercing crack of thunder. His words boomed and echoed throughout the small room.

"I found Elaine and Emily this morning," John hollered. "I'm the one that called 9-1-1. I didn't murder them!"

"Fine, fine," Douglas said. It was then he changed his stance, deciding that *he* would stay calm. He folded his hands on his desk and softened his voice. "Tell me your story. Tell me what happened." The man waited.

A couple of minutes passed. John didn't say anything, just looked at the floor. Out of pure boredom, the sheriff reached out and cracked his tight knuckles. Had there been a clock anywhere in the room, he would have watched it, studied just how slow time was actually moving. But there wasn't one in sight. In fact, there really wasn't too much in the man's office that was worth focusing on.

Douglas took in the space that was often referred to as his "second home." His surroundings lacked color, personality, life—in a word, motivation. His office didn't present any motivation to be a better husband, a better grandfather, a better sheriff. There wasn't even an item on display that inspired him to just be a better man.

It took all the energy he had to stop from tapping his black boots against the surface of the floor. Just because he was eager to hear John speak, the sheriff still didn't want to be too rude. Besides, fidgeting would probably only make John more nervous, possibly even clam up and not say anything else.

No, Douglas decided, he wouldn't rush the man. He wanted to know his story. He *had* to know it.

The air was thick, almost suffocating, and had a distinct, leftover food sort of stench. Now haunted by the fact that he'd eaten dinner at this very desk the past couple of nights in a row,

Douglas silently prayed that John didn't pick up on the smell of old grease.

If John had noticed the odor, he didn't show it. The man continued to sit still; his eyes were dark red and puffy, a direct sign that he'd shed a good amount of tears earlier in the morning. His light hair was messy and sticking up in odd directions. Maybe he'd nervously ran his large hands through it a few times? His green tie was off center and loosely hanging from his neck; sweat was already beginning to show at the collar of his dress shirt.

It didn't take long for Douglas to catch on: John Anderson was upset. He was a wreck. But the sheriff also knew that the overly obvious observation didn't mean that the man wasn't also a coldblooded killer.

"I'm not trying to pressure you, John, " the sheriff finally spoke. "But whenever you are ready to talk, is it alright if I record the conversation?" Douglas reached for the small black device that was sitting off to his left and then placed it evenly between them.

John started to open his mouth to answer, but then just gradually nodded his head up and down.

"Thank you." And to get the task done and over with, Douglas went ahead and hit Record on the machine.

Unlike Deputy Andrews, the sheriff preferred to play back the interview and listen to it a few times instead of writing out notes. Ben had argued that he got more out of the process if he took things down in his own handwriting. The sheriff didn't quite understand; why create more work for yourself? But he'd ultimately digressed — to each his own.

"I went to Elaine's this morning," John started. "Before work, to have coffee."

The sheriff nodded. "Was this a regular meeting for the two of you? Did you usually meet in the mornings before school?"

"No," John answered. "Today would have been the first time."

"And why is that?" The sheriff continued. He'd finally gotten John talking and now refused to stop. Douglas had checked his emotions, and was now on a mission to get to the truth. "What was so different about this morning?"

"We decided last night that I would come over before school."

"Via phone? In person?" The sheriff's patience was slowly starting to bleed out; he was getting close to empty. "Stop giving me these useless scraps, John. I want to help you. I *will* help you. But not until you give me the full story, okay? I want a play-by-play."

"A play-by-play?" John repeated. The man gritted his teeth, causing a painful grinding noise to fill the room. "Fine," he agreed. "Here it is, from the top. Last night, Elaine came over for dinner. My daughter, Elle, later joined us. Emily, Elaine's daughter, wasn't able to make it because of cheerleading practice. Before Elaine left, we agreed that I would come to her house to have coffee and see Emily since I hadn't been able to the night before."

"To see Emily?" Douglas asked.

"Yes," John confirmed. "Elaine and I have... had been dating for several months; I'd met Emily a couple of times outside of school. Elaine met Elle for the first time last night. We wanted..." he paused for a moment. He seemed to be trying to find the right words. "We wanted to start bringing our families together."

"I see," Douglas said.

"Was that detailed enough for you, Sheriff?"

Douglas chose to ignore John's dark tone. On some level, the sheriff figured he deserved it. "And there was no problem at school? No policy against the two of you dating?"

"No," John quickly said. And then the man did something that surprised the sheriff—he started laughing. "There's no such policy. As a matter of fact, no one really knew about us. We weren't trying to hide anything, but we weren't exactly shouting it from the rooftops either. It was no one's business."

"Do you happen to remember what time Elaine left your place last night?" Douglas nonchalantly scratched his head. This was an important question, maybe even the *most* important one he would ask the man.

John closed his eyes; he appeared to be concentrating. "Around eleven, maybe a little after."

"Interesting," Douglas said. And as soon as the word escaped him, he immediately regretted it. He felt his hand rush to cover his open mouth, but the damage had already been done. There was no way he could retract it.

"What's interesting?" John asked.

Douglas didn't answer. Instead, he shifted uncomfortably in his seat, and then nervously craned his head to the left to completely avoid eye contact.

"What's so interesting, Sheriff Douglas?" John repeated. "The fact that I was most likely the last person to ever see Elaine alive? Or the fact that I was most likely the first person to find her and Emily dead?"

The sheriff quickly turned back to John. "You said that, not me."

"You were thinking it. Don't deny it."

Douglas had been thinking it—word for word.

"Tell me I'm wrong," John demanded.

Douglas didn't bother acknowledging the order. Instead, he asked a question that would undoubtedly open up another can of worms. "Is there anyone who can vouch for you? Anyone that can say you stayed home after Elaine left? This is, assuming you did stay home after she left."

"I didn't leave my house last night," John said. "And no, no one saw me stay in, either. Elle went to bed early, and I never saw her again."

"I see," the sheriff said. "You know…"

"What I want to know," John roughly interrupted, "is why I would want to kill Elaine and Emily. What would possibly be my motive? Or better yet, let's talk about Kim Sullivan."

"Excuse me?" Douglas sat up straight in his chair. "You better watch your words, John. You don't want to say something that you're later going to…"

"Regret?" John finished. "Look where I am, Sheriff. Look what's happened to me."

"Nothing's happened to you, John. We're just talking."

"Well, I want to talk about Kimberley Sullivan," John said. "You think I killed Elaine and Emily because I was the one that discovered their bodies? Because I was connected to both of them? Why would I have killed Kim Sullivan, though? The murders are obviously all intertwined; the same person committed them. I'm in no way connected to Kim, so why would I have killed her? Enlighten me, Sheriff."

Douglas didn't say anything. He couldn't. John Anderson actually had a point, but the last thing the sheriff intended to do was reveal that to his suspect. He'd made that mistake once already in this interview, and he'd be damned if he was going to do it again.

The sheriff and Deputy Andrews had briefly discussed victimology in the past couple of hours. The women had most likely been picked at random. After all, the three victims didn't share much, if any, physically characteristics. But that didn't stop the sheriff from revisiting the idea now.

His gut told him that the women could all be grouped together in some sort of manner. In the very least, they each had to have some minor link to the killer. But if John hadn't known Kimberley Sullivan, did that mean he could no longer be considered a person of interest? Someone who was responsible for all three murders?

Playing connect the dots had never been his forte, which is exactly why he'd already assigned the tedious task to another deputy.

"Sheriff Douglas?"

He turned at the sound of his name. Deputy Andrews was standing in the opened doorway, gripping the round brass handle. An interruption was the absolute last thing the sheriff wanted — especially now that he and John were finally getting somewhere.

"Deputy, I'm in the middle of something very important." The sheriff thought he had done a great job of combining anger, annoyance, and frustration all into one. He didn't approve of the distraction. And Ben needed to know that. "Whatever it is, it will just have to wait until later."

"Sorry, sir," Andrews said. He looked down to the ground. "This can't wait; I need to talk to you in private. Now."

Douglas scooted his chair back, causing a nails down a chalkboard-like screech. He jerked himself up, crossed his arms over his chest, and started towards the deputy. The sheriff was almost positive that a thick steam was pouring out of his own ears.

"Sheriff Douglas?"

"I'll be right back," the sheriff called over his shoulder.

"When you do, would you mind bringing me some water? My throat's dry."

"Sure thing," Douglas answered. The sheriff took a giant step forward, willing the deputy in front of him to step back. Exiting the room, Douglas slammed the door shut, causing the frame to noisily rattle.

"Sheriff, I hated to stop you, but…"

"Follow me, son. Now!"

Douglas led the way down the narrow hall. After reaching a deserted section at the back of the building, he placed his hands on his heavy hips and stared down at the deputy. He had the power. He was in control. Why couldn't Ben understand that?

"What the fuck are you trying to do, son?" Douglas roared.

"Sheriff, I apologize for…"

"You apologize?" The sheriff mocked. "I'm trying to solve a murder. *Three* murders," he quickly corrected. "I'm in the middle of questioning a suspect, the only suspect that we have, and you just barge in like it's no big deal?"

"Sir, this is important," Ben stated.

"Oh, it better be, son. Otherwise, you might just find yourself holding a new record here at the Gray's Lane Police Department: hired and fired in the same week."

"Sheriff, Mary Evans is…"

"Down at the high school doing a live broadcast of the latest murders, as well as releasing the fact that the killer's signature is candy corn?" Douglas enjoyed watching Ben's eyes grow to the size of golf balls. "Yes, I'm well aware of what Mary Evans is up to, and I've already sent someone to the high school to stop her."

"You know?" Ben asked. "How do you know?"

"Well, I am the sheriff of this town; it's my job to know what goes on here. Now, did you have anything else you needed to tell me that was so damn important it couldn't wait until after I've finished with John? Or was that all?"

"Do you know where this leak of information is coming from?" The deputy asked.

"I'm currently looking in to it," the sheriff said, balling his hands into impatient fists. "Was there anything else? Or can I get back to my suspect?"

The deputy didn't answer, but stood completely still, gaze once again glued to the floor. The sheriff wondered if the kid was trying to become invisible.

"Look," Douglas started. He suddenly felt a case of nerves attacking him. The tingling sensation that erupted throughout his body made him cringe. He'd never been good at apologies. "I shouldn't have snapped or cussed at you. You did the right thing by informing me of Mary's broadcast. I lost my temper. This case, these murders, I'm just... I'm out of my..."

"Sheriff," Ben said softly. "There is something else."

"Okay, son," Douglas said. "Go ahead."

"I've been talking with that girl that came into the station. You know, the one who said she had information about the murders."

"Yes," Douglas nodded.

"Well, it turns out that she's John Anderson's daughter. She's recently moved to Gray's Lane from New York, and she seems to think that the killer followed her here."

"Excuse me?" the sheriff felt his thin eyebrows shoot up. He didn't move an inch as the deputy quickly delved into a wild story that low budget horror films were often made from. But the sheriff continued to listen, nonetheless, not sure if he was supposed to laugh, cry, or scream.

"So this girl," Douglas finally said once Andrews had finished, "this Elle Anderson, who is John's daughter, actually believes the killer followed her here from New York to Ohio?"

"Yes," the deputy said and then nodded.

"And she knew about the candy corn?" the sheriff asked, nervously biting down onto his lower lip.

"She didn't know that the victims here had been scattered with the candy, not until after Mary's report."

The sheriff tilted his head to the right; he let the deputy's words fully sink in. Everything was starting to make sense now. "So, it wasn't until *after* Mary revealed the killer's signature that this girl, this Elle, told you that her mother was murdered under the same conditions in New York?"

"Sir, I know how it all sounds, but I've talked to her. I believe her. Not to mention, if John is the killer, then this is another woman he was once connected to. This is his ex-wife."

That was certainly true, the sheriff decided, but something was still off. Why would a killer travel from New York to Ohio? He wasn't completely sure that he believed what the girl had told his deputy. It all seemed so sudden, so convenient. But then again, the sheriff thought, why would Elle Anderson make up such an elaborate story? Why would she lie?

"Sheriff, if a killer *did* cross state lines, we need to call…"

"Don't get ahead of yourself, Andrews. We don't know for a fact that this girl is telling the truth. For whatever reason, she could be making all of this up."

"But why would she do that?" Ben argued. "Her story ultimately puts another nail in her father's coffin."

"She doesn't know he's a suspect, right?" the sheriff asked. "You didn't tell her that we currently have him in custody, did you?"

"No, sir, I didn't. But I still think we need to try and confirm what she said. Maybe I should call the police in New York, talk to whoever handled her mother's murder."

The sheriff glared at Ben. "Listen to me, Deputy Andrews. We don't have time for wild goose chases. And the last thing I need is some fancy, city cop telling me how to do my job. I don't need an outsider's help; I can protect my town."

"I'm sorry, Sheriff Douglas. I just thought…"

"The girl is yanking your chain. She's still upset about her mother's death, so she's linking it to the murders that have happened here. Elle Anderson is lying, and I don't want to hear anymore about it."

"Alright," He whispered.

"I've got real leads to follow, and a real suspect to question. Drop this New York angle," Douglas ordered. "Forget what that girl told you, and forget about calling anyone outside of this department for help. Understand?"

Sheriff Douglas never got an answer; his cell phone began chirping. He abruptly reached into his pocket, gripped the device, and brought it up to his ear.

"This is the sheriff," Douglas answered.

"Sheriff Douglas, this is Deputy Hall. I went to the high school like you asked me to, but Mary was already gone."

"Good work, sport," the sheriff said, leaning up against the wall. "I'll pay her a little visit later myself. Now, were you able to find anything else out on that little matter we discussed?"

Sheriff Douglas listened carefully as the other man spoke. He promptly felt a warm smile spread across his face. "Thank you, Deputy Hall. Thank you very much." The sheriff ended the call and returned his phone to his pocket.

"Is everything alright, sir?" Ben asked.

"Everything is just perfect," Douglas answered. "Everything is finally falling neatly into place."

"What do you mean, sir?"

"Follow me, Deputy Andrews, and I'll show you."

Douglas led the way back down the hall and into his office. He resumed his seat behind his desk, leaving Ben to stand against the closed door.

It was then that the sheriff remembered John's request for water. But now, that request would just have to wait.

"Sorry about that, John."

"It's okay, Sheriff," John said. "I was wondering…"

"I was wondering why you lied to me," Douglas interrupted the man. He stared into John's dark eyes, refusing to blink. He had a role to play now — tough cop — and he was going to make sure that he nailed it.

"Lied to you?" John asked. A confused frown overtook his face. "Lied to you about what, Sheriff?"

"Kimberley Sullivan," Douglas swiftly said. "You said that you had no connection to that woman."

"I don't!" John screamed.

"You're lying again," the sheriff said coolly. "You better start telling me the truth, and I mean right now."

"I am telling you the truth! I've *been* telling you the truth," John pleaded.

"Okay," Douglas shrugged. "Then tell me about Kim Sullivan, because I know that you used to date her."

SEVENTEEN

HE HATED TO HEAR THAT TWO MORE women had been murdered. He'd seen Mary Evans' live broadcast from Gray's Lane High School this morning, and a rapid, gut-wrenching pain had immediately erupted throughout his entire body. There was a real, active serial killer in his hometown.

However, there was a bright side to all of this madness, and Jeff Sullivan had been quick to see it: he was officially off the hook and completely in the clear! Hallelujah, praise the Lord!

Jeff stood barefoot in his petite kitchen, the cold tile pressing into his skin. The rich, French roast scent lifted from the white mug he held hands and rose up to his nostrils. He wasn't sure which he enjoyed more about the caffeine: the smell or the taste. Either way, the coffee was a morning ritual.

He slowly began pacing. He started at the side-by-side black refrigerator, walked to the edge of the countertop, and then repeated the movement.

When he reached the counter for the second time, he set his now empty mug down and thrust his calloused hands into the pockets of his striped pajama pants. Events seemed to be moving at NASCAR speed; he needed a quiet moment to digest everything that had recently happened.

He was grateful that Niki was back at school. Though she had most likely seen Mary's report first hand, front and center, and would later need to be consoled because of the journalist's heartless ways, he was thankful for his time of solitude. He needed it.

Jeff propped himself up against the empty sink and crossed his arms over his tight chest. He was almost one hundred percent positive that he had dodged a bullet. If Sheriff Douglas hadn't already erased his name from the list of possible suspects, Jeff knew that it had to now be permanently gone. What had happened last night should have guaranteed it.   Though someone could have *maybe* found a reason for him to want his wife dead, Jeff knew that there wasn't one rock anywhere of any kind to be overturned that could prove he wanted Elaine and Emily Jacobs dead, too. He didn't care about them. He didn't even know them. Not to mention, he had an alibi.

He felt a growing smile stretch across his face. He couldn't remember the last time he had actually smiled, probably some time before Kim had been killed. The gesture felt foreign to him, even awkward, but he couldn't help but take pleasure in it.

The murders had nothing to do with him, nothing to do with his family, and nothing to do with his immoral actions. His wife had just simply — unfortunately — been chosen by some crazed psycho to be stabbed to death. The action had been uncontrollable. And for the past five days, he'd worried himself into a frenzy for no reason at all.

Jeff ran his fingers through his unkempt brown hair, relieved that he'd taken the day off of work, and had absolutely nowhere to be and nothing to do.

He contemplated calling *her*. It had been about a week since they'd last spoken, and he truly did miss her. He also forgave her, Jeff suddenly realized. He no longer was upset. He deeply wanted to tell her that now.

Later, he ultimately decided. He would give her a call later. After all, Jeff was well aware of the fact that she was a busy woman. So busy, he considered, that she might not even be able to take his call at the moment.

So, he would wait, be patient, and just make the call sometime later.

He contemplated pouring himself a glass of champagne, but there were two things wrong with that idea: he didn't have any bubbly, and he wasn't a monster. So instead, Jeff settled for another cup of joe. He then set out for the back living room, deciding that he would enjoy his brew while lounging on the sofa.

He took a seat and crossed one leg over the other. He assumed that this was what peace felt like—being in his quiet home, lavishing in a morning cup of coffee, knowing that his life was on the verge of changing for the better.

Sure, Jeff thought, as he leaned back into the comfortable cushion of the couch, he missed his wife and was genuinely disturbed at the way her life had ended. However, he didn't love her, hadn't for quite some time, and part of him was thoroughly happy that she was gone and officially out of his way.

Caution would still be a major factor, Jeff admitted to himself. He wasn't about to have his dirty laundry aired out all over town; he still cared what the community thought of him. The last thing Jeff wanted was to be known as a 'bad guy,' especially in the town he had grown up in. Therefore, he'd still have to be careful with his secret, and also hope that Robbie Douglas continued to keep his mouth shut.

Jeff closed his eyes; he only wanted to see darkness.

It was difficult to keep an affair hidden. It was even more difficult to keep an affair hidden in such a small town. A town where everyone knew everyone and gossip was just another sport. But when your teenage daughter's boyfriend unexpectedly became aware of your affair, well, then keeping your infidelities hidden became next to impossible. But so far, Jeff was pleasantly surprised to have accomplished such a feat. And to his knowledge, Robbie had still remained silent.

Jeff remembered the day vividly, too vividly, actually. It seemed to constantly play in his mind like a nightmare. And as much as he'd desperately tried to forget it, he was simply unable to. The day he'd been caught, the day he'd started living on that slippery slope, being continuously worried, was something Jeff had feared would always be with him.

Well, until now maybe. Now, none of that mattered. *Almost.*

He thought he'd been smart, sneaky, but in reality, he'd just been plain cocky. The actions now played out in his heavy mind. Jeff swore that he could even feel the burning sensation of tears slowly swimming into the corners of his eyes as he saw *that* day, the day he so badly wanted to flip off like a light switch.

It'd been several weeks ago, more accurately, closer to a month, Jeff decided. He was supposed to have had the house to himself that Saturday morning and into the afternoon. But Jeff had painfully come to realize over the years that things seldom worked out the way in which they were planned.

Kim had gone shopping for the entire day, some new, big time mall that was a couple of hours away. Niki and Robbie had had a college visit scheduled somewhere, the next state over, Jeff had believed, leaving him *supposedly* alone to have a "free day" to spend with a certain lady friend.

Jeff had called her the night before to arrange the meeting. They'd never used his house as a meeting place, and she'd been fast to voice her opinion about doing so now. In the past, they'd used her home or a discrete motel for all encounters. What if they got caught? What if his wife or daughter came home unexpectedly? What if she unknowingly left behind a distinctive strand of hair on a pillowcase? She didn't have a family to worry about, not like he did.

But he'd waved off her concerns, almost as if they'd been annoying flies buzzing around an open garbage can. But Jeff now realized that he'd been stupid, childish, and regretted that he hadn't listened to her.

He'd wanted to be with her in his own surroundings, have breakfast in bed — among other things — and not have to worry about a checkout time, or her abruptly kicking him out so that she could get to work on one of her new projects. Jeff had wanted to be comfortable, and he'd insisted until she had finally given in and agreed to drive out to his house.

Her vehicle had been parked in the two-car garage, her expensive heels had been kicked off at the front door, and she'd been standing half naked in the kitchen watching him scramble eggs when the teenager's voice had loudly rang out.

"Mr. Sullivan? It's Robbie."

Jeff still could recall the needle-sharp stab that had exploded in his spine. He'd immediately dropped the plastic spatula, reached for his discarded plaid boxers on the floor, and had tried to motion to his guest to find a hiding spot.

"We didn't make it very far. Niki left her ID."

A thick wave of panic had then smothered him. He'd looked over to his left, already knowing what he would see: Niki's pink wallet sitting right where she had left it, on the counter, directly in front of his lady friend.

"Mr. Sullivan, are you here?"

He'd known then what was going to happen; there would be no way to fight it. Jeff had been directly hit in the jaw with the inevitable: he was going to get caught. Robbie's voice had been getting closer, the teenager *himself* was getting closer; there would be no time to react.

"Niki said her ID was…" Robbie's words had trailed off as he'd entered the kitchen, and Jeff had tried like hell to avoid eye contact.

He'd wished for the power to become invisible, Jeff now recalled. Just like when he'd been a toddler and would get caught sneaking cookies before dinner from the ceramic dish in the kitchen. Only this time, he'd been well aware of the fact that his punishment would be much more severe. This time, the consequences for his wrongdoing would be like nothing he'd ever experienced in his entire life.

"Mr. Sullivan," Robbie had started, eyes wide and jaw hanging dangerously open. "I didn't mean… I'm sorry… please forgive me for interrupting."

Jeff had been fast to notice that Niki was nowhere in sight, assuming that she'd decided to wait in the car. At least there'd been a silver lining in the whole mess — albeit, a small one.

After moments of an achingly long silence had passed, Jeff had begged Robbie to stay quiet. He'd even gone as far as offering the teenager money for his discretion. Robbie had turned the offer down, making Jeff only flush more with guilt and embarrassment. But Robbie had also agreed not to talk. Jeff had been utterly relieved, because he hadn't only been terrified about what he was doing getting out, but also who he was doing it with.

His not-so-secret relationship had pretty much ended there. It had rattled his nerves, as if some minute bug or pest was underneath his skin, crawling around, constantly causing his skin to itch. But a break had definitely been in order, and she'd completely agreed with him.

But ultimately, a cooling off period hadn't mattered. Kim had still found out about his affair. She'd even confronted him about it last Saturday afternoon.

"How stupid do you think I am, Jeff?" she'd screamed. "Did you honestly think that I wouldn't find out?"

"How did you find out?"

"That doesn't matter!"

"Did Robbie tell you?" he'd asked.

"Robbie knows?" Her face had shown a genuine look of surprise. "Why does Robbie know, Jeff?"

He'd sidestepped her question, much like she had done to his. The argument had continued, only growing more fiery and intense. Kim hadn't known whom exactly he'd been sleeping with, but just that he had been sleeping around. Jeff hadn't been so sure if that was a good thing or bad thing, but still had been curious as to how she'd figured it all out.

"How long has it been going on, Jeff?"

"Why do you care? How will knowing that make anything different?"

She'd cried a lot. Her face had become a dark red tone, and when she'd spoke, her voice had been hoarse and almost unrecognizable. "Break it off, break it off *now,* Jeff. If you don't end it, I will divorce you, and I'll take everything you have."

"I hope you die a slow, painful death," Jeff had bellowed. He'd then left the bedroom and walked out of the house. It had been the last time he'd ever seen his wife alive. Those horrible eight words had been the last words he'd ever spoken to her. He'd come back home hours later to find that Kim had multiple stab wounds, and that her lifeless body had been littered with pieces of candy corn.

Jeff now regretted the way he had handled things with Kim. He knew that he should have been up front with her, left her, and only then started a relationship with someone else. And what he had said to his wife, the irony of it all, assuming that she really had suffered a slow, painful death, well, they were words that he'd never be able to take back.

Yes, the grinding torment of regret was something that easily flooded Jeff's veins, even if he really was glad to be rid of Kim.

However, the main thing now was moving ahead. And if Robbie continued to stay mum about what he had witnessed, then Jeff knew that he was definitely home free. What he had done and who he had done it with had had nothing to do with his wife's untimely demise. Like he'd already reasoned, it was all just an ugly coincidence. But as a result, he was now officially free to resume his relationship with *her*.

Jeff suddenly stood up, deciding to end this nasty trip down memory lane. He'd reminisced enough for one day. He power walked back to the kitchen. He traded his half full coffee mug for his cell phone, punched in the number he had long ago committed to memory, and hit Send.

Jeff waited.

"Yes?"

"Hello," he said. He promptly felt his entire body begin to tingle. He noticed that the hair on his arms had even started to rise. "It's me."

"Me?" she repeated. "Who is this?"

A frown replaced his crooked smile. He was taken aback. "It's Jeff. I guess it has been a little while."

"Jeff," she said. And then in a rough, disgusted tone, she added, "Jeff, I don't understand what you're doing. Why are you calling me?"

"I was hoping that we could talk, maybe even meet."

"After everything that's happened lately, you think we can just start back up again? You're not serious, Jeff?"

He felt his head bob from side to side; he didn't quite understand her deal. Maybe she was just having an off day at work. "Well, I do forgive you. In no way do I hold a grudge or believe that..."

"Forgive me for what?" she interrupted.

"For what you did following Kimberley's murder."

"Jeff, I'm not sorry for what I did, and I'm definitely not looking for forgiveness. It's my job, plain and simple. I'm good at it, and I enjoy it."

The last thing he wanted to do was fight, especially over the phone. He had to see her in person, and then maybe she would see how much he really missed her, how much he really wanted to be with her. Her attitude would change if he could just get her to agree to a meeting somewhere.

"Look, Jeff," she said, cutting off his needy, desperate thoughts. "I've recently met someone else."

"You're dating someone else?" he asked, quickly realizing that his question was soaked in surprise.

"No," she corrected. "I'm sleeping with someone else."

"I'm sure that if we were to get together…"

"The story is finally heating up. Don't call me again," she ordered. "It's over."

Jeff dropped his cell phone; the device landed on the hard countertop. He had no control over his numb body, as he slowly melted down onto the cushioned barstool. He felt like he couldn't breathe. Jeff hadn't been expecting this outcome. But apparently, his relationship with Mary Evans was now officially dead and buried.

EIGHTEEN

"WHO WAS THAT ON THE PHONE?"

"Is it any of your business," she hastily fired back, "who I speak to on my cell phone?"

"When you're speaking to someone on your cell phone in the middle of the day while we should be working," Henry started, "then yes, it is my business."

Mary angrily crossed her arms over her chest; she was not going to let Henry ruin this day. She was on a high now, and refused to come down from it. Her breaking story had been a hit; she just knew it. She didn't have time to argue with Henry Wren, or listen to Jeff Sullivan's whiney pleas. A reporter's job was never done, and Mary was well aware of the fact that it was time to search for a new story. And she knew just where to start.

"I need to know who the suspect is," Mary said. "I *have* to know."

"Well, why don't you give Baby Always a call," Henry suggested with a sly smile. "I'm guessing that wasn't him just now on the line."

"Do you enjoy being an ass? Does it make you feel good?"

"In a word?" Henry asked. Then he nodded, "Yes. It does feel pretty good."

She rolled her dark eyes, and then brought both of her small hands up to cover her face. Mary shook her head; the morning had started off so great, so perfect. And now, well now it was quickly going downhill.

As annoying as Henry was, she still found it difficult to complain. She'd been able to report live at the high school without a single interruption. Mary had seen that dopey Deputy Hall drive through the parking lot, eyes intently searching, as if he really stood a chance at stopping her. Hall had just missed her and Henry speeding away. Not that she'd been worried; there wasn't a chance in hell that he could bring her down.

She'd updated Gray's Lane on the double homicide, informed the town of the candy corn signature, and had even released the privileged information that Sheriff Douglas had a suspect in custody. But it still wasn't enough. Mary had a deep hunger clawing within her. She needed that suspect's name.

"So," Henry pestered, interrupting her private thoughts and concentration. "How about it? You going to call your source? Or what?"

"It's not that easy," Mary informed. She fused her hands together and placed them behind her neck for support. "I think that well has pretty much run dry."

She hadn't spoken with her informant, not since her broadcast, but she was willing to bet that he wasn't too impressed with her. She'd reneged on their deal, broken their tight agreement, and ran with the story despite her promise not to do so.

Mary had already taken into consideration that she might have hurt herself in the long run, but she'd accepted that fact. Though she might not get any more insider tips from Baby Always, Mary had ultimately decided that the story she had was too big to sit on. So she'd shared it, and she'd shared it well.

But now she was suffering. Her head was throbbing, quickly ticking as if it were a bomb ready to explode. She wanted to know who was in custody. But how could she get that information? It wasn't like she could storm the police station and make demands. Or could she?

Mary jumped out of her chair, eyes wide, body on fire, excitement pulsing throughout every vein. She had a new idea.

"I recognize that look in your eyes, Mary," Henry said, still calmly sitting in the chair in front of her desk. It was almost as if he didn't have one care or responsibility in the entire world.

He made her want to vomit. "And what look would that be, Henry?"

"That nasty look, like you're getting ready to fuck someone's day up."

She shrugged. "I guess that's just the way it goes. I'm sure as shit not going to wait around here for something to happen. I'm going to make it happen."

"Alright," he said and took a deep breath. "What's the new plan, then? Do I get to know? Are you dragging me down with you?"

Mary didn't respond to the insults, she didn't see the point. He enjoyed getting in his little digs at her. Oh, well. She knew that she would eventually have the last laugh. And besides, she was already busy putting out feelers for his replacement.

"Well?" he prompted.

"I'm going to the police station," she said, finally giving into him. "Do you want to join me or not?"

"Why in the hell would you go to the police station?" Henry barked. "Do you want to get arrested? Is that your plan? *Becoming* the news?"

"Why would I get arrested?" she asked innocently. "I haven't done anything wrong; I haven't stabbed anyone to death."

Henry sat straight up. "You really don't think that your little stunt at the school today warrants…"

"I think my little stunt," Mary mocked, "was just me practicing my right to freedom of speech. Plain and simple."

"And if Sheriff Douglas demands you give him the name of your source? Then what?"

She laughed. The throaty sound echoed around the room. Mary felt her eyes begin to water, and was pleased that she was wearing waterproof mascara. Honestly, Henry could be so mind-numbingly stupid.

"Did I say something funny?" he asked.

"Journalism one oh one," she said, trying to compose herself, at least long enough to educate him on the lesson. "A reporter doesn't have to give up her sources."

Besides, she thought, what was Douglas going to do? Arrest her? Not that that would be completely horrible, she considered. The Gray's Lane Police Department wasn't that big, there was probably only one unisex cell. And then she'd get a one on one interview with the suspect himself, so to speak.

Hmm, she contemplated. She used her forefinger and thumb to lightly rub her silky-smooth chin: how fast and easy could she commit a white-collar crime?

"Mary!"

"What?" She snapped her head back around to look at Henry. Why was he yelling at her — and in her own office? If she'd had a Pulitzer sitting on her tidy desk, she'd have picked it up and thrown it at him. "What do you want?"

"You're not listening to me, are you? I don't think it would be wise to go visit the police station."

"And why is that?" Mary's eyes traveled the length of her desk again, searching for another object this time. Damn, her mind screamed. Where was her traveling coffee mug? Probably still in the van from earlier, she assumed.

"Well, it did us absolutely no good the last time we went, remember?" Henry offered. "Sheriff Douglas practically threw you out, while all of the other deputies stood by and stared in amusement."

She did remember, quite clearly actually. But she also knew that that visit hadn't been a complete waste. Her impromptu rendezvous had scared her little gossip guy right into her arms, where he'd gotten comfortable and had willingly fed her more facts pertaining to the case.

Maybe it would work a second time, she wondered. If she unexpectedly showed up once more to the station, maybe fear would consume her source, and she'd get the name of the suspect.

"Are you hearing me, Mary? Or are you off in your own little world again?"

"Yes, I'm hearing you!" she hollered back. "I'm just not *getting* you!"

"Let me try another tactic then," Henry suggested.

"You can talk till you're blue in the face," she offered, "but nothing you say is going to prevent me from going down to the police station to see what I can uncover."

"Even if that means sacrificing whatever little credibility you have left? Not to mention if you make a fool of yourself, then the broadcast from this morning will be forgotten." Henry nodded, "You will definitely be the laughing stock of this town. That is, if you're not already."

"Excuse me?" Mary asked in a soft whisper. He now had her full attention. She slowly began sliding back into her leather chair, considering what he'd just said. As far as she was concerned, Henry had spoken fighting words. And now she needed to know *exactly* what he was getting at.

"Think about it," Henry said. He brought his elbows down to rest on his knees. "If you start making threatening remarks towards Sheriff Douglas and his deputies, he's going to arrest you. He'll say you're interfering with his investigation or something."

"So?" She exploded and threw up her hands. Mary prayed he got to the point and fast! Though a Gray's Lane jail cell wasn't one of her most desired destinations, she figured she could still handle it. After all, it wasn't Alcatraz. The hardest part of survival would be not dying of boredom.

"Well, then you'll be known as just another sleazy, tabloid reporter. Not that you're pretty much not that already," Henry corrected. "But even more so, your arrest will over shadow your broadcast. Residents won't be talking about the new murders or the candy corn. They'll be talking about the woman who broke the news and how she was thrown into the slammer. They won't trust anything you report ever again."

Silence suddenly overpowered her. Mary became aware that her jaw was hanging unattractively open. The inside of her mouth was as dry as a desert, and she craved water as if it might be the only thing that could possibly keep her alive. But at the moment, she couldn't move. Mary didn't have the energy to go in search of a drink.

"Did I make any sense at all?" Henry asked. He leaned back and crossed one leg over the other, repeating his position from earlier. "You're looking at me like I just lapsed into Chinese."

Henry had made sense, and she completely understood and agreed with everything he had said. But she didn't want to appear weak; Mary didn't want Henry to think that she needed him. She didn't want Henry to know that he'd actually been right, and that she saw his point quite clearly.

The truth, she now admitted to herself, was that a big blowup would only make her look bad. And the last thing Mary wanted to do was look bad. She'd worked way too hard, and her efforts were just now starting to pay off; she didn't want to counteract that now.

Mary reached down to the floor, grabbed the black strap to her Italian leather purse, and pulled the bag up to her lap. She began digging through the contents, grazing each and every item except for the one that she wanted.

"What are you looking for?" Henry asked. "Do you think you're going to find the solution to your problem in that knockoff designer purse?"

She was well aware of what Henry was trying to do—push her buttons even further, probably hoping to make her go completely crazy. But she wasn't going to fall for it. Mary was going to save her sanity, and not get into a yelling match with him.

Finally, she found what she needed—a brand new pack of chewing gum. She pulled a stick free, unwrapped the foil, crumpled up the trash, and then threw it into the wastebasket underneath her desk. The warm sensation of cinnamon immediately filled her mouth, and the heated scent caused her to smile and take a deep breath so that she could enjoy the vice even more. Mary didn't bother to offer Henry a piece of gum.

"You know, on second thought, I don't think I'll be going down to the station today," Mary said nonchalantly. She placed her purse back onto the floor, picked up a loose ink pen from her desk, and began looking for a piece of paper to write on.

"Oh, really," Henry said and then shrugged. "I'm just curious, Mary, but where did you get an idea like that from? It couldn't have been from, well, me?" A wide smile spread across his face. "Right?"

She threw the pen down and watched as it hit the surface of her desk, bounced, and then rolled out of sight. Much like her relationship with Jeff, she considered: out of sight, and hopefully, very soon, out of mind.

Their fling had been fun while it had lasted, but she was now moving on up to bigger and better things. She still cared about Jeff, and had enjoyed her time with him, but she didn't *need* him. He couldn't do anything for her or for her career. And now that she was completely certain that his wife's death hadn't been a direct result from their affair, Mary felt no guilt whatsoever for thoroughly cutting the man loose. Easy come, easy go.

"You should know by now, Mary, that ignoring me won't work."

"I'm not ignoring you, Henry," she argued. "I'm just thinking."

"Oh, okay," he nodded. "And are you thinking about how lucky you are to have someone like me around to offer you such great advice?"

"You were right, Henry!" Mary hollered. The words left a sour milk taste in her mouth. "Now, do you feel better? Will you get off of my damn back? I admit that you were right, okay?"

"Just say it one more time." He cupped his hand to his ear. "I want to make sure that I hear you clearly this time."

"Go to hell!" she ordered and then shook her head. Mary had been stupid. She recognized that now. She'd actually thought that giving in to Henry would have made him shut his mouth;

she'd been utterly wrong. In the end, Mary had only fueled the fire and given Henry more ammo, allowing him to further gloat.

"But seriously, Mary," Henry started, "all kidding aside, I'm glad we can agree on something. It's like we're officially a team. You know?"

"Yeah, sure, whatever," she said. She reached for her cell phone that was in the center or her desk. "You can call us whatever you want, Henry, but you still owe me a hundred bucks."

"So you keep reminding me," he said. "Who are you calling?" he asked with a frown.

"Just worry about getting me my money," she said, sidestepping his question. She stabbed in a number and waited. It was time to take back some control. Well, she reconsidered, *all* of the control.

"Yes?" a voice finally answered on the other end. She was positive that he was whispering, trying not to be heard.

"Hi," she said. She attempted to make sure that a certain amount of sweetness coated her voice. Mary was well aware of the fact that it sometimes took finesse to get what you wanted. "It's me. Are you busy?"

"I'm very busy," he said, the tone of his voice deepening, definitely dripping with anger. "Why are you calling me? You know I'm at work. I told you never to call me while I'm working."

And then, Mary quickly decided, there were times that in order to get what you wanted, you needed to be a total, raging bitch. That was some-thing she was *definitely* familiar with.

"Are you still there?" he asked. "Do you remember me telling you that?"

"I remember you telling me a lot of things," Mary backfired. "For instances, candy corn, the double homicide, and something about having a suspect in custody. How could I possibly forget something like that?"

"Alright, alright," he said. His voice was back to a whisper.

"Good," she said as she leaned back into her chair. She brought her long legs up, crossed her bare feet at the ankles, and placed them on the corner of her desk. "It seems like we have an understanding then."

"No," he argued, "we *had* an understanding and you broke it. You were supposed to wait until the case was closed before you reported anything on the murders. You lied to me. You used me. You *played* me."

"What can I say?" she said with a shrug. "I guess I'm just not a very patient person. I couldn't wait any longer, and made an executive decision to go ahead and run with the story. Sorry," she mumbled.

"Well, you can lose my number, because I'm not giving you anything else. That includes in the bedroom, too."

"Oh, honey, get real," she said, desperately trying to muffle an oncoming fit of laughter.

"You're not that great of a lay, and I'm pretty sure you're going to continue giving me whatever I want."

"Excuse me?"

"Think about it: I've got you right where I want you," she said. "If you don't continue to feed me information about the case, then maybe I'll be forced to give your superior a little phone call and update him on our arrangement."

"Seriously, a threat? Are you sure you want to blackmail a man of the law?"

"I've done a lot worse for a lot less," she said. "And don't act like you're innocent."

"Fine," he said. "What do you want?"

"I want to meet you. Tonight," she ordered. "We need to talk in person. Your place, seven-thirty."

"Okay," he agreed. "But it has to be later. I've got something else going on. I can meet you around ten."

"You better show up. Otherwise, you're done in Gray's Lane." Mary didn't wait for a response. She ended the call and threw her phone down onto her desk.

"Baby Always?"

She almost fell out of her seat. Until he'd spoken, she'd forgotten Henry was in the room. She'd thought she'd been alone. Mary brought her feet back to the ground, and rested her elbows on the surface of her desk.

"Don't repeat anything you just heard. Clear?"

"Another threat?"

"No," she corrected, "an order from your boss."

"I was wondering, Mary, do you think the killer is following your work?"

"What do you mean?" she asked.

"Well, I'm just thinking out loud, but you've got a pretty big mouth. I mean, you've reported information that no one else in town has really been privy to until now."

"So?"

"So," he repeated, "the killer may not want all of his secrets revealed to the public. Therefore, he or she may come after you. Have you given much thought to that idea?"

An ice-covered jolt of pain pierced her flat stomach. Mary hadn't given much thought to Henry's idea. She'd never once considered that she could actually be the next victim.

NINETEEN

THE CUL-DE-SAC WAS APPROPRIATELY DEC-
orated for the season and upcoming holiday.
Unfortunately, the festive decorations didn't
set too well with the string of murders that had
recently taken place.

Studying the houses that lined her street,
Elle couldn't help but notice the various ghosts,
tombstones, severed limbs, and masks from
famous scary films that had been intricately placed
throughout yards, in trees, and on the sidewalk.

Ironically, a terrifying Halloween seemed to
be the common theme for the entire community —
literally. Even the pumpkins that had been carved
appeared to have sharp teeth and angry eyes.

She pulled into the driveway and killed the
engine. Elle doubted her father's vehicle was in the
garage, making the assumption that he was still at
school. He was most likely still dealing with the
chaos Mary had created this morning. Or maybe
he was sitting alone in his dark office, grieving for
the sudden loss of his girlfriend.

Elle was positive that he'd heard the breaking
news by now, and though she wasn't sure how

close or how much in love John and Elaine had really been in, she knew that her father had to be upset, even confused. After all, the previous night he'd been sharing a meal with his girlfriend. And this morning he'd discovered that both she and her daughter had been butchered, the latest victims of what was shaping up to be the work of a serial killer in Gray's Lane.

Elle felt sorry for her father, which instantly caused tightness to form in her chest. But overall, it wasn't just sadness that was consuming her. Elle couldn't help but feel a tad bit curious, and the heaviness of that curiosity was starting to lead to guilt. She couldn't stop from wondering if her father had also heard about the candy corn signature, and if he'd then connected the murders in Ohio to her mother's murder in New York.

Maybe now he'd believe what she'd said earlier, after reading about the first victim, Kimberly Sullivan, in the local newspaper: "It's happening again."

Elle wanted to speak with her father. She *needed* to. But the task was proving to be impossible. She'd asked Deputy Andrews to help her get in touch with him, but the man hadn't succeeded. Elle had then tried making a few phone calls herself. She'd first used John's office number and then his cell. But when both attempts had proven to be unsuccessful, she'd eventually given up, deciding that speaking with her father would just have to wait.

She opened the driver's side door and stepped out. The smoky air hit her almost immediately. Again, someone somewhere close by was taking advantage of the dry, late morning air and burning leaves. Specs of ash danced around, staining the surroundings, only aiding to the backdrop of horror that had recently unfolded.

Elle should have gone back to school. She knew that, even accepted the fact. Skipping classes seemed to be an ongoing pattern for her, a bad habit that she needed to break. But with everything that had been revealed that morning, sitting in a classroom and concentrating was just not something she could handle at the moment.

Beside, if her theory panned out, then someone had followed her from New York to Ohio — a killer. And not just any killer, Elle reminded herself, but the same person who had murdered her mother less than a month ago.

She didn't bother with her bag, just slammed the car door shut and started for the front door. Niki suddenly flooded her mind.

Was her friend still at school? Was she with Robbie? Was she confused or angry, or scared after hearing about the new murders? Probably, Elle figured, a combination of all three. That was how she personally felt, anyway.

After hearing Mary Evans announce the candy corn factor of the murders, Elle had abruptly left her group of friends without much explanation.

Kyle had even chased her down, followed her to her car in the parking lot. He'd wanted to know where she was going, if she was okay.

She'd made up some lame excuse, something about forgetting a research paper at home, and had left Kyle staring after her in total disbelief. But she hadn't wanted to confess anything about New York or the similar details to her mother's death, not until talking to the police. And now that she had spoken with Gray's Lane's finest, well, Elle wasn't quite sure what to think.

Elle wasn't one hundred percent positive if Deputy Andrews believed her story or not. He was a hard person to read, but seemed to be on the fence about some things. Maybe he was just protecting himself and the entire police department until he received more information? The sheriff hadn't been available, so Elle hadn't been able to get his opinion on the matter, which now only left her father.

Would the man doubt her? John knew all about her mother's murder in New York Would he, too, connect the dots, and understand that there was a huge possibility the same killer could be at work and responsible for both groups of slayings. Or would he ignore the facts? Try and sweep them under the rug? Chalk it all up to a word Elle found to be bitter and useless, coincidence?

The front door was unlocked. Elle blamed it on pure forgetfulness. She entered the house, and an overwhelming silence quickly smothered her. The eerie stillness caused her body to grow shockingly cold, and then segue into complete numbness.

A creaking sound exploded to her right. At breakneck speed, Elle turned. No one was there — just an old house that sometimes made random noises. But now Elle couldn't help but wonder if she was really alone.

She considered the idea for a moment, but then managed to somehow put the heavy feeling off to the side. Because even if a killer had actually followed her across state lines, she still didn't understand how she fit into the scenario or why.

Maybe she didn't. Maybe it really had nothing to do with her. Elle had no way of knowing for sure that she was a part of this, whatever *it* was, or who the killer was going to come after next.

So she promptly made the rash decision to not be afraid — of anything. Being afraid was no way to live; Elle knew that eventually she would end up driving herself crazy.

Elle was starting to feel dizzy; she closed her eyes and randomly saw dark spots. Making a diagnosis was easy: she needed to eat something. Even though she wasn't hungry and food was the last thing on her mind, she still made her way to the kitchen. She had to take care of herself.

She swung open the door to the refrigerator and peered inside. Her eyes roamed the various shelves, taking in cheeses, various lunchmeats, a carton of eggs, and a foul odor that could only be bad onions. Elle went with a green apple from the crisper.

Next, she made herself a sandwich, using a slice of wheat bread and crunchy peanut butter. She grabbed a bottle of water and paring knife for her fruit, and headed up the stairs to her bedroom.

She surprised herself by finishing the sandwich at lightening speed, and then washed it down with most of the bottle of water. Elle sliced off several pieces of the apple, ate them, and then placed what was left of it and the knife on her nightstand. And because it was there, almost begging for attention, she picked up the glass frame and stared at the picture of her mother and her.

An icy tingle began coursing its way through her entire body. Her mind seemed to be screaming, high-pitched shrill that begged to be released. She wasn't exactly sure what it was or how to explain the feeling, perhaps an intuition, but something was telling her that she'd been right all along, since the very beginning: it *was* happening again.

She used her thumb to wipe away the tears that had gotten loose and fallen down onto the glass of the frame. What was happening again? She didn't know. Why was it happening? She didn't have an answer for that one either.

But she wanted to know. She *needed* to know. Her mother had been murdered, and a month later, in a completely different state, women were turning up dead, killed in the exact same manner, and signed the exact same way.

Only one thing made sense to Elle: the killer had to be one in the same.

So what was the big picture here? What was she missing? What was the killer's agenda, and why did she suddenly appear to be at the middle of it all?

She set the picture back down, stretched out on the bed, and rolled over. She faced the bare wall, and was quickly hit with the hard realization that she was completely alone.

The Gray's Lane Police Department didn't seem to believe her; she doubted her father would believe her. And if he did, he would most likely want to keep the truth to himself, let it stay buried, just to uphold his so-called wholesome image.

And then there was Niki. Elle surely couldn't inform her new friend of this disturbing theory. What would the girl say? How would she react knowing that Elle had accidently led a killer to Gray's Lane.

In spite of everything, the truth remained the same: the town had only experienced its first murder after she had moved to Ohio to live with her father.

Elle slammed her eyes shut, but the damage had already been done. Once again, she gambled with the truth of the situation: if the killer came after her, and all signs seemed to point that he would, she was entirely alone.

She had to get her mind off of this subject, off of the killings and on to other things and ideas. But the task seemed virtually impossible. How could she honestly be expected to focus on something other than the multiple murders that had plagued the small town, not to mention, her life?

The thought of her father and his dead girl-friend forced its way into her train of thought. Elaine Jacobs, the name floated into Elle's mind and stuck there. She'd just met the woman last night, and now she and her daughter were both gone. Elle's heart bled for the victims, their family and friends, and of course, for her father.

She grouped her hands together and placed them under her soft pillow, giving more support to her neck. Elle wished now that she'd been able to get a hold of her father. Was he alone? Was he suffering? Was he thinking about the fear and brutal pain that Elaine and Emily had undoubtedly experienced?

That had always been what she'd get stuck on when contemplating that night in New York: what exactly had her mother felt? Had she been scared? Had she known she was going to die?

Elle would have to be there for her father. As soon as John was ready, Elle would put her own feelings and worries aside and give her father the support he needed, the support that he had given her when she'd first lost her mother.

Her focused changed again, this time landing on Kyle. The pathetic look that had been etched on his face when she'd left campus this morning appeared in her mind; she couldn't quite shake it away. Elle hadn't wanted to hurt him, and desperately hoped now that she hadn't.

Maybe a relationship would eventually blossom. Maybe not. Either way, she thought of Kyle Burke as a friend, and the last thing Elle wanted to do was upset a new friend. She made a quick mental note to apologize to him and explain the situation. Well, as best as she possibly could.

Elle felt her body leisurely drifting towards a state of sleep. Her head felt hazy as more images started unconsciously attacking her mind. Images of a guy, another guy, a guy she knew quite well. Or *had* known quite well.

His thick dark hair that was usually swept to one side, his rich brown eyes, and his hard cleft chin all acted as jagged puzzle pieces that formed together into one clear image. It was almost as if Elle was staring at a photograph of Brian. She saw his tall, lean body, olive tinted skin, and the crescent-shaped birthmark that he carried on his right shoulder. She could even smell the deep oak scent that he always splashed onto himself.

Elle tried to get the memories to vacate her mind, but instead, the opposite happened. She now recalled the rushed and random way in which they had met, and even the extremely short time period that they had dated. But the most looming memory she had of Brian Gleason from New York was their breakup.

He'd been the one to end it, almost immediately following her mother's murder. He'd said something on the lines of how she was going to be stressed, even disturbed, and that she would need a lot of alone time. Brian had also brought up that she was moving to Ohio, and had then used the old excuse that long distance relationships never worked out.

In short, Brian had abandoned her during her time of need, and she hadn't seen or spoken to him since then. She'd rarely even thought of him in the past month.

But as a dark sleep began taking over, Elle had one last conscious thought: where was Brian Gleason now?

———

Killing Elaine and Emily Jacobs hadn't been part of the plan. Not both of them anyway, not at the same time. But he'd been surprised. He'd been completely caught off guard, which had led to him having to make a fast decision. He didn't regret that decision now.

He'd been confronted with the unexpected once before. He hadn't been completely prepared a month ago, and as a result, he'd made a huge mistake. *That* mistake had not only cost him time and money, but it had also forced him to change his entire course of action and ultimately kill again.

He'd learned from the mistake. He'd discovered how to adapt to the unexpected.

He'd stabbed Emily to death first. For a brief moment, he'd thought that she was going to get away, and he'd panicked. But in the end, he'd caught her, taken her life, and scattered her body with candy corn.

Next, he'd murdered the mother — Elaine. He'd just finished up with the daughter and had been getting ready to leave, when Elaine had surprised him by entering the house through the back door. But instead of fleeing this time, he'd gone into repeat mode: he'd raised the knife, pressed it into supple skin, and then added a little candy.

Of course, the double homicide had made the morning news. Both victims' names had been revealed, along with his sugary signature. It would only be a matter of time now before the New York angle was made public, which ultimately meant things would need to be heated up. He'd been pushed into the fast lane. His plan was in full effect now, and an ending was finally in sight.

Soon he'd have what he wanted, what he'd been searching for. And soon, Michelle Anderson would be dead.

TWENTY

"SO, YOU DATED KIM SULLIVAN, YOU WERE dating Elaine Jacobs at the time of her murder, and Emily Jacobs was a student at Gray's Lane High School where you just happen to be the principal. It looks to me like you're connected to all three victims. You might want to start explaining yourself, John."

"Of course I knew all of the victims," John agreed. "This is Gray's Lane, Sheriff. Everybody knows everybody. I'm sure you won't find one person in this town that *wasn't* connected to all three women."

"Well," Douglas disputed, "so far you're the only one."

"Have you even started looking for anyone else?" John asked. "Or did you give up? Call off the search party once you discovered me in the Jacobs' house this morning?"

"I've already warned you about your attitude, John. Calm down," the sheriff's voice heatedly rang out.

Douglas didn't blink; he stared into the suspect's eyes. He was going to get to the truth — one way or another. Andrews was with him now, standing directly to his left. It was now two against one, and Douglas was going to get what he wanted.

"I can't be calm, not anymore," John stated. "I already told you that I didn't kill anyone!" He banged both tightly formed fists down onto the sheriff's desk.

"You lied to us!" Douglas hollered. To show his own fit of rage, he matched John's motion and brought his own fists down onto the desk, but evoking an even bigger bang.

"Fine," John started, returning his hands to his lap. "I dated Kimberly Sullivan," John admitted. "I dated her in high school."

"Excuse me?" Ben spoke up.

"You dated Kim in high school?" Douglas asked, hearing the bitter surprise in his own voice. His body quickly stiffened; he sat straighter in his chair. "Not since high school?"

"That's right," John confirmed. He leaned back, appearing to get more comfortable. "We graduated together. We dated a few months at the beginning of our senior year, and then…"

"Then?" Douglas prompted.

"That's it," John answered. "We remained friends the rest of the school year and then went our separate ways."

"Did you stay in contact with each other while in college?" Douglas asked, hoping, *praying,* that

John would give him the right answer. The sheriff knew now that he was most likely grasping at straws, but he finally had a leg up on the case and refused to give up on it.

"No."

"And recently?" the Sheriff tried. "Had the two of you spoken? Spent any time together at all?"

"No," John said, repeating his single word answer.

Douglas released a heavy sigh. His body was growing intensely impatient, and to keep busy, he crossed his feet at the ankles. "You mean to tell me that you haven't seen or spoken to Kim Sullivan since high school? Thirty some years ago?"

John shrugged. "Yes.

The sheriff frowned. "Seems kind of odd to me."

"Why is that?" John asked.

"Because," Ben rapidly fired off, "just a second ago you told us how small Gray's Lane is, remember? But now you expect Sheriff Douglas and I to believe that you and Kim have lived in Gray's Lane your entire lives, but haven't seen or spoken to each other since you were both in high school?"

"Well…" John started.

"Well what?" Douglas asked, well aware of the sly smile that had formed across his wrinkled face. Once again, the power had shifted hands, and he found himself on top — right where he belonged.

Excitement rushed his bones. "Are you lying to us again?"

"I didn't lie!" John argued. "I'm not lying. Of course I saw Kim around town. The grocery store, gas station, sometimes even at the high school. We were always friendly towards one another, a wave or a smile. Perhaps even a 'hello.' But that's it. I swear."

Douglas didn't like where this was headed. He felt his body flush, and on instinct, lifted his hand to touch his cheek. It was warm.

The last thing he wanted was to be made a fool, especially in his hometown. The sheriff knew that if he were wrong, if John Anderson wasn't the person responsible for the multiple murders, that he would definitely be laughed right out of his high ranking position. In a manner of speaking, Douglas knew that he'd be left with nothing more than runny egg smeared all over his face.

"Where were you last Saturday night?"

The sheriff spun his head around to look at Ben. The deputy had been the one to fire off the no nonsense question. Douglas was surprisingly proud, and even felt a new jolt of energy burst through him. Andrews obviously favored John for the slayings, too. And clearly, the deputy wasn't planning on letting the suspect off that easily.

"Are you asking for my alibi?" John whispered.

"Do you have one?" Douglas demanded.

It was then that the sheriff discovered something: he trusted Ben. And though he knew that the deputy could more than handle the situation on his own, Douglas was ready for his turn again; he enjoyed playing the bad cop. As he rested both aging elbows onto his desk and stared the suspect down, he came to another conclusion: he was playing the role quite well.

"I was with Elaine last Saturday," John said.

"Times?" Douglas asked.

John shrugged and then closed his eyes, most likely trying to concentrate. "I think I got to her house around three. We had kind of a lazy day. We watched movies, ate an early dinner, and if I remember correctly, went to bed around ten. Maybe a little after."

"Did anyone see you?" Ben asked. "Maybe your daughter?" he offered. "Someone who can confirm you were at the Jacobs' home the entire evening and didn't leave until the next morning?"

"No," John shook his head. "I mean, no one other than Elaine."

"Hmm," the sheriff started. He swiftly looked over at Ben, and then turned his attention back to John. "I find that to be a little funny."

"Please, Sheriff, enlighten me," John ordered. "Because so far, I haven't found anything about this experience to be funny."

Douglas let the comment slide. John was upset, rightfully so, leading the sheriff to believe that he had the suspect right where he wanted him. Douglas didn't bother wasting his breath and saying it out loud, as he was sure that everyone in the cramped office was already thinking it: John Anderson's only alibi for the murder of Kim Sullivan was Elaine Jacobs, who had conveniently died the night before.

Hook, line, and sinker, the sheriff thought. Excitement was starting to set in; he quickly began tapping his foot onto the floor. All he had to do now was be a little patient, wait, and then reel John in. Finally, Douglas sighed, something good had happened in the case — they'd been met with a lucky break.

A steady silence began filling the room. The sheriff's tapping had gradually transferred from his foot on the floor, to his fingers on the desk, to now nothing at all. Douglas refused to speak first, and he'd already warned Andrews with a sharp glare to keep quiet, too. They were now in for the long hall, and would just have to sweat this out.

So Douglas did the only thing he could think of doing: he tried to stay occupied. He started by studying his surrounding — again — but when that became tedious, he tried sitting back and humming. But eventually, even the buzzing sound annoyed him, and he stopped just as soon as he'd started.

He registered a bitter, coffee-like taste in his mouth, and quickly went to work searching for a piece of gum or a mint of some sort. He used both hands to check his right and left pockets, but came up with nothing. The sheriff didn't bother with his desk drawers, knowing that only candy wrappers would greet him. And then he considered asking Andrews for help, but then decided against it. He wanted to keep the surroundings completely quiet, hoping that John would be frightened or frustrated enough to start talking again.

As he felt sweat beginning to form at his temple, he realized that *he* was the one growing antsy. His senses even seemed to be heightened, as the dangerous stillness of the room sharply pierced his ears, and the putrid stench of his past dinners once again filled his nostrils. The muscles in the sheriff's neck became taut; Douglas knew then that his plan had backfired. He was the only one being tortured, and he couldn't stand to take it for one more second.

"Look, John," the sheriff began. He laid his hands flat and steady on the surface of his desk, as if offering up a truce. It was time for yet another tactic. "Let me help you," Douglas suggested. "Tell me what happened. Tell me what you know, and I'll try and…"

"I don't know anything, Sheriff Douglas," John stated calmly. "I've told you repeatedly that I didn't kill anyone; I'm innocent. And if you insist on continuing to harass me, then I think I should call my…"

"Tell us about your ex-wife," Ben interrupted.

Douglas didn't need to see a mirror; he was already positive that his eyes had grown wide, and were now ready to burst right out of his head. His ears felt as if they might be bleeding; his entire body suddenly grew fiery hot with rage.

Douglas couldn't believe that he'd heard the deputy correctly. What in the hell was Andrews thinking? What was his motive?

The sheriff stared at him now, tried to get some sort of clue as to what this was all about. But Ben's focus stayed on John, clearly trying to avoid eye contact.

"Sherry?" John asked with a frown.

"Do you have more than one ex-wife?" Ben asked.

"No, of course not," John answered. "But Sherry lived in New York. She died a month ago. I don't understand what she would have to do with any of this."

"Just enlighten me, please," Ben said. "Tell me a little bit about her."

This was absolutely ridiculous. Douglas wanted to scream; he wanted to stand up, grab Deputy Andrews by the throat, and throw him up against the wall. How was any of this at all relevant? The sheriff had his own problems to worry about; he couldn't care less what had happened to another woman in another state, regardless of the story the Anderson girl had cooked up.

John shrugged. "Okay," he began. "Sherry and I met at college, a small school a couple of hours away from here. We were married for a very short time. Right after our daughter was born, Sherry moved back home to New York. I came back to Gray's Lane."

Douglas rolled his eyes, not caring about the disrespect it showed or how childish he looked. This was nothing but a complete waste of time, and they were getting only further away from the important agenda at hand. The deputy would have a lot of explaining to do, perhaps even a suspension coming, the sheriff contemplated. He hated being blindsided, especially when this was his town and he was supposed to be the one in charge, the one on top on things.

"After that," John continued, "we kind of lost contact. Sherry was a full time bank manager at some branch, married to her career. I stayed in touch with Elle, even visited her several times. And then when Sherry was killed last month, my daughter came to live with me in Ohio."

"Do you know any of the details regarding your ex-wife's death?"

"A few, I suppose. I mean, just what Elle has told me. She's the one that found her mother murdered. Sherry was murdered."

"I see," Ben said.

"She was stabbed to death," John offered. "Sherry had multiple stab wounds. The killer had also placed..." his words suddenly trailed off.

Douglas immediately noticed the recognition on John's face; the suspect had made the connection, realized that there were similarities between the New York murder and the ones in Ohio.

The sheriff suddenly leaned forward and rested his chin on his right hand. He had to admit that this was all starting to get interesting.

"I never considered that, not once, not until now," John said, his face showing a tight, genuine look of confusion. "The candy corn," he continued. "Elaine and Emily's bodies had both been scattered with it; I saw it myself this morning." His hands were on each side of the chair, gripping the edges, like he was afraid to let go. "Are you saying that the killer from both sets of crimes is the same? That whoever murdered Sherry in New York also murdered Elaine and Emily in Ohio?"

"No, we're not saying that at all," Douglas said. He saw where this whole conversation was headed — straight for disaster. He knew it was high time for him to take the reigns and once again control the situation. So much for trusting Ben Andrews. "It's come to our attention that both cases do share some minor resemblances, but..."

""Wait!" John interrupted. "Are you trying to imply that I killed Sherry? Are you pinning her murder on me now, too?"

"We didn't say that," Douglas stated.

At least John was talking now. The sheriff prayed that he would slip up, reveal something useful. And while the edgy tone of the suspect's voice told Douglas that he just might get his wish, the man also knew that everyone needed to get back on coarse. Douglas wasn't concerned with the New York murder; it honestly didn't matter to him who had killed Sherry. He had his own murders in his own town to solve. That was his priority, and it should have been Ben's, too, the sheriff thought. Not trying to do someone else's work or crack open someone else's investigation.

"Then what are you saying?" John exploded. "I want to know *exactly* what you want from me. What do you want me to say?"

"Why did you murder three women?" Douglas shouted. He burst out of his chair. It fell backwards and collided with the floor. He gripped the edge of the desk and leaned forward. His nose was just inches away from John's. "Why did you kill Kim, Elaine, and Emily?" he asked, trying a new approach and personalizing the victims.

"I want a lawyer," John screamed. His voice echoed around the room. "I want a lawyer," he repeated. "Right now!"

The area was quiet again. Much like a stand-off, the sheriff stood as still as a statue and waited for John to make the first move. He instantly blamed this new predicament on Ben; Douglas wanted to physically rip the deputy apart. How was he supposed to finish the interview now that the suspect had lawyered up? How was he supposed to get the information that he needed to solve his case?

John Anderson was the killer — the sheriff just knew it. And now he was stuck, legally unable to say another word to the man. And it was all because of Deputy Andrews.

Douglas didn't speak, but reached into his pocket, pulled out his cell phone, and tossed it onto the desk towards the suspect. Before they'd started chatting, Douglas had requested that John turn off his cell phone, but John had informed the sheriff that he hadn't brought one with him. And now, well, John wanted to call a lawyer, so Douglas provided him with a way to do so. He really didn't have another option.

The sheriff watched as John reached out with his left hand, picked up the phone, and started punching in numbers. The suspect never said another word, just placed the device up to his hear and waited.

"Sheriff Douglas, can I speak with you out in the hall?"

Douglas turned toward the deputy, eyes wide and nostrils flaring — it was déjà vu. He'd just warned Ben about interruptions, yet here they were again, an hour later, in the exact same situation. Same shit, *same* day.

"I'll be right back, John." Douglas rounded his desk, walked passed Ben without so much as a glance at the man, and left the room.

Back in the same hallway as before, the sheriff was aware of Ben's presence; the deputy was standing right behind him. Douglas took a deep breath, collected his thoughts, and then he spun around on his heel and started yelling.

"Andrews, didn't we just have a talk about..."

"I didn't think it mattered, sir, not since the suspect requested a lawyer."

Douglas shook his head. "It does matter, Deputy Andrews. I make the calls, understand?" This kid was starting to get to him — badly. First, there were all of the interruptions. And now, the kid was back to cutting him off midsentence. Andrews clearly had no respect or manners; the sheriff had about reached his limit.

"Sheriff," Ben started, "John Anderson isn't our guy. He's not the killer."

Douglas threw his arms up into the air, and then surprised himself by breaking out into a soft chuckle. "So, all of a sudden you decide Anderson's not the killer? And do you mind filling me in on how you came to that conclusion?"

"The killer is right handed," Ben informed.

"I know that, Andrews," Douglas said and promptly placed both hands on his hips. "This is my investigation; I know that the killer is right handed due to the angles of the knife wounds." He

was angry. The thick disdain that was overly present in his voice was unmistakable. Did Andrews
really think he was that incompetent? He was the
sheriff, for crying out loud!

"John Anderson is left handed."

"Now, how could you possibly know that
John…" Douglas stopped himself. The cell phone, he
knew. The realization hit him like a large brick wall.

John had used his left hand to retrieve the
cell phone; he was left-hand dominant. The killer
was right-hand dominant. Therefore, the sheriff
shuddered to think, Ben had been correct: John
Anderson wasn't the killer.

This day was just getting better and better. So
much time had been wasted; they were now back
to square one. Or, in a word, they were nowhere,
nowhere even close to solving the murders.

"I wasn't sure if you caught him reaching for
the cell or not," Ben said. "I thought it needed to
be brought to your attention. Immediately."

Dammit! This investigation was going no
place, and fast! To hell with catching a so-called
lucky break, Douglas thought. Instead, they'd
only created more work for themselves, essen-
tially taking two steps back. Not to mention, the
humiliation. Douglas didn't even want to think
about what would happen if Mary Evans got a
hold of this information and reported it to the
community. He'd never be able to show his face
again. Anywhere!

"Sheriff, I think we should…"

"What in the hell were you trying to achieve, son?"

"Excuse me?" Ben asked.

"Bringing up that murder in New York and its similarities to this case," Douglas stated. "Seriously, what were you thinking?" It was petty, he knew, but the sheriff had to take the attention off of himself and his own faults and place it onto someone else. That someone was Ben and his over-active imagination.

"Sir, I didn't mean to cause any trouble, but I really believe…"

"I don't care what you believe, Andrews," Douglas interrupted. "I know you've only been with this department for a few days, but I'm in charge around here. And we've got enough problems on our own without you chasing down random murders that happened across state lines."

"I didn't chase down anything," Ben argued. "Elle Anderson came to me, and you have to admit that the candy corn signature proves…"

"I don't have to admit anything, Andrews." The sheriff took an oversized step toward Ben. He knew he was getting older, but hoped that he could still somewhat pull off intimidation. "I want you to keep your mouth shut."

"What about the candy corn?" Ben pleaded. "Why candy corn? And how can you honestly believe that it's just a coincidence that two killers are using the same calling card? Especially after you factor Elle Anderson into the equation?"

"Look, son," Douglas lowered his voice and shifted a step back from the deputy. "I'm going to tell you one last time: leave New York alone. I don't know what happened there, and I don't want to know. I've got enough on my plate; Gray's Lane is all I care about. The New York theory is just that, a theory. It *is* a coincidence. And quite frankly, I'm extremely tired of hearing about it, so knock it off!"

"I understand, sir," Ben said. He looked down to the ground.

"We're done," Douglas ordered. "We're going to focus on what's happening here, meaning that I don't want you calling anyone in New York. Do not try to get a hold of the detectives that worked Sherry Anderson's murder. Clear?"

"Clear," Ben repeated.

'This is my town, and like I've already told you, I don't need any outsiders' help running this investigation. The Gray's Lane Police Department will solve these murders without the assistance of anyone else."

Douglas watched closely as Ben turned and walked down the hall, his shoulders slumped. The deputy rounded the corner and then fell out of sight.

Supposedly, Andrews was going to go study the case, search for a new lead, something useful.

But the sheriff took a deep breath and slowly shook his head; he wasn't so sure he believed the deputy.

Though Ben had agreed to keep the details of the murders in-house and not seek information from anyone or anywhere outside of the department, Douglas still couldn't help but sense a flutter of heavy panic sweep through his body.

In fact, he expected trouble out of Deputy Ben Andrews.

TWENTY-ONE

SHE WAS GOING TO SCREAM, SHE WAS almost sure of it. If he asked her one more time how she was feeling, Niki knew that she would just lose it. She appreciated Robbie's concern and the fact that he was so worried about her, but she didn't like being treated as if she were some fragile, porcelain doll. Yes, she'd been through a lot the past few days, and the latest news of the double homicide had done absolutely nothing to help matters. But she was still strong. Niki was a big girl, and she refused to crumble under the weight of what had been unfairly thrown at her.

"Is your dad home?"

"No," Niki answered. "I'm alone."

"Do you want me to come over?" Robbie asked.

Niki took a long, deep breath, hoping the gesture would somehow calm her. She reclined back into the couch, allowing her body to completely stretch out and find comfort. Immediately, she melted into the soft cushion. Niki crossed her bare feet at the ankle, and with her cell cradled between her shoulder and ear, she was able to place her arm behind her head for support.

"You still there?"

"Yes, Robbie," Niki answered through gritted teeth. "I'm still here."

"Are you mad at me? Did I do something wrong?"

And just like that, a heavy wave of guilt smacked into Niki so forcefully that she quickly found herself sitting straight up and becoming as stiff as a rock.

It was amazing how Robbie had the ability to make her emotions do a three hundred and sixty degree turn. Instantly, her annoyance at her boyfriend had transferred into gratitude, and she felt a little embarrassed for not recognizing it sooner. Robbie was a good person, plain and simple. His only concern was her — clearly. And Niki knew that she should have been more grateful for the fact.

"No, I'm just tired," she lied. The excuse was lame and definitely dated, but she figured it would suffice. Robbie was being so caring, and Niki just didn't have the heart to tell him the truth.

Since her mother's death on Saturday, she'd had been completely surrounded by family, friends, and random grievers who had wanted to express their condolences. At the moment, she looked forward to change of solitude.

Of course, it was more than terrifying to think that a killer was on the lose, running around, most likely planning another murder. But fear was something she was quickly learning to live with — not that she had much of a choice. And she'd already lost her mother in one of the worst ways imaginable; there weren't too many more horrible things left to happen to her.

"You sound distant," Robbie said. "Are you sure you're okay? I know it's been another crazy day and…"

"It has," she agreed, cutting him off. "But I think I'm going to take a hot shower and probably just go to bed."

"At seven-thirty?"

"I told you I was tired," Niki reminded him. She had no intentions of going right to sleep, but didn't feel that Robbie needed to know that, either.

She simply just wanted to be alone for a while. And not knowing where her father was or when he was coming home, Niki knew that her chance at privacy could evaporate at any moment. So why was she wasting precious moments on the phone with Robbie, when she'd just seen him a few hours ago?

"Well, I guess I'll let you go," he said. His voice seemed to be breaking in and out.   "I'll see you tomorrow morning," she tried to assure him, figuring that she had only half accomplished the task. "We'll meet in the parking lot before school."

"Hopefully," he whispered.

"What does that mean?"

She waited, slowly counting the seconds in her head that seemed to pass at a snail's pace. Why wasn't Robbie answering her? And what in the hell had he meant by his comment?

Like a strong, thick smoke, anger was beginning to build up inside of her and linger. She couldn't help but remember that he had been the one to call her, not the other way around. And now he was staying silent and ignoring her. What the hell?

"Robbie," she started, voice heated, "I asked you a question."

"I know," he quickly answered. "I didn't mean anything by it. Just forget I said anything."

"I won't forget about it," she argued. "I want to know…"

"I'm scared, alright?" he hollered into the phone, causing Niki to jerk her cell away from her ear. "So much has happened. I didn't expect to wake up this morning to find that two more women had been stabbed to death. Did you?"

"Of course not!"

"And who knows what we'll wake up to tomorrow morning. That's *if* we wake up."

"The way I see it," Niki snapped, "you don't have anything to worry about. Whoever the killer is, he's obviously choosing to just go after women. You're basically saying that I could be next, right?"

"No, I didn't say that," Robbie countered.

"That's how it came off." Her body felt as if someone had lit a match and thrown it directly at her. The couch was smothering her. She had to stand.

"I'm sorry," Robbie offered. "I'm scared," he repeated. "I overheard my grandpa talking earlier. The suspect who was in custody today has been released. He didn't kill anybody, and there are no other leads."

"That's comforting," she mocked. Niki wasn't sure why, no one could see her doing it, but she gradually started shaking her head.

Were the local police really that incompetent? How hard could it be to catch the killer? Niki had a difficult time believing that a single man could continue to outsmart the entire department. What would make the murderer to stop?

"I'm sure it's upsetting to hear."

"It is," Niki agreed. "And not just for my dad and me, but everyone in Gray's Lane. What happened to our safe, boring town?" She felt her throat immediately tighten, pain erupted in her chest. As she clutched at it, she undoubtedly knew what would be coming next: tears.

Her emotions were completely all over the map. And though Robbie had seen and heard her at her worst several times in the past week, Niki didn't want to reveal that vulnerable side now.

"Are you sure you don't want me to come over?" he asked. "We could watch a movie or something."

"No, I'm fine," she half lied. Niki wanted to be alone, but she wasn't fine, not by a long shot. So much for trying to be brave and strong, for acting as if she really did have it all together.

As she stood still and stared into the round mirror hanging on the wall in front of her, reality reared its ugly head and looked back at her. She realized then that she seriously wasn't fine; she was a mess. Between her dull, sleep deprived eyes, cracking lips, and disheveled hair, she saw the truth: a frightened little girl who missed her mother.

"Niki…"

"I'm going to go, Robbie," she said, forcing down the thick lump that had formed in her mouth. "I'm going to go, but I'll see you in the morning."

"Yeah, okay," he muttered. "But please," he quickly added, "don't forget to lock all of the doors."

"I won't forget. I promise." Niki ended the call and tossed her phone down onto the couch. She ran her fingers through her tangled hair, and left them resting at the base of her stiff neck.

Confusion invaded her, and she had a difficult time shaking a certain, sickening thought. It was almost as if Robbie expected for the killer to come after her. But why?

Niki rolled back her shoulders. She couldn't think about murder anymore, not tonight. She needed to distance her mind from the events that had plagued her and her hometown, if even for an hour.

Niki left the living room and started for the kitchen. She wasn't particularly hungry, but thought food might be the distraction she needed. But as soon as she opened the refrigerator door, she instantly discovered that it wasn't.

She stepped out of the kitchen, trading the cool tile for the soft carpet. For the first time, she noticed the heavy musk scent that hung in the air. Niki recognized the smell as her father's favorite cologne. He obviously hadn't left too long ago, and probably wouldn't be back for a while.

Niki stood in place, brought her arms up to her chest, and wrapped them around herself in a tight bear hug. She'd gotten what she'd wanted; she was alone. Only now, she decided, she no longer wanted to be alone.

She went back into the living room, grabbed her cell off the couch, and punched in Robbie's number. Hopefully, he'd laugh off her inconsistencies. After all, above everything else, Robbie was very understanding. Niki figured that he would be no different now. If she knew Robbie, and she thought she did, he'd be in the car and over to her house in the next ten minutes.

"Hey, it's Robbie. Leave me a message and I'll get back to you. Thanks."

Something didn't seem right. Robbie always had his phone on him, and he almost always answered it, especially if she was the one calling. And she'd just spoken with him. What was going on?

Niki knew that she couldn't keep freaking herself out like this. She was creating fear and speculation that didn't exist, and she was going to eventually drive herself insane. It was time to stop. Right now. Besides, she tried comforting herself, Robbie was probably just eating dinner or in the shower or something.

She reached for the remote and started flipping channels, but nothing caught her interest. The growing pile of homework sitting in her bag didn't thrill her either, so she picked up her phone again. Elle was probably home, maybe she'd want to get together or at least talk.

Halfway through dialing, Niki changed her mind. She was overreacting, yet again. She was a big girl; she could more than handle one night at home by herself. Plus, she hadn't seen or heard from Elle since this morning when the girl had abruptly fled campus after Mary's broadcast.

Niki took a deep breath and closed her eyes. I'm safe, she thought, trying to convince herself. No one is after me. Nobody wants me dead.

A loud sound caused her to open her eyes, quickly stand up, and jerk her head to the left. The noise had to have come from the coat closet that was directly off to the side of room. But then doubt rapidly found her. She wondered if the noise was in fact real or if she'd just imagined it.

"Dammit!" she muttered. She had one eye glued to the closed door, and the other on her phone. Did she call the police? Try and get help? Or did she investigate herself?

Robbie, she decided. She'd try calling Robbie again. Hopefully, he'd answer this time. He'd either tell her what to do or at least calm her down.

After three painfully long rings, she finally heard a distraught, muffled "Hello" on the other end.

"Robbie, it's me," she whispered.

"Oh, hey," his voice mimicked her own soft, barely audible tone. "Sorry I missed your call earlier, I was…"

"Robbie, I think someone's in the house."

"What? Why?"

"Because, I heard a noise." Niki tried with everything she had to be as quiet as possible. If someone really was in the closet, just feet away from her, the last thing she wanted to do was tip that person off.

"What kind of noise?" Robbie asked. "Are you sure that…"

"It was a noise, Robbie! A strange one!" She hastily threw her left hand over her mouth, but knew that the damage had already been done. If she wasn't alone in the house, Niki realized that whoever was with her had undoubtedly heard her almost shrieking outburst.

"Just calm down, Niki," Robbie ordered. "You don't want to panic. Are the doors locked?"

"What's it matter if the doors are locked?" she asked. "If the killer is already in the house, I don't want to lock him in here with me!"

"Okay," Robbie said heatedly. "Get in your car and drive to the police station. I will stay on the line while…"

Niki never heard the rest of Robbie's command; her deep scream immediately cut him off.

"What's going on? Niki, are you okay? Answer me!"

Everything was happening so fast. She could barely process it all. Niki seemed to see things in dull, blurry flashes instead of one big picture. Only one conscience idea was perfectly clear to her: she needed to get out of the house. Now!

Someone had charged out at her. A dark figure was getting closer, closing the distance between the two of them. But Niki was not going to let the blackness consume her. It was time to prove she was a fighter, a survivor. She would fight.

"No!" she ordered. "Stop! Get away from me!" Niki dropped her cell phone. It fell to the floor and slid out of view. That's when she first noticed the knife—it seemed to rise out of nowhere. The tool glistened. Niki knew the sharp point of the blade was intended for her.

A killer, the same killer that had brutally murdered her mother, was now after her, in the *exact* same house he'd killed in before.

He lunged at her, but Niki didn't miss a beat. A quick shuffle to her right had the weapon barely missing her, as the killer lost balance and fell face first into the couch.

There was no more time to waste. Niki was too determined to live. She was running. She sidestepped her attacker's feet and fled the living room. Her own home was like a brutal obstacle coarse that she so desperately needed to find a way to escape.

She found the hallway and began sprinting down it as if it were a wide-open track field. But she instantly became stalled. Her feet seemed to act as two magnets and forcefully came together and tangled, causing Niki to fall to the ground. She promptly rolled onto her back; she wasn't giving up that easily.

He'd rounded the corner. He was closing in on her. He dove, and just like that, he was on top of her, straddling her. The knife was threateningly close to her chest. A whimper escaped her quivering lips. She realized that she was trapped.

"No!" she hollered. "Please," Niki tried begging. "Don't do this!"

He didn't listen. Niki felt a sharp pain as his knees tightened, squeezing into the sides of her stomach. He was locking her into place. His knife went up fast. And she was well aware of how it would come down—hard!

She lifted her hands and tried pushing on his chest. She had to get him off of her. But the gesture didn't work; he was too strong. Niki hastily decided to go with another plan.

She raised her right leg, bringing it up as high as she could, and connected it to the stranger's groin. The knife fell out of his hands. He slid off of her and immediately began clutching himself.

Niki was on her feet. She stared down at the man, noticing for the first time that he'd brought something else with him: a plastic bag of candy corn.

He was moaning, swaying back and forth on the ground. She knew it would only be moments before he was up and after her again.

She didn't give him the chance; her path was lit from the bright light that was hanging from the ceiling above. She ran the rest of the way to the front door, threw it open, and embraced the chilly air.

Niki never looked back, not even once. She jumped into her dark blue car, started the engine, hit the auto lock button, and floored the vehicle into reverse and out of the driveway. She didn't give the killer another opportunity to succeed. She was long gone.

TWENTY-TWO

"I CAN'T BELIEVE YOU TOLD SOMEONE. After I specifically told you not to, you…"

"Dad, please. Just hear me out. Let me explain…"

"And not just someone," John corrected, "but the sheriff. You actually told Sheriff Douglas about what happened in New York."

"I didn't tell the sheriff anything," Elle said, searching intently for the right words to use to explain the situation to her father. "I told Deputy Andrews about mom's murder, and that was only because…"

"Yes," John interrupted, "Deputy Andrews." Elle watched as he used his thumb and index finger to gently rub the edge of his chin. "I remember him quite well. He was the man who indirectly accused me of murdering your mother."

"What?" Elle asked. She took a step backward. "You were questioned about…" her words trailed off; she needed a moment to think. "Why were you questioned about what happened to Mom?"

"Oh, it wasn't just Sherry the police wanted to know about," John informed. "They were also very interested in hearing about Elaine and Emily."

"But why would they ask you…"

"Well," John started, "besides the fact that I was dating Elaine at the time of her death, I would say it probably had something to do with the fact that I was the one that found both of their bodies this morning."

Elle's hand immediately went to her chest. She took a deep breath, feeling her eyes grow wide. "You found their bodies this morning?" She needed to know more.

"Yes," John said and then nodded. "And then, of course, I was asked about Kim Sullivan. We dated briefly in high school, about a hundred years ago."

Elle didn't have the strength to stand anymore. She quickly found herself falling onto one of the bar stools that faced the kitchen, where her father stood in front of the refrigerator, his arms crossed over his rising chest. "Are you saying that you're the suspect? Today, when Mary Evans reported that the sheriff had a suspect in custody, she was talking about you?"

"I *was* the suspect," John said. "I guess so, anyway. But before I could even call my lawyer, I was released. Apparently, just being connected to all of the victims wasn't enough to charge me with anything or keep me overnight."

Elle shook her head. When she finally spoke, she made sure that her tone was as soft as possible. "You can't honestly blame me for what happened today. Just because I told Deputy Andrews about the similarities between Mom's murder in New York and the murders here, doesn't mean I'm responsible for your interrogation. I know you're not the killer, Dad."

"But you didn't help matters with your little story," John said. He uncrossed his arms, stepped up to the counter, and gripped its rounded edge. "In fact, you made them worse. You made me look even more guilty by making your mother's murder a part of this whole mess."

"You were released," she argued, her voice starting to rise. "And it wasn't just some story I told the police. Mom is a part of this. The details of her death match…"

"Coincidence," he interrupted.

She bit down on her lower lip; Elle was beginning to hate that word. "Why are you so worried about keeping my past a secret?" she demanded. "You don't want me to talk about Mom or her death or what happened back in New York. Why is that?"

"I'm doing it for you," he said. He lifted a finger and pointed it at her. "I'm trying to help you get over what happened. If you could forget the events that happened a month ago, then I think you'd be able to move on and enjoy life a lot more easily. You might even learn to be happy."

"It's only been a month!" she yelled back and jumped up to her feet. "I'm not happy. I'm not going to be happy for a long time. And as for me just *forgetting* what happened in New York, that will never happen. I'll never be able to just forget about it."

"Fine, fine," John said quietly. "I understand that it is something that will always be a part of you, but why involve other people? Why make your mother's murder a part of everyone's life in Gray's Lane?"

"Do you really believe that's what I'm doing?"

John shrugged.

Elle released a heavy sigh. "I only told Deputy Andrews the truth. The fact that candy corn was used in New York and now in Ohio has to mean…"

"Nothing," John said. "It means nothing," he repeated. "Do you really think the killer traveled from New York to Ohio? Why? How does that make any sense?"

"I don't know," she admitted. "But the faster the police answer that question, the faster they'll find the person responsible for all of this."

"Elle, honey, listen to yourself. I know you want to find your mother's killer, but attaching her murder to the murders here is not the right way to go about it."

"You know what I think?" she asked, looking directly at her father, refusing to blink. "I think you want to sweep Mom's murder under the rug. You care so much about what people in this damn community think about you, and you would just hate for them to know that you have a skeleton hanging in your closet. A skeleton like a murdered ex-wife!"

"That's not fair! It's also *definitely* not true!" She watched as his hands balled into tight fists.

Elle resumed her seat, and changed her focus to the floor. The staring contest was over. She couldn't stand to look at her father anymore, and really didn't want to. John could be so caring and supportive when he wanted to be, but then there were other times, like right now, where he was completely self-centered.

"Look," he began, "we've both had a very long day. I lost my..." she heard his voice break, and he quickly moved on from the thought. "I think it would be best if we stopped for the evening and just talked in the morning. I'm exhausted."

She agreed, but she didn't respond. Elle tilted her head and closely watched as her father walked out of the kitchen, passed her without another gesture, and started for the front of the house.

Without turning around, Elle said, "I'm so sorry about Elaine and Emily."

But her father didn't say anything back. In fact, she was only sure that he'd gone up to bed after hearing the creaking of the stairs.

Elle rested her elbows onto the countertop, and then promptly pressed the palms of her hands into her eyes. The pressure almost felt soothing.

Elle wasn't tired; she'd slept most of the day away. But she was happy to be alone once again. Even though things with her father had ended on a low note, she was getting used to being by herself. She was kind of enjoying it, finding comfort in it.

She slowly swallowed the lump that had formed in her throat, and then lowered her forehead onto the cool surface in front of her. So much had happened, so much was *still* happening. And as Elle feared what would happen next, she felt sharp tears sting the corners of her eyes. It was hard to say for sure.

She brought her head back up and faced the kitchen. Nothing in the room was dirty or out of place. The way her father insisted on keeping everything perfectly clean and in place sometimes drove her crazy. Now was one of those times. Elle swiftly turned in her seat, stood, and started for the living room.

Besides, she was tired of sitting, and found relief in pacing the area and stretching her legs. But Elle really wasn't sure what to do now, though. She stopped in the middle of the living room. She let her bare feet sink into the soft carpet and placed both hands onto her hips. Had her father seriously been a suspect in the Gray's Lane murders?

Elle struggled with the idea that her father had even been considered a suspect. Why had he even questioned — just because he'd known all of the victims and had had a connection to all of them?

She took a moment to let what her father had previously said sink in and completely register. John had found the two victims this morning. Maybe that did warrant her father giving a statement, but that didn't mean he had killed anyone. He'd simply been in the wrong place at the wrong time. He'd loved Elaine. At least Elle assumed he had loved her. There was no way that he'd stabbed her to death.

Not to mention, Elle decided, lowering herself onto the couch, her father hadn't been in New York the night her mother had been murdered. He'd been home, in Ohio, hours and hours away. Elle knew her father, loved him, *trusted* him. There was absolutely no way that he was a killer.

She sank back into the inviting cushions and let her eyes gradually close. Perhaps she was still a little tired. Maybe she did need more sleep. She felt her breathing begin to slow for a moment, but then almost instantly, it found its rhythm again.

Her father. Elle opened her eyes. There was a possibility that John had been right, she decided. The candy corn could have been just a coincidence. Someone else, someone other than the person who was killing women in Gray's Lane could have murdered her mother in New York.

Was she really that desperate to find her mother's killer? Was she turning something into nothing, making connections out of simple similarities? Not only was candy corn common this time of year, but it was also sold everywhere.

Was the candy corn even enough to go on? To make it plausible that the killer from New York and Ohio was one and the same?

To stop them from shaking, Elle ran her fingers through her hair. She knew that the only way her theory could be a fact was if someone had been in New York at the time of her mom's murder, and then in Ohio when Kim Sullivan had been stabbed to death.

She closed her eyes again. She let her mind take her back to New York, back to the night her mother had been killed. That dark, suffocating feeling immediately found her once again.

Elle could see the thick, scarlet trail that had led her into the kitchen. The metallic smell had been heavy, sickening, and even now almost caused her to gag. The subtle glow from the orange, white and yellow pieces of candy even stood out in her vision. She could see her mom, lying face up on the tile floor, covered in blood and numerous stab wounds.

Elle's cell started ringing, bringing her back into the empty living room, back into reality. She stood up, managed to dodge the large gray footstool, and quickly dug her phone out of her front right pocket. She wiped her eyes, clearing away the wet tears that had arrived unexpectedly and stained her face. She looked down at the caller ID, and immediately recognized the New York area code.

"Hello?" Her voice sounded rough, even to her, and it was the only word that escaped her before her breath caught and she became silent.

"Elle? Elle, it's Brian." His voice hadn't changed, still deep and intoxicating.

"Brian," she softly said. Brian Gleason, she thought, her ex-boyfriend from New York. She'd just been thinking about him earlier this afternoon, and now he was calling her. What were the chances?

"Listen," he started. "I know it's been like a month, but I'm in Ohio. I'm in Gray's Lane, and I'd really like to see you."

TWENTY-THREE

HE HADN'T LISTENED TO THE SHERIFF. THEN again, he hadn't had any real intentions of doing so in the first place. The deputy was trying to solve a murder, not create long lasting friendships. Sometimes the rules had to be bent, or more appropriately, broken. And that's exactly what Ben had done; he'd broken the rules, gone against the sheriff's orders, and had made a few phone calls to New York.

Ben shrugged his shoulders, now thinking about his actions and how the sheriff would react. Douglas would either get over it, or he'd fire the deputy. Either way, Ben had no regrets. He could feel himself getting closer to unmasking the killer.

Trying to be as quiet as possible, he stretched his long arms over his head. Ben bridged his fingers together and lay still in a pencil-like pose. He was completely aware of just how uncomfortable he really was, and not because of his position, but because of the hard mattress that was underneath him.

Ben hadn't expected much when he'd signed the month-to-month lease of the rental, but he'd at least hoped for a soft bed. He'd wanted some place cozy and inviting, a place he'd be able to go at night to kick back and forget the workday. But his home didn't offer that. He wasn't getting any sort of rest, and instead of forgetting the workdays, he was constantly reflecting on them.

Ben knew that this was ultimately just another lesson to be learned. The next time, he'd make sure to be entirely satisfied before putting his signature on any dotted line.

He avoided his deep craving for a beer by closing his eyes and telling himself that he didn't want a drink. And when that didn't immediately work, he changed his stance on the subject by telling himself that he didn't *need* a drink.

Ben's mind traveled back to earlier when he'd talked to the homicide detective that had worked Sherry Anderson's murder. Doubt suddenly found the deputy, slowly crept in, and annoyingly caused Ben to wonder if he really had done the right thing. Not that there was any going back now, and he hated to question himself, especially since he'd been one hundred and ten percent positive his measures had been justified, but he realized that his great ambition could easily blow up in his face. And though he wasn't sure how long he'd be staying in Gray's Lane, he knew that he really did care about being fired.

Making an arrest would definitely clear up any doubt, so Ben concluded that that was what he was going to have to do. And after having gotten a quick overview of what had taken place some six hundred miles away, Ben was certain that the killer from New York and Ohio was one in the same.

I did the right thing, he told himself, trying to be as convincing as possible that he really had.

"Yes, the woman's body had been scattered with candy corn after being stabbed to death." Detective Michaels' words from earlier seemed to rewind and play again in Ben's mind.

He pulled the thin blue sheet up higher to cover even more of his bare chest. The complete conversation he'd shared with Michaels began spinning in his head, rotating around like a large turning top. Ben listened intently as if their words were booming from a speaker somewhere, rather than inside of him. And even with the striped cloth covering most of his body, an icy chill still managed to find and invade him.

"Why are you so interested in the Anderson murder?" the detective had asked, a certain New York drawl in his voice.

Ben had remembered taking a moment's pause, contemplating the best way to answer the question. His cell had been stationed between his right shoulder and ear, as he'd balanced a small tablet on his lap, all the while sitting in the seclusion of his vehicle. Treading carefully had been a must.

"Deputy Andrews? You still there?"

"Yes, Detective Michaels," Ben had answered, "I'm here. There have been some recent murders here, murders that seem to mimic Sherry Anderson's."

"And when you say 'mimic,' you mean…"

"Three women have been stabbed to death," Ben had interrupted. "Each body was then littered with candy corn."

Though Detective Michaels had then taken his turn to pause and contemplate, Ben had had no trouble interpreting the other man's thoughts.

"Detective?"

"Yes, sorry," Michaels had apologized. "Where was it you said you were calling from, Deputy Andrews?"

"A small town in Northern Ohio. Gray's Lane. Ever hear of it?"

"Can't say that I have," Michaels had admitted. "How did you find out about the candy corn? That aspect of the crime was purposely kept out of the papers and hidden from the press."

"Sherry Anderson's daughter, Michelle, told me. She's currently living in Gray's Lane with her father."

"Excuse me?" Michaels had asked.

"Do I really need to repeat myself, Detective Michaels?" Ben had been getting tired of saying it out loud. The case had snowballed, with the irony of the situation being very cruel and hard to swallow: he'd run from his own past, but had only traded it for a darker, more dangerous present.

"Doesn't this all seem like a very complicated coincidence?"

"You have no idea," Ben had eagerly agreed. "Not to mention, I don't particularly like coincidences. They're too sloppy, too…" he'd let his words trail off for a minute while he'd considered how to form his opinion and accurately put it into words. "I feel like coincidences let us take the easy way out, if you know what I mean."

"Perfectly," Michaels had answered. "So, either someone slipped up and revealed details on the Anderson murder, meaning there's an original killer in New York and a copycat in Ohio…"

"Or…" Ben had jumped in, taking over for the detective. "… there is just the one killer who traveled from New York to Ohio."

"I don't mean to play devil's advocate," Michaels had started, "but why would the original killer from New York be in Gray's Lane?"

"Well, why would there be a copycat killer in Gray's Lane?" Ben had asked, deciding to answer the man with yet another, hair-raising question.

"Touché."

Ben had come to terms with his less than desirable situation, knowing that, bottom line, he needed the other man's help. Starting a pissing contest would get him nowhere—and fast. He'd reminded himself that he was already running out of time as it was, and had half expected the sheriff to come out to the parking lot in search for him.

"Look, I need your help," Ben had finally admitted. He'd heard the desperation in his own voice almost immediately. "I think it's clear that Michelle Anderson is involved in all of this, I just don't know how or why," Ben had confessed. He'd known that his cards had already been shown, and that an honest, upfront approach would only aid him into getting what he wanted and so badly needed.

"Okay," Michaels had agreed. "What can I do to help? Should I fax you my notes? Do you want to see the case file?"

"No!" Ben had instantly called out. The forceful jerk of his body had caused his tablet to fall from his lap and hit the floor of his vehicle. He'd then taken a deep breath and cleared his throat. "I'm sorry, Detective Michaels, I didn't mean to snap at you. It's just that my boss, Sheriff Douglas, well…"

"He doesn't know you're calling me, right? He doesn't know that you're getting outside help on *his* case, in *his* town?"

Ben had felt his jaw fall wide open. "Yeah, that's exactly it. How did you know?"

"Because I have a boss, too. He also happens to have a very large ego."

"I don't mind if I'm out on the limb alone," Ben had stated. "I know these murders are related.

I need your help," he'd repeated his plea from earlier. And then he'd hurriedly added, "Please."

"Alright, I'll help you," Michaels had said. "From one man of the law to another, I know what it's like to have a case that offers more questions than answers. And truth be told, Sherry Anderson's murder still haunts me. I'd love to officially close the case. Maybe we can help each other."

"Thank you, Detective Michaels, thank you."

"Now, what would you like to know?"

At that moment, Ben's heart had began pounding so loudly that he'd been positive the other deputies in the station some fifty feet away from his vehicle would have been able to hear it. He'd then quickly wondered if this was the break he'd been looking to find?

"Deputy?"

"Right. Sorry." Ben had then shaken his head to clear his mind of any and all outside thoughts. "Anything that originally stood out in the case would be helpful. Did you ever have a suspect?"

"Yes, we had one," Michaels had swiftly answered.

Ben had abruptly reached down and grabbed his notebook before the other man had had a chance to say another word. When he'd had his pen ready, he'd said, "Please, continue."

"In the beginning, we were looking at Brian Gleason, Michelle Anderson's boyfriend. The two had only been dating for a short while, and something just didn't feel right about him. Something was off."

Ben had felt a sharp pain in his wrist from the speed it had been moving across the paper. But he still hadn't stopped writing. "And what happened? How did you determine he wasn't the killer?"

"Had an alibi," Michaels had answered through a thick sigh. "He'd been on a date with Michelle at the time of her mother's murder."

Ben had stopped taking notes then; he'd wanted to focus all of his attention on piecing together what Michaels had said. Or, more importantly, what Michaels *hadn't* said.

"So," Ben had started, "just to be clear, the victim's daughter just happened to be the only suspect's alibi?"

"There's more," Michaels had continued. "A few months prior to Anderson's murder, there had been a string of local bank robberies. Nothing fancy, a couple of guys in black ski masks with guns. We thought we might be able to catch them with counterfeit money from one of their hits, but so far, no luck with that."

"I'm sorry, Detective Michaels, I don't mean to stop you, but what exactly do bank robberies have to do with Sherry Anderson's murder?"

"After her murder, the robberies ended. I mean they completely came to a halt, which wasn't these guys' MO. They were hitting a bank every two weeks."

"I hate to say the 'C' word, Detective Michaels, but…"

"Do you think it's also a coincidence that Sherry Anderson just happened to manage one of the banks that was robbed?"

Ben had thought he might actually swallow his tongue before he could get a word out. "Okay, Detective. You've got my full attention. I'm hooked."

"There were several thousands of dollars in Sherry Anderson's account that couldn't be accounted for, not to mention, she was living slightly above her means."

And just to make sure he'd connected the dots correctly, Ben had asked, "And the robberies completely stopped after her death?"

"Completely," Michaels had repeated.

"You're thinking Anderson was involved with these bank robberies."

"I could never prove it. There was no hard evidence that directly linked her to the robberies," Michaels had admitted. "But that was my theory at the time of her murder, and it still kind of is today."

Ben had closed his eyes then. He'd called the homicide detective to get answers, not more questions. He'd felt like he was drowning. A group of murders had somehow transformed into a group of bank robberies.

"Thank you, Detective Michaels. You've given me a lot to consider. I appreciate…"

"Wait," Michaels had called out. "There's just one more thing."

"And what's that?" Ben dared to ask.

"Sherry Anderson had a life insurance policy. Guess who's a half a million dollars richer because of her death."

"Who?"

"Her daughter, Michelle Anderson. The girl who just happens to be in Gray's Lane where other women are turning up dead, and the girl who also just happened to know about the candy corn detail of the original murder."

The lingering scent of the vanilla candles brought Ben back into the present, back into his bedroom. His head was beginning to angrily pound, and he quickly reached up with both hands and started massaging his temple.

Could Elle Anderson really be involved with the murders? Ben knew she was obviously connected somehow, that much was as clear as day. But was she connected as a killer or a potential victim?

More questions seemed to form and appear out of thin air, and Ben knew that he was solely responsible for the aggravation. He'd called New York, he'd gotten himself into this sticky situation, and now he was wondering if he'd made a terrible mistake.

Maybe Elle was the killer. Maybe she'd partnered up with someone and had murdered her mother for the money. But then why was she killing women in Ohio? And if she was behind everything, then why did she even bother bringing the New York angle to his attention?

Something wasn't adding up. Ben used his right hand to lightly scratch the top of his head. What was he missing? And how in the hell did these bank robberies fit in? If they even did. Could the unaccountable money in Sherry's account and the fact that the robberies had stopped at the same time of her death really just be a big coincidence?

The sudden buzzing of his cell phone had Ben frantically sitting straight up. As he reached for the nightstand, there was a slight movement to his left. He knew the damage had already been done.

He gripped the phone, looked to see who was calling, and then answered it. "This is Andrews." After a few moments, he said, "The hospital? Yes, sir, I'll be right there."

"Who was that?"

He knew that his guest had been disturbed, and would expect an explanation for the late night call. But he didn't particularly care what she wanted. He barely had time to get dressed, let alone have a conversation.

"Get your clothes and the rest of your things," he ordered. He stood from the bed and began looking on the floor for his pants. "I have to go."

"Ben?"

"I'm serious," he said through clenched teeth.

Ben bent down, but then quickly brought himself back up to a full standing position. Though darkness surrounded both of them, he still met her gaze and stared deep into her green eyes. He never once blinked.

"And so help me God, if you report anything I've shared with you tonight, I'll kill you myself, Mary."

TWENTY-FOUR

"NO, I DIDN'T SEE HIS FACE."

At least she'd answered his question, even if her voice had been filled with rage. Niki was clearly on edge, and for good reason, Jeff concluded. Less than an hour ago, his daughter had been attacked and almost butchered.

And where had he been during all of the excitement? Not at home, not where he was supposed to have been.

He stood completely still. With his hands shoved deep into the pockets of his jeans, he slowly shook his head back and forth. He realized all too well that he'd almost lost his daughter, and in the exact same way he'd lost his wife.

He hadn't been there when his family had needed him the most. He hadn't done his job; he hadn't protected them

"Dad, where were you?" Niki asked.

Jeff wasn't exactly sure how to answer her question. He hadn't actually done anything wrong. He hadn't even done anything illegal or morally inappropriate, for that matter. But he knew for a fact that Niki wouldn't approve of his response.

After all, his wife had died less than a week ago; he should have been at home with his daughter. That was his place, his responsibility.

"Dad?" Niki repeated, only much louder this time. "Did you hear me? I asked you a question."

"I was out," he quickly cleared his throat before he answered her. He knew that his daughter was a determined person; Niki wasn't going to give up until she got what she wanted. "I was trying to clear my head, so I stopped over at the Arches for a beer."

"You were out drinking?" Niki asked, straightening her position in the small bed. "I was alone at home and almost stabbed to death, and you were out at the bar?"

"I thought you wanted to be alone. I offered to come over, but you made it quite clear that you didn't want me there."

At the sound of his voice, Jeff turned to face Robbie. The last person he expected to have his back was his daughter's boyfriend, especially considering the last conversation he'd shared with the teenager, the one that had taken place at the funeral for Kim.

"Why are you sticking up for my father?" Niki asked, her voice rising. "You're supposed to be on my side, Robbie."

Silence quickly filled the cramped room. Hoping to somewhat blend in with the beige corner, Jeff took a few steps back. Not daring enough to look at Niki or Robbie, he made eye contact with the clean vinyl flooring.

A nurse had gotten in touch with him after his second beer. The woman on the other end of the line had seemed calm, even a little unconcerned. But as soon as he'd heard the words "attacked" and "unknown assailant," Jeff had grabbed his car keys, knocked over his torn leather barstool in the process of getting to the entrance of the bar, and had sped towards the hospital.

Jeff had then been escorted to a corner room. He'd found Niki sitting in a light blue dressing gown, obviously done with the routine checkup. Robbie had been standing by her side, his arms tightly crossed over his chest. And though Niki had been sporting a look of bitter annoyance, and Robbie one of deep sorrow, all had appeared to be in order.

Niki was okay. His daughter was alive, and without one visible scratch anywhere on her body.

"Robbie, whose side are you on here?" Niki asked. Her voice echoed around the room, only adding to the thick tension that had already created. "You're dating me, remember?"

"Niki, I'm not on anyone's side," Robbie protested. "And I really don't want to fight with you, but I think you need to calm down."

"Calm down?" she repeated. "How do you expect me to calm down? I was almost murdered tonight.

"But that's not our fault," Jeff argued. "Believe me," he said, taking a small step toward the bed, "when I got that phone call from the nurse telling me what had happened, I was terrified. I can't tell you how grateful I am that you're okay. But you can't blame Robbie or me for what happened. It's horrible, yes, but the only one responsible is the person who attacked you."

"I could have been next," she whispered.

"I know, honey," Jeff agreed and took another step, inching closer to his daughter. He stretched out his right hand, ready to grab Niki's. "But how were Robbie and I supposed to know that the killer was going to target you? Let's just be thankful that you weren't next."

The quiet returned, and instead of continuing to preach, Jeff decided to let his last comment hang in the air.

For the first time, he noticed the heavy stench of sanitizer that had most likely been used by every person who had walked through the door. The rich alcohol scent was almost unbearable, and Jeff quickly recalled why he hated hospitals and usually tried to avoid them.

He felt a thin breeze, and the few hairs he had on the back of his neck suddenly stood up, causing his entire body to tingle. Cold air was blowing in from somewhere. Jeff determined then that this space wasn't that accommodating, and definitely not for someone whose life had just been threatened.

There wasn't even anything comforting to focus on in the room, Jeff noticed, taking in the area. There were windows along the far wall, but whatever view that was offered was blocked by long, rectangular blinds. A closed door, which most likely led to a bathroom, a small flat screen TV, a faux wooden table on wheels, and a lumpy brown chair completed the room. Not so much as a single painting hung on the wall, and Jeff silently wished the television had been turned on. It would have made for a nice distraction.

"I'm sorry," Niki offered. "I really didn't mean to snap. It was just so… I mean, I actually thought that I was going to…" her words trailed off.

"I *am* sorry I wasn't there, Niki." Jeff closed the distance between himself and his daughter. He grasped her hand, not minding that he had to brush Robbie out of the way to stand where he wanted to. This was ultimately about family, and as far as Jeff was concerned, Robbie wasn't officially part of their family just yet.

"I'm sorry, too," Robbie said. "You didn't deserve what happened to you, especially after…"

"We don't need to bring up the past, Robbie," Jeff hastily jumped in, stopping the teenager from finishing the thought. "Niki's been through enough for one night."

"She's been through enough for one lifetime," Robbie fired back.

Jeff craned his neck around to stare at Robbie. The teenager's eyes were wide; it seemed as if he was refusing to be the first one to blink. A staring contest, Jeff thought to himself. How pathetic.

But he somehow couldn't help but believe that he'd sort of created this little battle for himself. While Robbie had originally stuck up for him, Jeff had reacted by throwing the kid under the bus. And now, Jeff concluded, turning back to Niki to offer her the warmest smile he could muster, the game had begun. It was every man for himself. Who would Niki choose as the winner?

"Well, thank you both for being here right now," Niki said with a half smile. "And please stop apologizing. You're right: no one is to blame. Well, except…"

Jeff immediately picked up on the hint. He provided more support by attempting to change the focus of the conversation. "Have the police been here to get your statement?"

"No," Niki said and shook her head. "I'm kind of surprised, too. I'm sure they've been notified. I really thought they would have been here by now."

"They should have been," Jeff said. The disgust in his voice acted like a sharp knife that tore into his opponent's soft flesh. He faced Robbie once more, this time with a prominent smirk stretched across his face. "Have you talked to your grandfather this evening, Robbie?"

"No, I haven't," the teenager answered. "I'm sure he's on his way, but…"

"Maybe you should try and get some rest," Jeff said, looking back at his pale daughter. "Don't worry about the police; I will take care of them. They should have been here by now, anyway."

"Who's doing this, Dad?" Niki asked. "Why is this happening?"

"I don't know, sweetie," Jeff answered. He bit down on his lip and shook his head; she'd asked the million-dollar question. Two of them. "But if Sheriff Douglas and his deputies had been doing their jobs this whole time, you wouldn't have to ask those questions. You wouldn't have been attacked tonight."

"I think my grandfather and his team are really doing everything they can," Robbie spoke up. "Nothing like this has ever happened in Gray's Lane. There hasn't been much to go on at the crime scenes, and they did have a suspect in custody.

"You're right," Jeff agreed, turning completely around to face Robbie. "They *had* a suspect in custody, 'had' being the key word. But I do have a question," Jeff started. He used his thumb and index fingers to slowly rub the short bristle of hair on the end of his chin. "Just how exactly do you know what has and hasn't been found at the crime scenes?"

"Well, I…"

"What?" Jeff interrupted immediately. He couldn't help but believe that he was definitely winning, and decided to push the teenager even further. He crossed his arms over his chest, and managed to conceal a full-blown smile from completely covering his face. "Have you personally been to these crime scenes? Or does your grandfather just share confidential information with you for the hell of it?"

"Dad, stop!" Niki ordered. "Don't blame Robbie. He's not the bad guy here."

"I know he's not, Niki. But I don't think he's helping matters; he's not making anything easier."

"What do you want me to say, Jeff?" Robbie demanded. "What should I say or do to make all of this better?"

"Well, for starters, you could call your grandfather and tell him to step on it."

"What's the point?" Robbie asked and then shrugged. "It's not like Niki saw anything. She already said that she didn't see her attacker's face. Or weren't you listening?"

Jeff felt his throat tighten; he became speechless. On instinct, he reached up and ran his fingers over his taut neck. Robbie had successfully turned the tables on him, and Jeff knew that he was in trouble. The ball had swiftly bounced into Robbie's court. Jeff figured that he only had minutes to react.

What it all came down to, Jeff concluded, looking back down at the ground, was that Robbie was a problem. The teenager could smile, act polite and cooperative, and even pretend to be useful when it came to comforting Niki, but he was still a ticking time bomb. Robbie possessed something that terrified Jeff. The boy had knowledge. Robbie knew his secret, and Jeff promptly felt his entire body quiver as he came to terms with the fact that Robbie could release that secret at any given minute.

Bottom line: Robbie Sullivan needed to be taken care of. Right now!

"Maybe you should go home, Robbie," Jeff suggested, tilting his head slightly to the side. "It's late, and you seem…" he let his words hang in the air as he thought for a moment. "Tired."

"What are you trying to do, Jeff?" Robbie asked.

The boy wasn't going to back down, Jeff thought. Robbie was definitely in the game now, and he was clearly trying to win Niki over. Jeff couldn't let that happen. He wouldn't.

Jeff took two massive steps forward; he was nose to nose with Robbie. In fact, he was so close that he was positive he could have reached out and pulled the kid's tongue. Jeff could even smell the teenager's breath, and estimated that he'd had something with garlic in it for dinner.

"I'm not trying to do anything, Robbie." Jeff flawlessly combined his smooth tone with an open- jaw look of surprise. "I'm not sure what ulterior motives you're implying I have, but I'm honestly only concerned with Niki's well-being."

"Same here," Robbie agreed.

Jeff was amazed to see Robbie stand painfully still, rather than move backwards. The teenager wasn't backing down. "Well, that's good, but I think Niki needs her rest."

"What I need is for you two to stop fighting over me," Niki called out. "Please."

"Sorry, Niki. Again." Robbie said. "I really do want to be here for you. You should decide who stays and goes, not your father."

"He's just trying to look out for me," Niki argued. "Maybe he's right. Maybe you should go."

"Excuse me?" Robbie asked.

Jeff quickly brought his right hand up to his mouth to conceal his impromptu smile.

"I think I do need to rest," Niki answered. "And I think my dad probably knows what's best for me."

"Really?" Robbie started. "You think your father knows what's best for you?"

"You heard my daughter," Jeff cut in. He hadn't mistaken the anger in Robbie's voice; this bomb was seconds away from exploding. "She wants you to leave."

"Hold on, Dad," Niki ordered. "Robbie, what are you holding back? What are you trying to say?"

"Do you honestly want to know?" Robbie asked.

"Yes, I do."

"No!" Jeff shouted. He pushed Robbie backwards with his fingertips. "I want you to go. Now!"

"No, Dad. I want to hear what Robbie has to say."

"Okay, fine," Robbie agreed. "Tell me, if your father really knows what is best for you, then why was he having an affair?"

"An affair?" Niki repeated.

"Yes," Robbie went on. "Your father was cheating on your mother with Mary Evans."

"What?" Niki cried out. "Why would you say that, Robbie?"

"Because it's true," Robbie answered.

"Oh, really? And how would you know something like that?"

"Because, Niki, I saw your father and Mary together." He paused for a moment. "I saw them in your house, and she wasn't conducting an interview."

Jeff felt a sharp pain explode in his right side. He reached down and put pressure on the mark. He had to remind himself to breathe—a deep inhale through his nose, followed by a long exhale through his mouth. Damage control was in order, but how could he possibly get out of this mess?

"Is it true, Dad?" Niki's voice was thick; Jeff almost didn't recognize it. "Is Robbie telling the truth?"

"Yes," Jeff admitted. He'd decided to go with the truth, hoping he'd get the chance to explain the situation to her. Maybe Niki would find some way to understand, maybe even forgive him.

"And you knew all along, Robbie? You saw my father and Mary together and didn't bother to tell me?"

"Your father asked me to keep it quiet," Robbie explained. "And I wasn't sure how to tell you that…"

"You lied to me! You've *been* lying to me."

"It's not like that," Robbie argued. "I didn't want…"

"Leave!" she ordered.

"What?"

"I want you to leave, Robbie. I don't want to see you again. We're done!"

Jeff was almost positive that he was dreaming; he hadn't expected Niki to react this way. She'd actually dismissed Robbie, and he silently prayed that he wouldn't receive the same fate. Niki was, after all, his daughter, his only living family member. They would surely get past this.

Robbie's dark boots made a squeaking sound across the floor as he turned and fled the room. Jeff watched until the teenager's hooded sweatshirt and jean-covered body faded out of sight. He then shifted, closed his eyes for a moment, and then opened them wide to stare at Niki. It was time to accept whatever punishment he had coming to him.

"Niki, I'm so sorry." An apology, he knew, was the only way to start. "I never wanted you to find out, and definitely not like this. I didn't want to hurt you. And believe me when I say that the affair is over. I swear."

"Well, it wouldn't really be an affair anymore, now would it?"

"Excuse me?"

"I mean, Mom is dead. So technically, you wouldn't be cheating on her. Right?"

"Niki, please…"

"You can leave, too," she stated. "I don't want to see you any more than I want to see Robbie."

"What?" Jeff asked, hearing his own voice go up an octave.

He knew that Niki was one hundred percent serious. She wouldn't even look at him. She wasn't just mad, she was furious, and he didn't have one idea as to how he was going to be able fix it.

"You were seeing someone else when Mom was…I don't want to be around you. I need you to go; I need you to leave me alone."

"Niki," he tried. Not knowing how she would react if he touched her, Jeff chose to ball his trembling hands into fists. "We can get through this, we just need to stick together."

"No!" she demanded. "I don't want to be around you. Go!"

There was no use in arguing with her. Niki had made up her mind, and Jeff knew that his daughter was stubborn enough not to change it. There was nothing left for him to do besides go, just like she had ordered.

No final speech was made. Jeff turned and followed the same path out of the room that Robbie had taken just moments ago. He was going to do as he was asked. Jeff would leave; he'd give his daughter the space that she'd requested.

TWENTY-FIVE

SHE ABSOLUTELY HATED BEING TOLD WHAT to do; he should have known that by now. After all, Mary hadn't gotten to where she was in life by taking orders. She always had and always would do what *she* wanted to do. The last thing on her agenda was to listen to some man, especially since that so-called "man" was actually her boy toy, Deputy Benjamin Andrews.

Mary hadn't taken Ben's threat seriously, of course. Through the years of the uphill battle that was her career, she'd been warned to back off numerous times. As a result, she'd quickly learned the most important trick of the trade: to not scare so easily.

"Time for another great story," Mary whispered aloud. And she had Ben Andrews to thank for it.

Their relationship may have gotten to a weird, ugly, flat out disastrous state, but she didn't regret that relationship now. In fact, as she threw her black leather purse and matching coat down onto her desk and took a seat in front of her computer, Mary decided that she had no regrets at all.

She could still recall every single detail of her first encounter with Ben. But then again, part of being an excellent reporter was having a top-notch memory. And that she did. Mary even remembered what she'd been wearing the night she'd abruptly shown up at the front door of Ben's rental house.

Mary had originally laid eyes on Ben at the Gray's Lane Police Department. How could she not have noticed the "new guy" in town? And she'd instantly formed a plan—sex for a story.

The rest had been history. She hadn't even felt dirty afterwards; it was simply just a chore that had needed to be done. Besides, she'd done a lot worse for a lot less. Her main rule of thumb was well known: do whatever it takes to get the story.

Not only could she still smell the stench of beer, but Mary could also see that utter look of confusion that had spread onto Ben's face upon her original arrival. He'd been genuinely surprised to find her at his front door, offering a bargaining chip.

But her time with him hadn't all been bad, she'd concluded. Ben was hot; it wasn't as if she wouldn't have slept with him anyway. And by doing things her way, she finally had something to show for her assets: a big fat boost into the limelight.

Because of the paper and impromptu live report at the school, even more people knew who she was, and were now eagerly waiting to hear or see what she would uncover next about the Gray's Lane murders.

Using her perfectly manicured right index finger, she pressed the power button on her computer and waited for the device to come to life. A new article was practically bursting out of her; she anxiously drummed her nails on the wood of her desk, creating an irritating clicking sound. Time seemed to creep by at a snail's pace. Patience was a virtue, and in no way, shape, or form did Mary posses such a virtue.

After her coverage at the school, Mary had pretty much assumed that Ben's well of information had run dry. And she had been willing to settle for that. Baby Always, or Benjamin Andrews, had given her more than enough material to go on: the candy corn, the double homicide of Elaine and Emily Jacobs — the fact that there had been a suspect in custody. Not to mention, he'd consistently given her day-to-day updates regarding the investigation.

But being ballsy was one of her most favorite traits, and Mary had made the decision to call Ben after her broadcast to see if there was anything else she could possibly sink her teeth into. Of course, he'd been angry, even rude. And as a result, she'd had no other choice but to take control of the situation and lay down the law.

Her threats towards the deputy had worked. Ben had been scared into revealing the latest information about the case. And now she had a new angle for the newspaper.

"Yes, it's time for another great story," Mary repeated aloud, her smile somehow growing even wider.

She bit down onto her lower lip as she contemplated the latest leak. So, Kimberly Sullivan my not have been the first victim, but the second. This New York woman, was she actually involved? Sherry Anderson, Mary remembered, was she the original victim — the one that had started this whole killing spree? But why would the killer travel from New York to Ohio a month after committing one murder, only to start killing again — and with the same MO?

Mary almost exploded with laughter at her own questions. She knew that if she could answer them, then she'd be able to solve the entire case. Mary took a quick moment to indulge in how *that* would affect her shiny career.

The New York and Ohio connection, Ben had shared, was Michelle Anderson. Gray's Lane had only become a death destination *after* the teenager had moved across state lines to live with her father. Clearly, she was involved, Mary decided. Or maybe her father, John Anderson, was the one to blame. After all, John had been dating one victim, and had been her boss. He'd also been the principal to another, and he would have certainly known the details regarding his ex-wife's murder.

Mary hit the backspace key on her keyboard, deleting the few points she had just typed out. She leaned back into her chair and ran both hands through her tangled hair. She reminded herself that she was strutting down a dead-end road. Ben had already shared with her that John Anderson had been brought in, questioned, and released. He wasn't the killer; that angle of the story was D.O.A. It was time to move on.

There was still something to be said about Michelle Anderson and her mother. But what that was exactly, Mary wasn't quite sure. She suddenly closed her eyes and let the darkness surround her. She had to choose her words very wisely. That was a given.

Ben had thought that Sherry Anderson was hiding something. He had called a New York detective, the same one that had worked the unsolved Anderson murder. But instead of getting answers, Ben had only received more questions. He'd been so kind to have divulged that much, but Mary couldn't help but feel that she hadn't gotten everything from her source.

She stood up, kicked off her heels, and with frustration, placed her hands on each side of her waist. Her thick hose was making her legs itch; she now wondered why she had even bothered putting the garment back on.

She suddenly wished that she'd taken a quick shower at Ben's before coming into the office to pull an all-nighter. The smells of his lavender fabric softener and cheap, spicy cologne still consumed her body. She knew that the combined, nauseating stench could only be weakened with soap and water.

Mary told herself to focus on the positive. Ben had still revealed plenty. Though a little light, she did have something she could work with and write up for the paper. Besides, she thought, resuming her seat and letting her fingertips hover hungrily over the square keys, it wasn't her job to reveal *everything*. Mary's main goal was to keep the residents entertained and thirsty for more.

Ben had mentioned that there were concerns with Sherry Anderson's financials; Mary decided that she would segue into that. First, she would play connect the dots and draw attention to Michelle. The teenager had found her mother murdered. And then a month later, women baring the same conditions were turning up dead in a small town some six hundred miles away, where the young girl just happened to move to live with her father. Definitely a fact, and *definitely* worth reporting.

She began typing, her hands dashing across the keyboard, knowing that she would next dive into the questions regarding Sherry's bank account.

Mary wrote about the suspicious amount of money the woman had, followed by the string of bank robberies that had taken place. Then, she blatantly pointed out that the Anderson woman just happened to be a bank manager, and that the robberies came to a surprising halt after Sherry met her untimely death.

Mary took a long, deep breath; she exhaled slowly. This wasn't where she had expected the feature to go. In fact, as she reread her words on the screen, Mary couldn't help but feel like she'd gotten off track. She'd launched into a whole other story. It was almost as if there were two separate news articles that she was attempting to carelessly splice together with a weak piece of masking tape.

She rolled her neck to the left, letting her negative thoughts and concerns fade away. Mary knew that she was good at her job; she could very easily get her audience to see whatever it was that she wanted. And deep down, she knew that Ben wasn't that far off base. Therefore, she wasn't either.

It was all quite simple: Sherry Anderson had secrets, secrets that in some capacity had to do with the New York bank robberies. Sherry had been butchered because of those secrets. And in some odd, unknown way, Sherry's daughter, Michelle Anderson, was involved, too.

"But is Michelle a victim or a villain?" Mary asked aloud.

A noise burst out from somewhere in the main lobby. She quickly looked up, trying to place it. Mary thought it had been some sort of popping sound, as if someone was chewing gum and then had blown and popped a large bubble.

She suddenly wondered if she was really alone.

Mary pulled away from her desk and stood up. She dodged her discarded heels, and treaded as softly as possible across the floor of her office. She reached the glass door and peered out into the darkness. She hadn't bothered to turn on any lights when entering the building, clearly knowing her way around the "L" shaped obstacle coarse. But she now wished that she'd turned on something. The only thing providing light in her office was her computer screen, and she was well aware of the fact that it was timed to go off in a matter of minutes.

It wouldn't be long before she was completely in the dark.

The popping sound again—loud and close! Then that sharp, piercing thought once again: maybe she wasn't alone.

Mary couldn't see anything, but she knew the layout: square desks accompanied by cheap and uncomfortable chairs scattered throughout the space, a few more offices, a set of bathrooms around the corner, a typical break room. Thick carpet was spread throughout the rest of the building. She wouldn't be able to hear if someone was walking towards her.

She checked her office door, making sure the lock was in place, but continued to stare out

at nothing. Mary knew that she wasn't technically safe, taking in all the glass that surrounded
her. If someone desperately wanted to get in,
they could.

She squinted, trying to search the area and
determine if someone really was watching and
waiting for her. Her breathing became heavy, causing the glass to start fogging up.

"That damn Henry!" she muttered through
gritted teeth. All of this was his fault; he had her
completely paranoid.

Mary chose the wrong time to remember his
lame ass comment from earlier, something about
possibly being the next victim, and just because
she'd exposed details about the killer. Henry was
definitely the one to blame! He was the only reason
she was acting like some little girl who searches
under the bed for a boogeyman that doesn't exist.

Her mantra flashed in front of her eyes,
causing her to go dizzy for a second: don't scare
too easily.

"If you want me mother fucker, come and get
me!" Her shout echoed throughout the room. Mary
stuck out her tongue, pivoted on her bare heel,
and then turned around and walked back to her
computer.

If someone really wanted to kill her, well, there
was just no getting around that. When her time
was up, it was up. And at least she'd die doing
what she loved to do.

She resumed her seat and went back to work. Mary managed to get over the scare; she began thinking about how the town would react tomorrow morning when her article hit the stands. Though many would be racing through paragraphs to read her latest scoop, she knew that there was one person in particular that wouldn't approve: Ben Andrews.

But Mary shrugged off the idea. She'd figured that Ben was pretty much done with her anyway, and she actually didn't mind. He'd barely shared the latest info with her, and hadn't even bothered to say why he was rushing off to the hospital. But that, too, didn't bother her.

Now, going to the morgue or an actual crime scene, *that* would have been newsworthy. But a hospital? Amateur stuff, she decided. The whole survivor façade was dead, over. What people really wanted were blood and guts, the nitty gritty. And that's exactly what Mary planned on giving them with the Sherry and Michelle Anderson angle. A story full of dirt and crime that most small town reporters wouldn't dare to write, but Mary knew that she was a far cry from 'most.' And when the paper came out the next morning, she didn't plan on batting one, perfectly long eye lash.

Ben could pout or yell out threats all he wanted; she wasn't going to back down. She had come too far. Besides, she determined with a roll of her shoulders, he could very well be replaced.

First, Jeff Sullivan and then Ben Andrews. Mary figured that she could find someone else to...handle her business. She wasn't completely positive that she'd find another source as helpful as Baby Always, but Mary had learned early in her life to never say 'never'.

Not to mention, there were plenty of other men in useful positions that could get her what she wanted. The time had come to reveal everything she knew about the Gray's Lane murders, and she would be damned if she was going to pass up *that* opportunity.

Mary typed her closing statement, and then printed out a copy of the article. She stood, stretched, and wiggled her tight fingers to release the built up tension. She had a phone call to make. Though her editor wouldn't enjoy the late night interruption, she was sure that he'd be pleased once she started explaining her breaking story.

But first, she had an errand to run. Mary wanted to celebrate and treat herself with a rare indulgence: a candy bar. There was a convenience store on the corner, and she couldn't wait to unwrap and bask in the rich, creamy chocolate-taste of victory. She'd more than earned it.

TWENTY-SIX

ELLE STILL HAD TROUBLE BELIEVING WHAT she was actually seeing: Brian Gleason was in Ohio. He was in her home, sitting on her bed, and staring at her with those intense brown eyes that she'd originally been so severely drawn to. Part of her wanted to scream, but out of excitement or horror, she really didn't know yet. And the other, more logical half of her wanted to pinch herself on the arm to make sure that this wasn't some strange, cruel dream she was currently trapped in.

She chose to do neither, deciding to wait out the next few moments and hear what Brian had to say. Then, she knew that she'd be able to determine what was really happening here.

"You can sit down. There's plenty of room on the bed." She watched as he raised his arm and softly patted the space beside himself.

"That's okay," Elle answered, waving off his offer. "I'd rather stand."

"By the door? Are you preparing to bolt?"

"No, I just…"

"Elle, are you afraid of me?"

He'd hit the nail on the rusty head, but she wasn't quite sure how to respond to the question. Maybe "scared" wasn't the most accurate word to use, Elle considered, eyeing the door that was half ajar with a fast, sideways glance. "Unsure" was a more appropriate for the impromptu visitor. After all, Brian had conveniently shown up to Gray's Lane when women were mysteriously turning up murdered. Elle didn't know how long her ex had been in Ohio. Not to mention, he was yet another connection to New York and what had taken place there.

"You don't have to be scared of me, Elle; I'm not going to hurt you. I promise."

She felt a slight smile spread across her face. She instantly raised her right hand to try and conceal it. Elle silently prayed that Brian hadn't seen the gesture.

"What's so funny?"

Dammit! The smile hadn't gotten passed him. She was fully aware that her face was flushed, and almost positive that her whole body was now turning red. Elle immediately felt foolish.

"Nothing, really," she finally answered after a few seconds. "I was just thinking that if you were the killer, you probably would tell me not to be scared, even try to convince me that I'm safe and you have no intentions of hurting me."

"Excuse me?"

"Well, I mean, you wouldn't come right out and say, 'I'm going to kill you, Elle.' Right?" She felt her smile return; a small snicker even escaped her dry lips.

"So," Brian started, a wide frown appearing on his pale face, "you don't trust me, do you, Elle?"

Elle shrugged. "I don't know who to trust or what to believe. I *want* to trust you," she stated, a certain thickness in her voice. She realized that she was starting to choke up. "But put yourself in my shoes. You unexpectedly break up with me in New York, and then you randomly show up in Ohio when…"

"I've only been in Gray's Lane for a few hours," he interrupted, "and I just found out about the other murders today. I swear. Please, just hear me out; let me explain."

She considered his plea, and after a long moment, slowly nodded. Elle opted to hear him out. Besides, she thought, leaning up against the wall for more comfort, her father was just in the next room. Elle didn't actually believe that Brian could attack her that quickly without John hearing the struggle.

"A deputy from the Gray's Lane Police Department contacted me today," Brian started. "Deputy Ben Andrews called me this afternoon, said he got my number from a detective in New York. It was during our conversation that he revealed the murders that have taken place here."

"Ben called you?" she asked, a frown appearing on her own face that matched Brian's from earlier. "I spoke with him today, too. What exactly did he say? What did he want from you?"

"He asked me a lot of questions about Sherry."

"About my mother?" Elle heard her voice go up an octave. "Like what? Did he think you had something to do with her…"

"Murder?" Brian finished. "No, well, I don't think so, anyway. I told him that we were together during the time your mom was… you know…"

"Right," Elle jumped in, "I know what you mean." She figured that she'd avoided some awkward tension by not making Brian finish his statement. After all, she also sometimes had trouble using certain words to describe what had taken place a month ago.

"The deputy also wanted to know if I remembered anything strange about that night. You know, if I noticed anything out of the ordinary when I picked you up and then took you home. The same stuff I was asked by that New York detective."

"What did you say?"

"No, of course," he answered. "I told the deputy that had I known about what you were going to walk into, I never would have let you go inside the house alone."

Elle took a deep breath. "Thanks, Brian, but you had no way of knowing what had happened while we were gone."

"It doesn't change the fact that I'm sorry and still regret the way it all played out."

She felt the tension in her shoulders release, as she folded her hands together. Elle was well aware of what was happening; she was beginning to feel safe with Brian. Maybe he really was the person she'd thought he'd been all along.

"So, what's going on here now?" Brian asked, breaking the thick silence. "Tell me what's been happening in Gray's Lane since you moved here?"

Elle became confused. "Didn't Deputy Andrews already fill you in?"

"Yes," Brian nodded. "But I want to hear it from you. Your version, your thoughts."

"Okay," she agreed, taking a long, hard look at Brian.

Elle found herself staring at her ex. His thick dark hair was longer than the last time she had seen him; it now almost covered his eyes. He sat tall and lean on her perfectly made bed, and looked quite attractive in faded jeans and a form-fitting black shirt.

She glanced down at her own attire, now wishing that she hadn't chosen something so comfortable after Brian had called and she'd invited him over. There was nothing appealing about gray sweatpants, a white v-neck t-shirt, and a disheveled ponytail.

But this meeting wasn't about impressing one another, Elle understood. She wanted answers, and apparently so did Brian. So, she decided, tonight would be about exchanging information and nothing else.

"It all began last Saturday. A woman, Kimberly Sullivan, was murdered," she started, already aware of the minor tremble in her voice. "And then last night, two more women were murdered. Elaine and Emily Jacobs, a mother and daughter. My father was dating Elaine."

"That's what the deputy said," Brian admitted. "Three women in five days. But I had no idea that your father had been... I'm so sorry, Elle. That had to have brought up some terrible memories for you."

"All of the murders have," she stated. "It's been like a bad nightmare coming true." Elle considered addressing his comment further, but knew that she couldn't. Her strength could only go so far, and if she wanted to finish her story, she had to keep moving forward.

"Then," she continued, choosing to avoid eye contact and instead stared at the blank space above her bed, "a local reporter revealed something about all of the murders. All of the women had been stabbed to death, but they also had something else in common." Elle finally stared Brian directly in the face. "All of the women were found with candy corn scattered on their bodies."

"Just like your mother," Brian slowly stated. "I was informed of the new murders, but to only some extent." He jammed his hands into his tight jean pockets. "I was really confused by the deputy's phone call. I mean, I assumed there was some connection to New York, and that that's why I was being contacted. But I thought that the connection was you, Elle. I thought you were in danger, and so I hopped on the next flight to Ohio. I wanted to be her for you this time, since I wasn't last time."

She shook her head. "There's no reason to bring all of that back into the present," Elle said. "It was a scary time; we hadn't even been dating that long. I'm not even sure how I would have reacted had the circumstances been different. I may have bailed, too."

"Well, I'm not bailing this time," he informed. "And from the sounds of it, you traded one nightmare for another one. Or maybe it's still the same nightmare. The candy corn?" he asked. "I had no idea there was a connection like that linking your mother's murder to the murders that have been happening here."

"That's why I decided to speak with the deputy as soon as I heard about the killer's signature, the candy corn."

"And did he believe you?" Brian asked.

"He must have," she nodded. "That has to be why he called you. It's just too bad that Deputy Andrews may be the only one who believes me." She quickly recalled the earlier conversation she'd had with her father.

"I believe you, Elle. It's pretty obvious to me that whoever murdered Sherry murdered the women in Gray's Lane. The candy corn is just too big of a coincidence." It was as if he were reading a script that had been typed up from her own thoughts. "And you're clearly, for some reason, at the center of it all. I think the killer followed you from New York to Ohio.

"But why?" she asked. Elle suddenly felt as if all of the blood had just evaporated from her head. Her knees started shaking. "None of this makes sense to me."

"You need to sit down," he said.

Elle didn't bother arguing. Instead, she did what she'd been told. She moved over to the bed, lowered her body down onto the comforter, and took a seat beside Brian.

"Should I get you some water?" he asked.

"I'm fine," she said, declining his offer. "I guess it's just a little overwhelming to hear all of this out loud. That, and to actually have someone else believe me," she added.

"Of course I believe you," Brian said. "It's the only logical thing that makes sense."

"I know, but…" Elle stopped short of her argument; her cell phone was beeping. She reached into her pocket, pulled it out, and looked down at the screen. "It's a text from my friend Niki."

"Well, it's good to know you've made friends."

"My God!" Elle screamed.

"What is it? What's wrong?"

"Niki's in the hospital; she's been attacked."

"Is she okay?"

Elle couldn't take her eyes off the screen. She just kept rereading the message.

"Elle?" Brian asked.

"She's fine, but she needs a ride. She said that she would explain everything in person." Elle stood and began searching the floor for a pair of shoes.

"I'm going with you," Brian stated. "Right now, I'm not comfortable letting you out of my sight. A killer is still out there."

"Fine," Elle said. She walked over to her dresser and grabbed her car keys. She tossed them to Brian; he caught them with his right hand. "I'll give you directions to the hospital; you can drive."

"Okay," he agreed. "Let's go."

Elle followed him to the bedroom door, but before turning out the light, she looked back at the picture of her mother and her, still sitting on the nightstand. So much happier, simpler times, she thought.

As Brian led her down the stairs, she couldn't help but feel a little confused; the tiny hairs on the back of her neck were standing straight up. Though he'd talked a good game and had seemed genuinely concerned about her, she was still unsure about Brian Gleason's motives for being in Ohio.

The conversation had been entirely focused on her. Elle's past and present had been discussed, but not one detail of Brian's life had been mentioned.

She couldn't stop herself from wondering if she'd just put her life into the hands of a killer?

———

Mistakes had been made, that was for certain. He'd underestimated the Sullivan girl's strength, and as a result, the bitch had gotten away.

But it would all be okay, he decided, standing naked in front of the full-length mirror, accessing the damage. Luckily, there were just a few tiny bruises that could easily be covered. And at least she hadn't seen his face.

He reached into the shower, turned the knob, and let the hot water rain down. He then stepped into the tub, taking instant pleasure in the hard stream that hit him. He told himself once more that everything would be okay.

His game plan was picking up speed. And tomorrow would finally bring forth the ending he'd been waiting to execute.

TWENTY-SEVEN

THERE'D ACTUALLY BEEN A SURVIVOR. HE was still having trouble wrapping his mind around the fact. Ben took a long sip of coffee from his travel mug, and let the strong scent of hazelnut fill his nostrils. He wasn't sure of the last time he'd actually smiled, most likely days ago, but the deputy was fully aware that he was now grinning from ear to ear.

He rounded the corner of Glenwood, and the large brick building came into view — the Gray's Lane Police Department. Ben turned right, drove over the cracked asphalt, and pulled into an employee marked parking spot.

He brushed off a few crumbs of his toast breakfast from the bottom half of his khaki uniform, pulled the key from the ignition, grabbed his coffee mug, and then stepped out of his truck. Even the daily ritual of taking inventory of the rust and dents that stained the red vehicle couldn't stop Ben from smiling. Nothing was going to rid him of the warm, tingling sensation of hope.

Ben knew quite well that there was no guarantee the killer would be caught anytime soon.

But he wasn't about to let *that* negativity drag him down. The killer had slipped, and because of Niki Sullivan, the good guys had finally been awarded a point.

The key word was 'closer,' Ben decided. The police were *closer* to catching the person who was responsible for at least three and possibly four murders. Simply put, they now had some information about the son-of-a-bitch.

As Ben balanced his coffee mug in his left hand and used his right to open the heavy glass door, he started making mental notes about last night's meeting with the lone survivor.

Niki had given a very useful description of her assailant, having been able to estimate both his height and weight. Ben was also pleased to know the attacker's wardrobe: black pants, sweatshirt, and boots, complete with a black ski mask. According to Niki, he'd smelled sour, like sweat, and he'd brought a bag of candy corn to the scene.

This was the real deal, the man that the Gray's Lane Police Department had been searching for — Ben was sure of it.

Not even the regretful screw up that was Mary Evans was going to cause him doubt today, Ben realized, stepping into the thick, dry atmosphere of the station. He'd fallen into her trap — again — and had repeated the same mistake of giving her privileged information about the case. And though it hadn't *technically* been factual information pertaining to the case this time, but more of his own personal theories on it, Ben still recognized that he'd slipped.

And now, the selfish, desperate, no good reporter would never get another word out of him. Period.

Mary was quite persuasive, but he would be stronger, prove that he had will power. It also helped that he just so happened to be a man of the law, and the next time she handed out threats, he'd take out his handcuffs and throw the bitch in jail.

He was officially done.

Sure, he thought, keeping a steady pace as he headed toward his desk, the encounter with Mary had been fun, exciting, and he'd willingly taken part in it. But he had to end it. He'd put both his job and the investigation on the line. And the sharp pains of guilt that now pierced his sides had him regretting that decision.

She'd just been so damn hard to resist that first night she'd shown up at his house. He'd been new to town, had had an overwhelming first day at the office, and of course, had been half drunk. Not that those were good excuses, Ben admitted to himself, but they were the real, piss-pour reasons for the decision he'd ultimately made.

Sleeping with Mary had been interesting, to say the least. And like a stray cat that gets fed once, he'd eagerly gone back for more. But then she'd wanted something in return for her "services."

He'd obliged, of course, and now knew that he was standing knee deep in a pile of horse shit.

Mary had broken their agreement. Instead of waiting until the killer was caught, she'd gone ahead and run with the story, revealing the candy corn signature, double homicide of Elaine and Emily, and that there'd been a suspect in custody. And instead of telling her off, he'd only shown weakness by falling onto his knees like some trained puppet. She'd won, and had gotten more material out of him.

But he was serious this time — no more. After all, he'd been rather lucky. So far, no one knew that he was the leak. Ben was smart enough to know his limits, and he was getting out while he still had the option. Never one to gamble, he'd come to the conclusion that he sure as hell wasn't going to start now.

"Andrews."

He hadn't even reached his desk yet. He continued the few steps to his personal space, set down his coffee mug next to the framed picture of his mother, and then spun on the heels of his black boots to see who had called for him this early and why.

"Deputy Hall," Ben said, sizing up his colleague.

Hall had on the same tan uniform and dark boots as Ben. The other deputy's hair was cropped short and neat; he seemed to be in decent shape.

Ben saw a smug, almost superior look on the man's face. Though close to the same age, it was easy for Ben to notice something he and Hall didn't have in common: Ben was damn good at his job, and Hall simply wasn't.

"Is there something I can do for you, Deputy Hall?" Ben asked.

"Not me *personally*," Hall answered, his smiling starting to grow obviously wider, "but for Sheriff Douglas. He wants to see both of us in his office. Now."

"Fine, after you." Ben waved the other deputy forward, and then fell into step behind him, staying in place until they reached the open door of the sheriff's office.

"Come in," the sheriff ordered, "and close the door behind you."

Ben waited for Hall to enter. Then, just as he'd been told, he closed the door behind himself. He took a few steps forward, but unlike Hall, who took an immediate seat, Ben remained standing. He placed his arms behind his back and connected his hands. The scent of tobacco immediately became nauseating.

"Well, park it, son."

"Yes, sir," Ben said softly. He lowered himself down into the uncomfortable chair. "How are you doing this morning?"

"Not too damn good, son," the sheriff's voice roared out, filling the small, enclosed space. "I'm guessing you haven't seen this morning's paper, otherwise you wouldn't have asked that question."

A lump the size of a baseball formed in Ben's throat. He tried to swallow it, but the gesture was useless. "Excuse me, sir?"

"Take a look." Ben watched with wide eyes as Douglas tossed a thin copy of the Gray's Lane Examiner onto the desk. "Do me a favor and read fast."

Ben glanced down at the bold headline; his gaze didn't have to travel any further. The words 'Local killings may have originated in New York' stared back at him. He didn't need to see a mirror to know that his face had turned red. His breathing became heavy, and for a slight moment, he saw stars.

"Do you have anything to say about this article, Andrews?" Douglas asked. Ben was almost positive he could see fire dripping off of each one of the sheriff's words.

"Why would I, Sheriff?" Ben asked, praying silently that playing stupid would somehow work to his advantage. "Is that why you called Deputy Hall and me in here?"

"No," the sheriff answered and shook his head. "It's why I called *you* in here. Mary Evans didn't mention Deputy Hall in this piece of trash, but she did name you."

Ben lowered his head; he began scanning the page once again. He saw his name in print at least five times.

"Now, do you have anything to say, Deputy Andrews?"

Ben bit down onto his lower lip. He only lifted his teeth when he tasted the bitterness of his own blood. "You don't believe her? I mean, what she wrote, you can't think that it's…"

"What else am I supposed to think, son?" the sheriff interrupted. "To my knowledge, you are the only person in the entire department to both know about and accept this ridiculous New York connection."

"Right," Ben nodded. "But that doesn't really matter…"

"Actually, it does," Douglas disagreed. "You see, son, Mary's little tips have obviously been coming from the department. Whoever gave her the latest leak truly believes that this killing spree began with Sherry Anderson in New York. And like I already mentioned, the only person who actually believes that is you."

"But…" Ben's thoughts trailed off. He looked up at the stained ceiling, hoping to find the right words to say. But then he quickly realized something: there weren't any.

"And before you try to come up with another lie, Deputy Hall has something to say to you."

Ben turned to his left, remembering for the first time that he and Sheriff Douglas weren't alone in the room. Deputy Hall's blue eyes seemed to almost be sparkling; his nasty smirk was back in place.

"Go ahead, Deputy Hall," the sheriff's eyes shifted to the other man. "Tell him."

"Last night," Hall began, "on my way to the hospital to help question the witness, I drove by your house."

"So?" Ben shrugged. Though he wasn't exactly sure where this was all going, he still felt a line of sweat beginning to form at his left temple. Something told him that this wasn't going to end well.

"I saw Mary Evans walk out the front door," Hall said, clearly trying to conceal a full-blown laugh.

Ben took a moment to try and process what the deputy had said so that he could prepare an appropriate answer.

He held his breath for a few seconds and then released it. "Is my house even on your way to the hospital?"

"Ben," Douglas said, with a certain sharpness present in his tone. "You're fired."

"What?" Ben felt his eyebrows come together to form an angry scowl. He didn't understand; this couldn't be happening. "Fired?" he repeated the sheriff's word. "How can you… why?"

"You put this entire investigation in jeopardy," Douglas answered, not once blinking his heavy eyes. "You made this whole department liable for a lawsuit. *And,*" he put a hard, emphasis on the word, "most importantly, you lied to my face."

No! Ben's mind screamed. How could this be happening? And right now, when he had a new suspect in mind?

"You're done here," Douglas continued. "Leave your gun, badge, and clear out any personal belongings you may have stored in your desk these past five days. And though I can't legally force you out, it might be wise for you to get out of Gray's Lane. Permanently."

Ben didn't have control of his body; he suddenly found himself standing. "Sir, please! Don't do this. I'm begging you!" He started gripping the edge of the sheriff's desk with both of his hands. "I think I might know who the killer is," he blurted out.

"What?" Hall exploded.

"Who?" Douglas asked.

"Well," Ben wasn't one hundred percent sure how to proceed, but he knew that he definitely had to give it a shot. "I did call a detective in New York. I'm telling you, Sherry Anderson is a part of this, and I think her daughter's former boyfriend may be involved."

"Get out of my office!" Douglas ordered.

"Sir, please. Just hear me out." Ben knew that he was drowning; he tried to rush his theory. "Brian Gleason was a suspect in New York. I got a hold of the guy, and something just seems off about him. He said that…"

"Who are you talking about?" Douglas asked.

"Michelle Anderson's ex-boyfriend in New York, Brian Gleason," Ben answered, almost out of breath. "I think we need to do a background check, maybe even see if he really is in New York."

"You want to waste time, money, and resources on some dead-end theory that I've repeatedly warned you to drop?"

"Sir, if we…"

"No!" the sheriff said, raising both of his hands. "Your pleas aren't going to work; I don't have to hear them anymore!" Douglas' lips firmly tightened. "Get out!"

Ben shook his head; he knew that any other attempts to change the sheriff's perspective would be useless, and he didn't want to waste another minute arguing the matter. He figured that if he left immediately, he might even be able to some dignity.

He started for the door, but turned around for one last glance at Sheriff Douglas and Deputy Hall. Ben wasn't surprised, not in the least. Deputy Hall was grinning from ear to ear.

TWENTY-EIGHT

"I DON'T WANT TO HEAR IT, KYLE. I'M NOT getting back together with Robbie."

"I know that he let you down, but he wanted me to call you and see…"

"Stop!" Niki ordered, increasing her tone, hoping that Kyle would get a clue and quit trying to convince her to forgive her ex. "Robbie didn't just let me down, he lied to me. I'm not even sure for how long, but it was about my mother."

"I'm sorry," Kyle said softly. The last thing I want to do is upset you. I hate being in the middle of all this. I mean, both of you are my friends."

Niki took a deep breath. She suddenly realized that her body was becoming very hot, and she now felt guilty for telling off her friend. Deep down, she knew that Kyle really had been trying to help. He *was* in an awkward place.

"Niki," Kyle started, "are you still there?"

"Yes," she answered and then cleared her throat, "I'm here. You don't need to apologize. This isn't your fault." Niki propped herself up on her left elbow. "I'm just going to need some time separated from Robbie.

"I guess that's understandable," Kyle agreed.

"I never thought he would betray me like that," she confessed. "Well, in all honesty, I never thought my dad would either."

Niki slowly closed her eyes and let her head fall down onto the soft blue pillow. She stretched her legs out, not even coming close to reaching the end of the queen-sized bed, and once more reminded herself not to cry. It was a hard act to accomplish; she'd never felt more alone in her entire life.

Niki knew that she had herself to blame, kind of. After all, she had dismissed both Robbie and her father last night, saying that she didn't want to see either of them ever again. And she'd gotten her wish: Robbie had left the hospital, her father had disappeared, and she'd bravely gone back to the house where she'd almost lost her life—completely alone.

But in her defense, at the time of hearing about the affair, she'd been completely overwhelmed. She'd just been attacked, her mother had been murdered five days before, and to top everything off, she'd found out that her father had been cheating on her mother and that her boyfriend had known about it all along.

Niki quickly concluded that there wasn't an appropriate way to act to a situation like the one she'd been forced into being part of.

Her eyes began burning and almost instantly became wet. Ultimately, she couldn't fight the tears and decided to let them roll down her already puffy red cheeks. She just didn't have the energy or the strength to fight anymore.

Pictures of friends and family hung around her spacious room, pictures that had captured wonderful memories. But there was nothing wonderful to capture in her life right now, Niki determined. She'd lost her mother, boyfriend, and father. She couldn't help but wonder how someone who'd recently had so much could lose it all in an instant.

"Niki, do you want me to let you go?"

She'd forgotten that she was still on the phone. "Sorry. No, please don't hang up." She gripped her cell phone tighter, and then pressed the device forcefully against her ear to remind herself not to zone out again. "It's really nice to talk to someone."

"Despite everything that's happened with your father and Robbie," Kyle began, "how are you doing? I can't believe you were attacked last night and lived to tell about it. That's..."

"Kyle," she cut him off. "I can't talk about that, not now. I hope you understand." Niki was only okay if she wasn't focusing on the fact that she was almost brutally murdered, that she was now considered a survivor in the Gray's Lane killings.

Though covered with the thick comforter, Niki's legs began shaking and frantically knocked together. The truth, she knew, was that until the killer was actually caught, there was nothing stopping him from coming after her again to finish what he'd started. She wasn't quite sure why she'd almost been a victim, but was positive that until the culprit was caught, she may not continue to be a survivor.

"Of course," Kyle said. "I wasn't thinking."

"It's fine," Niki said. She scooted up to rest against her headboard, and brought her knees up to her chest.

"So," Kyle began, clearly trying to find another subject, which caused Niki to produce a vague smile, "are you going to the funeral today?"

Not a complete stray, she considered, but she appreciated the attempt. "Yes, I am," she answered.

The sad irony of it all was that school had been cancelled, but at the expense of two women's lives. She hadn't shared a relationship with Emily Jacobs or really even known Elaine, but she would pay her respects today, as would most of the town. Mourning would definitely be this morning's theme, Niki believed.

"Are you going with anyone?" Kyle asked.

"Elle and I are supposed to go together," she answered. And then Niki knew that she had some explaining to do. It was her turn to be placed between a rock and a hard place.

"Oh, Elle," Kyle whispered.

She frowned. Niki instantly felt her entire body cringe; she knew what she would have to do next. "Kyle, I…"

"Is something wrong?" he interrupted.

Niki shook her head and then closed her eyes; she would just have to come out and say it. "Last night, Elle picked me up from the hospital, but she wasn't alone."

"What do you mean?" he asked. "Who was with her?"

She inhaled deeply, and then in one big blow, released the heavy breath. "She was with her ex-boyfriend from New York. Apparently, he heard about the murders and came to Gray's Lane because he was worried about her."

"Niki, wait…"

"No," she said, "let me get this out. I need to finish it. Now, I'm not saying that he and Elle are going to get back together or anything like that, but I did see the way he looked at her. You're my friend, Kyle, and I know you like Elle. I just don't want to see you get hurt."

"You don't have to worry about me, Niki," Kyle stated. "I'm over Elle; she can get back together with her old boyfriend. I don't really care."

Niki pulled away from the headboard, hanging on Kyle's last word. Something was up. What exactly had she failed to notice?

"Seriously," he continued, "I don't want anything to do with her."

"Okay," Niki mumbled. She shrugged her shoulders. "Did I miss something?"

"You haven't seen this morning's paper, have you?" he asked.

She shook her head. "No, why? What has Mary Evans cooked up this time?"

"I think her article is legit this time," Kyle said. "She's even got a statement from that new deputy, Ben Andrews."

"Well, what's it say? What does it have to do with Elle?"

There was a thick pause before Kyle spoke again. "I think you need to read it, Niki. You know, for yourself."

The little hairs on the back of her neck immediately stood up. Despite the blanket and flannel pajama bottoms she was wearing, Niki's body temperature seemed to reach freezing. "Kyle, you're scaring me."

"Just go get the paper," he ordered. "I'll wait."

It was as if Niki didn't have control of her body. She stood from her bed, her cell held down at her side. And like a block of ice, she drifted from her room, down the stairs, and out the front door. She didn't mind if the neighbors happened to see her barefoot and in her t-shirt and pajama pants. Her only concern was getting to the end of the driveway.

The strong, almost overwhelming smell of freshly mown grass hit Niki. Someone had been busy this beautiful, fall morning. But not even the intoxicating scent was going to stop her from finishing her journey.

When she reached the spot where the paper had landed, she promptly knelt down, traded her cell for the paper, pulled off the rubber band, and released the thin sheets.

"Niki?" she heard Kyle's muffled voice from her cell. "Did you get it?"

She didn't answer him right away, she couldn't. Her eyes were swimming back and forth over the dark ink. Niki tried to absorb the story as quickly as possible, and once she'd finished, she knew that she finally had answers to all of her questions.

Niki crumbled the front page with her fist, reached for her cell phone from the pavement, and stood up.

It was now clear why her mother had been murdered, and why she, herself, had almost been stabbed to death: Elle Anderson. Her so-called, new friend was behind this entire nightmare.

Her throat became tight; she thought she might scream. Niki's body was shaking again, but this time, with rage. Her left hand instantly clenched into a fist; she wanted to hit somebody, a *specific* somebody.

Niki brought her phone closer to her face, closing the distance between the device and her mouth. When she spoke, her voice was deeper than ever.

"Kyle, I'm going to have to call you back."

TWENTY-NINE

ELLE WAS EVEN MORE CONFUSED ABOUT Brian than she had been the night before; Mary Evans' article had successfully caused that confusion. Now, Elle decided, adding a splash of sea breeze scent to her neck, not only was she unsure if her ex-boyfriend was actually involved with these murders, but she was also having strong doubts about her mother.

She let her hand rest at her neck, and gently ran her fingers over the Amethyst stone that hung loosely from the sterling silver necklace. Elle had often wondered how her mother had been able to afford such an expensive piece of jewelry. And now, she thought, slowly shaking her head, she may have just gotten the answer to that question.

Elle took a small step back so that she could see her entire self in the full-length mirror. Hair straightened and pinned back, black pinstriped pants and heels to match, and a white sweater — she definitely looked the part... to be going to a double funeral.

She flicked the switch on the wall behind her, causing the bathroom light to go out. Elle then rounded the corner, turned, and stepped into her bedroom. She took a seat on her bed and looked down at this morning's paper. She'd already read the story twice.

"Local killings may have originated in New York'" flashed before her eyes. Well, she thought, shaking her head—that was nothing new. She'd been the one to inform the police of her mother's murder in the first place, and share her concerns about the similarities of the New York murder and the local killings. That wasn't her issue.

The problem, Elle decided, glancing away from the piece, refusing to read it again, was that her mother had been made out to be some sort of monster. Just because there had been a string of bank robberies happening in the city that had mysteriously stopped at the time of her mother's death proved nothing. Elle refused to believe that her mother was involved in the handful of heists.

But then hesitation began gnawing away at the corners of her mind, much like a hungry rat. She instantly thought back to her jewelry, but that wasn't her only concern, she soon realized. There had been new clothes, home appliances, furniture, that one getaway weekend to the Hampton's, and even talk about a new car in the few months leading up to her mother's death.

Living in New York was expensive, to say the least. And Elle was well aware of the fact that her mother and she had just barely been making it on a bank manager's salary. But once all of the other luxuries were added in, well, Elle had had her suspicions at the time, but she'd ultimately ignored them. Her mother had told her not to worry, so she'd done just that. She'd had a good, open relationship with her mother; she'd fully trusted the woman.

Elle looked at the picture on her nightstand. That relationship now appeared to be false, or highly misconstrued. Even the bank that her mother had worked at had been hit. So, was that only further evidence that Sherry had somehow been entangled in everything?

Elle quickly wrapped her arms around her shivering body, hugging herself. She was too afraid to answer that question.

And then there was Brian; something no longer added up about him, Elle concluded. They'd met in the midst of the robberies, he'd abruptly broken up with her after her mom had been killed, and now he was in Ohio at the exact same time women were being stabbed to death. She desperately wanted to know his angle.

He'd been helpful last night, even comforting, but he'd also gotten aggravated when she'd told him he couldn't stay with her and that he needed to go back to his hotel room. It'd been after they'd dropped Niki off, and at the time, she'd wished that she hadn't been alone with Brian. His eyes had grown wide and angry, and it had been then that

Elle realized she wasn't completely sure what he was capable of doing.

A panic abruptly washed over Elle, and she didn't need a mirror of any size to know that her face had turned bone white. She could no longer tell who was trustworthy. Somebody had a secret, somebody had lied, and somebody was killing women that were connected to her.

With the sleeves of her sweater pushed up to her elbows, the small hairs on her arms were quite visible, as they stood straight up. Elle wished now that her father hadn't gone ahead to the funeral without her. Right now, she didn't like the idea of being alone.

Elle jumped up at the ringing sound of her cell phone. Her body became tense, and for a moment, she became completely still. She closed her eyes and slowly counted to three; she knew that she needed to calm down. Otherwise, Elle decided, walking to the nightstand to retrieve her phone, she was going to have a panic attack.

"Hello?" she answered, not bothering to look at the caller ID.

"It's Niki."

Relief instantly washed over Elle. Her body suddenly loosened, and her shoulders dropped; relaxation was beginning to settle in. "I'm so glad you called, Niki." Elle even felt a smile form as she said her friend's name.

"Elle, we need to talk."

"Okay," Elle agreed and nodded. "We can talk about anything as long as it has nothing to do with current events." A soft laugh escaped her lips. Well, at least she'd *tried* to make a joke. "Can we talk in person?"

"What?" Niki's voice seemed somewhat hard, even a little snappy.

"I know I'm not supposed to pick you up for another hour, but I was hoping I could come over now. My father already left for the church, and I really don't want to be alone."

"No, Elle," Niki said. "We're not going to the funeral together."

"Excuse me?" Elle asked. She bit the side of her cheek in confusion, and then shook her head. "I thought we agreed last night to go together, remember?"

"Yeah, well, that was before I saw this morning's paper," Niki answered. "Have you seen it?"

Elle quickly sighed; her confusion was easily replaced by frustration. This couldn't be happening. "Niki, please, you can't…"

"So, you have seen it, then?"

"Yes," Elle admitted, "I have." She felt weak and off balance all of a sudden, and in fear that her legs might give out, she lowered herself onto the edge of the bed. "Will you give me a minute to explain?"

"I don't think there is anything left to explain," Niki argued. "You lied to me. That pretty much sums everything up."

"I didn't lie to you," Elle tried. She lifted her left hand and pinched the bridge of her nose; how was she going to fix this?

"You withheld the truth," Niki said.

"Niki, in all honesty, when I came to your house that first time, I had no idea that my mom's murder was related to your mom's. I swear. I only connected the dots after Mary's reveal about the candy corn."

"Why didn't you tell me then, after you'd put the two together?"

"I don't know," Elle answered. She shook her head again, and felt her dangly earrings spin in the movement. "I told a deputy down at the police station, but at the time I wasn't sure if he believed me. And then my dad didn't want anyone to know and…"

"I had a right to know," Niki interrupted. "I lost my mother, too, and…"

"Niki, I'm so sorry." Elle felt tears beginning to burn the corners of her eyes. "I don't know what else to say."

"What about the bank robberies that were happening in New York up until your mother's murder?" Niki asked. "The article was kind of vague, but it seems to me that your mom had some skeletons hanging in her closet."

Elle's eyes widened, and for a moment, her vision went blurry. "That's not fair, Niki. You didn't know my mom, and you can't believe what

Mary wrote. There isn't one piece of evidence any-where in her story to back up those accusations."

"You have to admit, it still makes for an interesting read." Niki's words were sharper than broken glass. "And there are too many coincidences to think that she wasn't involved in something illegal."

Elle gripped the comforter on the bed, actually thinking she might rip right through the fabric. "Stop, Niki!" she ordered.

"I'm not the only one that feels this way," Niki continued. "Kyle agrees with me."

"You've been talking to Kyle about me?"

"He called me this morning, told me to check out the paper. Good thing," she added, "otherwise, I might have missed it."

"Niki," Elle started, "I'm going to tell you what I know…"

"No!" Niki yelled. "Let me tell you what I know. I know that in New York, you and your mother were involved in something bad. As a result, your mother was murdered. Then, you came to Ohio with some sob story, all the while leading a killer to Gray's Lane. Your got my mother killed!"

"You don't actually think I'm responsi-ble for…"

"Yes!" Niki said. "You are responsible for what happened to my mom. You're responsible for what happened to Emily, Elaine, even what almost hap-pened to me. I hate you, Elle!"

"Niki, please, don't do this!" Elle begged. But she soon realized that her plea had gone unheard. Niki had hung up; the line was dead.

THIRTY

FIRING DEPUTY BENJAMIN ANDREWS hadn't been something that he'd really wanted to do. After all, the sheriff admitted to himself, Andrews had been good at his job. But Douglas' hands had been bound with a tight rope; he'd had no other choice but to let the deputy go.

Part of the problem, Douglas realized with a heavy sigh, was that Ben didn't listen. The sheriff had point blank warned the deputy to back off, to forget the whole nonsense about New York. Douglas didn't honestly believe the murders were connected. And so what if they were? He had Gray's Lane to worry about—that was his main concern.

The sheriff crossed his arms over his chest and leaned back into his chair. He stared down at his desk; he couldn't help but shake his head. In the past week, he'd spent more time in this office than he had at home, and he had nothing to show for it. He wanted to scream; he wanted to arrest someone.

No, he thought, immediately feeling the full smile spread across his face, he wanted to shoot someone.

In frustration, he rapidly began digging around in his top drawer; he craved something sweet. Ben had upset him deeply, and Douglas knew that a sugary snack would help to put him at ease. He located the small bag of candy corn, relieved that his search had proven to be successful, and ripped open the package.

Candy corn was a very common treat, he considered, chewing on the small, triangular pieces. Not only more so now, he knew, because it was close to Halloween, but because the candy could easily be bought year round. Why hadn't Ben been able to see that? Why had he made a bigger mess of the investigation by trying to get useless, outside help? And why in the hell had he slept with Mary Evans?

The woman was attractive, that was more than obvious. The sheriff could recall a time or two that he'd checked her out when she'd been wearing a short skirt or very tightly buttoned blouse. But that had been completely innocent, he figured. It had just *looking.*

Ben had jeopardized everything. And for what—some common whore? Had he really been trading information with the enemy? Or had she somehow tricked it out of him? Douglas assumed now that he would probably never know.

The sheriff crumpled up the half empty bag of yellow, white, and orange candies and tossed it back into his drawer. He felt a small burning pain in the side of his stomach. Partly, he knew, because of the sugar, but the other part had to do with another one of his deputies—Deputy Hall.

Hall was sly, sneaky, and had clearly wanted Ben out of the department. Hall had obviously been spying on Ben, waiting for him to slip up, just so he could come tattle like some little bratty boy. And as a result, Andrews was gone and Hall was still here.

Douglas noisily drummed his thick fingers onto the surface of his desk. Not only had he been forced to fire his best deputy, leaving him stuck with an incompetent one, but he also had a double funeral to attend. He'd be wearing many hats today; keeping Mary and her cameraman away from the church was at the top of his to-do list. The sheriff would also be grieving the loss of two town residents, as well as simultaneously trying to wear a brave face that hopefully implied the police department was close to making an arrest in the Gray's Lane slayings.

Though the latter was completely false, the sheriff did have an ulterior motive for attending the funeral. He just hoped that it paid off, because he was quickly running out of both steam and fresh ideas.

The community was small, and Douglas prayed that the little handicap would work to his advantage. He'd be watching closely from the first pew, taking note of those who showed up to pay their respects, but more importantly, those who didn't. And though guilt plagued him like a nasty canker sore, it had been the only option he could think of to possibly flush out the killer.

His office phone came to life, ringing loudly, interrupting his thoughts. He reached out for it, coolly answering with, "This is Sheriff Douglas."

"It's Deputy Hall."

Douglas rolled his eyes. "Good. Are you at the church?"

"No," the deputy answered. "I got a little sidetracked."

"Excuse me?" the sheriff roared. His entire body grew hot. "I gave you a direct order to get to that church and start watching for possible suspects. You're also supposed to be saving me a seat, remember? Where in the hell are you, son?"

"Over at the motel on Lane Street."

"What in the fuck are you doing there?" Douglas abruptly rose to his feet; his left hand formed a tight fist. And though he was right-handed, the sheriff childishly wondered if he could punch the deputy through the phone.

"I was headed to the church when something came over the scanner," the deputy answered. "There's been a murder, sir."

"A murder?" Douglas repeated. His words echoed throughout the room. "Who's been murdered? Is it like the others?"

"No," Hall answered. "Single gunshot wound to the forehead, and the victim is a male. I haven't been able to locate the weapon, either."

The sheriff bit down onto his lower lip; he closed his eyes. For some reason, the nightmare never ended, but only continued to get worse. Now, a new, completely unrelated murder had taken place — and when he was short-staffed, to boot.

"Sheriff?"

"Yes, son. Whose the victim?" he asked.

"An out-of-towner," Hall answered. "His ID says Brian Gleason. As far as I can tell, the ID matches the body."

Brian Gleason? Douglas thought. Hadn't he just heard that name from somewhere?

Dammit! His mind promptly screamed. Of course, he'd just heard that name less than an hour ago in this very office, from Ben.

"Deputy Hall, I'm on my way. Seal off the crime scene and don't let anyone touch a thing." Douglas threw the phone down, not giving a rat's ass that it hadn't landed in the cradle. He rushed for the door.

Things had gone from bad to worse at lightening speed. Not only was Brian Gleason in Gray's Lane, but Ben could have actually been right all along. About everything.

The sheriff slammed the door behind him, but then suddenly stopped in his tracks; his mind was racing.

If this Brian Gleason was behind the killings, then who had shot him?

THIRTY-ONE

ELLE QUICKLY SHIFTED HER CAR INTO PARK and killed the engine. One way or another, she was going to speak with Niki.

Her friend wouldn't answer the phone, causing a deep frustration to rapidly sneak up on her. Elle was tired of getting the other girl's voicemail. Therefore, she'd taken matters into her own hands, and had traveled to Brown Street, deciding to visit Niki in person. Elle had had a realization: maybe a face-to-face approach was the only way to deal with the mess that Mary Evans had created.

She stepped out of the Honda and slammed the door shut behind her. The sound erupted into the still morning air, and for a slight moment, goosebumps invaded Elle's body. She began rubbing her arms, hoping to generate some warmth. And though the sunlight was bright and almost blinding, Elle found herself wishing once more that she wasn't alone. Too much had happened, too many questions were still unanswered, and a thick fear overwhelmed her, knowing that anything could happen next.

Part of her worry, Elle knew, was Niki. Her friend had been so angry, so hurt, and Elle had no way of predicting how she might react to the impromptu visit. Would Niki ask her to leave? Tell Elle that she never wanted to see her again? Or, Elle couldn't help but be optimistic, would there be tears and hugs and apologies?

No matter the outcome, Elle was going to take a chance and continue on with her plan. She really had nothing to lose.

Her heels annoyingly clicked across the driveway; she approached the front door. Elle had checked the time before getting out of her car; she knew that there was only about a half an hour until the funeral was due to start. Therefore, Elle determined, slowly raising her right fist to tap on the door, this mission would have to move fast.

There was no answer. Elle repeated her action. Only this time, she made sure her pounding was harder and louder. Her hand immediately turned bright red from the rough surface of the wooden door; Elle knew that she had succeeded. The only way Niki wouldn't have heard her arrival was if her friend wasn't even home. Which was a good possibility, Elle figured; Niki could have already left for the funeral.

A sickening feeling cut deep into the pit of Elle's stomach; she considered another option. Niki could have seen who was at the door, and much like she'd done with the phone calls, chosen not to answer it.

"Niki," she called out. "Niki, it's me. We really need to talk. If you're in there, will you please open the door?"

Nothing. The silence was almost frightening, and Elle briskly spun around to make sure that no one was standing behind her. Her eyes widened, and her mouth gradually split, as if she were getting ready to scream. But no one was there; she was still alone.

Another knock. This time, Elle heard movement from somewhere in the house. She stood stone still as she tried to place the noise. Elle was only guessing, but thought that it had come from the kitchen or dining room area. As if in an attempt to hide, Niki had bumped into the table or knocked over a barstool.

So that's how this was going to play out, Elle thought. Niki was just going to act like she wasn't home. Like she hadn't heard her phone ring, or the piercing knocking at the front door. She honestly expected Elle to pretend like she hadn't just heard the commotion from inside the house?

No! Elle's mind screamed; she wasn't having it. Niki was her friend, and though the friendship had only been in effect for a few days, it was still a relationship that Elle wasn't ready to give up on. Not yet.

"Niki," she called out. Elle pounded on the door once more, and then decided to try the knob. To her surprise, the home was unlocked; she finally let a small smile spread across her face. Things were beginning to work in her favor.

"Niki," she repeated, "I'm coming in." Elle twisted and turned the handle until the barrier opened. She entered the house, and then quietly closed the door behind her.

The surroundings seemed surprisingly dark. Elle shifted her gaze, taking in the large windows to her left; they were completely covered by long, plain drapes. She shrugged, finding an answer to the darkness.

She started forward, down the long hall, and that's when déjà vu forcefully smacked into her. Elle recalled her first and only other visit to the Sullivan home. On Monday, when she'd initially met Robbie and Niki, she'd traveled this same path and had ended up in the back living room.

Elle kept moving. Her steps didn't echo, but were silent due to the thick carpet. She took a deep breath, wishing that a TV, radio, *something* was turned on and making noise. The house seemed too quiet.

"Niki," she tried again, her voice coming out thin and weak; she didn't recognize it. "Niki, I know you're here. I really want to talk to you."

Elle reached the end of the hallway and immediately closed her eyes. She feared what might be waiting for her. Why wasn't Niki responding? For support, Elle gripped the wall to her right. She let her eyes flutter open.

No one was in front of her; nothing was out of the ordinary. She shook her head and whispered aloud, "Get it together, Elle."

To her left, the living room area with the "L" shaped couch and flat screen TV appeared to be vacant—Niki wasn't present. Elle turned and faced the kitchen; she'd been accurate. A wooden chair was awkwardly tipped over on its side. But other than that, everything appeared to be in order. But where was her friend?

Behind the counter, Elle considered. Of course, her friend was probably ducked down low, trying to keep hidden. Well, Elle thought, taking a leap forward, a side smirk spreading across her face, she wasn't going to fall for it. Niki hadn't been that smooth.

"Come out, come out, wherever you are," Elle playfully taunted, stepping onto the hard tile. She lowered her gaze. She instantly fell into the wall behind her.

Elle's jaw dropped open. She tried to scream, but nothing came out. Tears quickly formed in her eyes. She used all the strength she had to keep from plunging to the ground.

Niki was dead. Her friend lay on the checkered-tile floor, a large pool of dark blood surrounding her. Stab wounds were present, along with several pieces of candy corn that had been placed all over her body. The thick metallic stench finally hit Elle; for a moment, she found herself caught in a disturbing flashback. Instead of seeing Niki's mutilated body, she was staring at her mother's.

Elle blinked, and just like that, she was back in the present. Niki's blue eyes were still opened, completely void of any life. Her hands were palm up and deeply cut, as if she'd tried to fend off her attacker. A trail of scarlet was swirling, slowly making its way toward Elle. She stood up from the wall, turned away from her friend, and lunged for the carpet.

"I'm so sorry," she whispered, bowing her head. Elle pinched the bridge of her nose, trying to get some control of the situation. She didn't bother wiping at her tears.

Suddenly, it hit her: the chair that had been knocked over. Elle had heard the disturbance, and then had entered the Sullivan home immediately following it. She lifted her head; her body became numb. The only noise she heard now was the uncomfortable clatter of her own teeth.

The killer could still be here, in the house, waiting. She had to move. She had to move now!

Her legs were heavy, but she managed. She ran. Elle rounded the corner to the hallway, thrust open the front door, and sprinted out into the chilly, late morning air.

She jumped into her car, smashed down onto the auto-lock button, and burnt rubber on her way out of the driveway. Elle never turned back, fearing what might be behind her.

THIRTY-TWO

THE NICEST THING ABOUT RENTING A FUR-
nished apartment was that he didn't have too much
to pack. Ben placed the rest of his clothing — a few
pairs of blue jeans, some flannel shirts, and mismatched socks — into his half full suitcase. This is
what his life had come to, he suddenly decided.
This was who he had become: the guy who moves
from town to town, no agenda or family or purpose, living life out of a box.

Ben eased himself onto the edge of the bed. He
let his head slowly fall down into his hands; he then
closed his eyes. He wanted to blame someone else
for his termination from the department — Mary
Evans, Sheriff Douglas, Deputy Hall — anyone,
really, except for himself. But Ben knew that he
was ultimately the only one to blame for what had
happened. He was responsible for his own actions,
his own mistakes. And it was solely his own fault
that the journey to Gray's Lane, Ohio had turned
into a failed attempt at a new start in life.

The real disappointment, Ben decided, lifting
his face and releasing a heavy sigh, was that he was
just starting to fit in with the small town. He was

even starting to enjoy Gray's Lane living, despite the gruesome murders.

At first, the killing spree that had exploded at the same time he'd arrived had been a major turn off, not to mention, a huge incentive to flea. But Ben had since gotten into the investigation, and had even found it to be a healthy distraction from his dark past and own mother's murder. He'd also been almost positive that he'd found the killer, or in the least, a person of interest. But now the gig was officially up, and it was time to move on.

The truth was simple, Ben concluded, Mary Evans had screwed him. The only difference this time, however, was that he hadn't had any fun in the act, and had immediately gotten fired afterwards. And now, because of the sheriff's over-powering pride and refusal to think outside of the box, a killer could go uncaught and continue to murder women. That, Ben couldn't help but to believe, was definitely Mary's fault.

Ben was aware of a lot of things. He was good at his job, and part of his job was to watch, to listen, and to understand.

Ben understood why he'd first slept with Mary, and then had gone on to repeat the task again and again. He understood the sheriff's old, set-in-stone ways and stubbornness. He even understood Deputy Hall being a tattletale, and the ex co-worker's selfish need to get ahead. The only thing Ben didn't quite get was Mary's dark, aggressive agenda.

He rolled his stiff shoulders, and then fell completely back onto the bed. Ben stared up at the ceiling, refusing to blink; his eyes slightly began to water.

How could one woman be so heartless — so righteous and cutthroat? She may not have only wrecked his entire career and set suspicion throughout the whole community on a teenage girl, but Mary could have also potentially caused the killer to run due to her reports and so-called journalism work.

Ben was more than aware of the fact that he'd been the one to give all of the information to Mary; he'd been the leak. But she'd reneged on their deal, printed and reported privileged stories, and could have ultimately tipped the person responsible for the murders, causing him to go into hiding.

How in the hell did she sleep at night? Ben asked himself. Wasn't helping to stop a madman from offing women in town more important than face time on TV, or bold headlines in the newspaper? Mary's game was obvious; she wanted fame and praise at any cost; she was another coldblooded psycho in the equation, just a different kind.

He needed to go. Clearly, there was nothing left for him in Gray's Lane. No job, no girlfriend, no friend of *any* sort, really. There'd be another town though, another place that needed a cop. There'd be other crimes, more action, probably even another murder investigation somewhere for him to focus on and sink his teeth into. It was starting to get easier to find distractions, different ways to get lost so that he wouldn't have to take inventory of his own life and his own problems.

His cell phone buzzed in his right front pocket. Yet another type of distraction, he thought, fishing out the device and reading the name that had appeared on the screen.

"You've got to be kidding me," he whispered through clenched teeth. He felt himself smile. Not because he found the situation funny, *definitely* not, but because he found it highly pathetic. He'd in no way, shape, or form seen this coming.

Ben debated on whether or not to answer the call, or to let it go to voicemail. He could almost feel his mind racing back and forth like a large fish stuck in a small tank, as he tried to determine the best option.

"Dammit!" he muttered. He'd known from the start how he was going to handle this. He was just too curious to think about the further complications that could possibly arise.

And hell, Ben wondered, maybe he'd get an apology, or in the very least, an explanation.

"What?" he asked angrily, his attitude thick and apparent.

"I'm so glad you answered," she said breath-lessly. "I'm in trouble, and I really need your help."

"You're not serious?" he asked. "I mean, are you really about to ask me for a favor?"

"Ben, you don't understand…"

"No, Mary," he interrupted, "I completely understand. You're a two-faced bitch that will do anything to get ahead, without bothering to worry about who you hurt in the process."

"I'm guessing you saw my article in this morn-ing's paper," she said.

"Yes," Ben answered. He brought himself up to a sitting position. His body burned with rage; for a second, he thought he might actually be on fire. "The sheriff was the one who brought your latest article to my attention. And I must say, Mary, you have the writing skills of an uneducated barn animal."

"You can crawl up my ass later, Deputy Andrews. Right now…"

"Sorry," he started, "but it's just Andrews now."

"What?" Mary asked. "You're not a…"

"Deputy anymore?" he finished for her. "No, I'm not; I've been fired."

"Why?"

"Well, sleeping with you and feeding you facts about the investigation is apparently frowned upon in the department."

"You can't blame me for anything, Ben" she stated coolly. "I never once admitted that you…"

"You used my name in this morning's article!" he shouted. As it turned out, confronting Mary and sharing his fury with her was somewhat comforting. "Not to mention, you revealed a lead that I'd been working on. I was the only one with that New York theory, and you printed it! You had no right to…"

"Ben…"

"You betrayed me!" he continued. "And for what? Just so…"

"I think I'm going to get arrested," Mary interrupted quietly.

"For what? Being the town whore?"

"Fuck you!" she screamed. "I'm not joking around here. There's a deputy standing in my living room with handcuffs; I convinced him to let me call you before taking me to the station."

Ben took a moment to run his fingers through his hair. Did life ever get easy? "What's going on, Mary?"

"They're saying the hundred dollar bill I used last night to buy a candy bar was…"

"Wait!" he ordered, stopping her. "Why in the hell did you use a hundred dollar bill to buy a candy bar?"

"That's not the point!" Mary fired back. "They're saying that the bill was counterfeit, but I…"

"You're home?"

"Yes," she said.

"I'll be right there." Ben jumped from the bed and started for the door. He knew his keys were already securely sitting in the ignition of his truck; his personal gun was stationed safely in his glove box.

There'd been no need for Mary to finish her sentence; he'd already known what she was going to say. And whether or not he was still officially a man of the law didn't much matter anymore.

Ben was going to solve this case; he would bring the killer to justice. And he now had a solid lead to help him do just that.

THIRTY-THREE

NIKI WAS DEAD! THE WORDS WOULDN'T stop screaming in Elle's mind, but she had trouble believing them. She didn't want to believe that her only friend in Gray's Lane had been stabbed to death. But Elle had seen the proof up close and personal. She'd seen the multiple knife wounds, the blood and gore, the candy corn; Elle knew the truth. Niki really was dead, the latest victim in a series of brutal murders.

Elle made absolutely sure that the front door was locked — sealed and bolted — and then sprinted up the stairs, and slammed her bedroom door shut behind her. She didn't know who to call or who to trust; and though she deeply hated to be alone, Elle knew that, at the moment, it was her safest bet. The only way she could stay alive was to be alone.

The whole town was most likely now at the church for the funeral of Elaine and Emily Jacobs: Sheriff Douglas and his deputies, her father, Robbie Douglas, Kyle Burke, Mary Evans. And that pivotal question floated to the surface: who *wasn't* at the funeral? Who had snuck off undetected, entered the Sullivan home, and ended Niki's life?

Elle thought she might know.

She dove onto her bed and quickly covered her face with her large pillow; Elle welcomed the darkness. What she really wanted to do was get completely under the bulky comforter and hide under the covers until this nightmare was over. But she knew that she couldn't do that; she wasn't a little girl anymore. Therefore, Elle needed a more realistic approach to dealing with this terrifying situation. But what that was, Elle wasn't quite sure.

She took a deep breath, and became aware of the thick tears that were still continuing to stream down her puffy, wet face. Someone had murdered her mother in New York, and then followed Elle to Ohio. They'd repeated the madness by picking off local women in Gray's Lane. And she knew who that someone was: Brian Gleason. Nothing else made sense.

Brian had been in New York at the time of her mother's death; he'd known about the specific and privileged details surrounding Sherry's murder. Brian had suspiciously shown up in Ohio, and for all Elle knew, had been in Gray's Lane this entire week, butchering women.

But Brian had also been with her at the time of her mother's murder.

So, where did that leave her theory of whom the real killer was? Had she just unmasked him? Or was she not even close?

Elle needed air. She tossed the pillow that was covering her head off to the right, and then exhaled slowly.

As much as Brian's random visit didn't add up, there was something else that was painfully pinching her regarding her ex-boyfriend: motive. Though she hadn't known Brian for that long, she still had trouble pegging him as a killer, or even having a reason to kill.

Another question arose, stinging Elle's mind, causing her to sit straight up and swing her legs off the side of the bed. What was the logic behind these murders? What *was* the killer's motive?

She ran her trembling fingers through her hair, but the act didn't release any of her tension. Elle bridged her hands together and placed them at the base of her neck for support.

A killer had followed her across state lines. Did that mean she was the ultimate target — the real reason that five women had lost their lives?

Elle shook her head back and forth; she refused to believe that she was responsible for the killing spree. And then, almost as if someone had taken this morning's newspaper and stapled it to her forehead, Elle was seeing Mary Evans' article, remembering it verbatim.

Just like that, she no longer blamed herself for the disaster that had exploded; she blamed her mother.

Elle couldn't help but wonder if Mary's words had been accurate? What if she really hadn't known her mother at all? Sherry could have had secrets, been involved with something illegal. Her mother's actions, for whatever reason, could have resulted in sending a psychopath over the edge and right into a gruesome, murdering frenzy.

She rolled back her shoulders, lowered her heavy head down towards her lap, and gently pressed the palms of her hands into her eyes. Elle hastily added more pressure; could her mother be the bad guy, the monster hiding in the dark closet — the sole person standing at the center of this bloodbath?

Elle lifted her face. "Why?" she whispered. "Why were you hiding something? *What* were you hiding?" Out of her control, her tone had deepened; she was no longer whispering, but full on screaming. Her throat began burning, as if someone had made her swallow a lit match.

She turned her head and looked down at the picture on her nightstand, the picture of her mother and her. Was her mother's smile fake, too? Had her mother really even loved her? How much of their relationship had actually been a front, a lie? Who was her mother? What kind of person had she been? And why in the hell had Elle been so stupid, so blindsided, so damn ignorant to see the truth?

"How could you have done this?" Elle yelled. "How could you have created such a nightmare?" Her vision was blurred from the tears; her entire face seemed to be running, sliding downward. She couldn't stop it.

She suddenly found herself rising to her feet. Elle was in motion; she had no power over her own body. She reached out for the silver picture frame, firmly grasped it in her hand, and in one swift movement, turned and threw it with every ounce of strength she possessed. The frame hit the wall to the left of her bedroom door; it instantly shattered.

"Shit," Elle muttered softly, and then shook her head. As if she didn't have enough to deal with, she now had another mess to clean up.

Using the back of her hands to try and clear her face, she wiped at her eyes. The gesture barely worked. And after taking a few moments to get her breathing under control, she released a heavy sigh, and then started for the broken glass that littered her floor.

Elle squatted down. She reached out with her right hand for a piece of the frame. But before she could grab hold of anything, she stopped. Her arm stayed in position, stretched out and frozen in midair. Something had caught her eye, something that had been placed inside the picture frame—something that didn't belong.

Elle felt the frown form on her face; she squinted to make sure she was accurately seeing what lay on the floor directly in front of her.

The four-inch flash drive was small and mostly flat, but its shiny white color and rectangular shape made it stand out. Elle picked up the memory stick, avoiding the rest of the debris, and resumed her seat on the bed.

She was positive that she'd never seen the flash drive before, and guessed that it had been her mother's. But why had her mother hidden the stick in the picture frame? And how long had it been there?

Once again, Elle's breathing became shallow; she could feel her heart beginning to race. The pounding had a rhythm, and it almost sounded like music. She needed to see what was on the device. What kind of photos or documents had her mother been saving?

She started the task. First, she retrieved her laptop from the top of her dresser; she opened it up, bringing it to life. Then, she pushed one end of the flash drive into a vacant slot on the left side of her computer. Her fingertips were sweaty; it took her three attempts to get the stick to fit just right.

Finally, an unnamed folder appeared on her desktop. She double clicked it. Altogether, there were fourteen documents and images to choose from. Elle chose the first picture, and then swiftly began sorting through the rest.

It took her a minute, she had to concentrate, but she finally realized that she'd seen the man from the pictures before. He'd been at the school. But who was he? How did he factor into this?

Elle continued looking at the picture, moving from one image to the next, and then she skimmed through the documents.

When she'd finally clicked on every option available, she was at last given answers to all of her questions. For once, she understood. Elle knew who the killer was. She knew why her mother had been murdered, and she knew why she'd been followed to Gray's Lane, Ohio.

Wait! There was one more picture to view; she'd somehow missed it. She double clicked on the option.

Her hands immediately began shaking; Elle thought she might lose balance of the computer. A new person's face had filled the screen. She recognized him at once; he was *definitely* not a stranger. Elle had already guessed his involvement, but now she had proof to confirm it.

Her body became stiff, and she had difficulty believing that she'd actually had this evidence the entire time the killings had been taking place. She'd unknowingly brought it with her from New York, all the while accidentally attracting a murderer to this small community. And though she'd been confused for so long, Elle was now fully aware of what she had to do.

She needed to get to Sheriff Douglas, and she knew right where to find him: the church, along with the rest of the town.

White, fiery-hot adrenaline seemed to course through every vein in her body. She started moving.

Elle removed her mother's flash drive from the computer, and shoved it deep into the front pocket of her pants. She didn't bother returning her computer back to its original resting place, but left it sitting on her bed. She dodged the glass shards and broken pieces of frame, still reeling from the fact that she'd stared at that picture of her mother and her at least once a day, never once guessing what it had concealed. She threw open her bedroom door, and darted down the stairs.

She reached the front entrance of the house, removed the deadbolt, and swung open the door.

"Hi, Elle," he said. "I'm guessing from the expression on your face that you've found what I've been looking for."

She caught her breath. Her body became as still as stone; her eyes painfully widened.

Elle was nose to nose with the man from the pictures, the man that she'd seen at school… the killer!

THIRTY-FOUR

"YOU," SHE WHISPERED, BARELY MANAG-
ing to get the word out. Elle hardly recognized her
own weak, panicked voice. "You did all of this. You
killed Kim Sullivan. You killed Emily and Elaine,
even Niki. And my own mother!"

He nodded. "If you're going to make a list of
my victims, you'd better include Brian Gleason,
too. And since I think we should be on a first name
basis, please, call me Henry."

Henry—Elle's mind registered. She'd seen him
on campus with Mary Evans the day the reporter
had done the live broadcast. He was the cameraman. Henry had been on the memory stick; he
was the killer, and he'd just admitted it. He was
the one responsible for the Gray's Lane slayings.
And now he was standing in her house.

"You killed Brian?" she asked. Elle didn't quite
understand. Brian had been the other face from the
photos, an apparent accomplice. But if that were
true, then why had he been murdered, too?

"Yes, I did," Henry answered. "I'm assuming
you know that he was my partner. Not in the stabbings, of course. Brian has, or *had*, a weak stomach.

389

But in the bank robberies, he was most certainly my right-hand man."

The bank robberies that had taken place in New York, Elle's mind raced. The heists that Mary had mentioned in this morning's article, the exact same ones that had suspiciously stopped at the time of her mother's murder. Henry and Brian had been working together, the pictures she'd seen had depicted as much. But where did that leave her mother in all of this?

"If you two were the ones robbing banks, does that mean my mother was…"

"Involved?" Henry finished with a smirk. He shook his head. "No, you're mother had nothing to do with the actual robberies. She's just the greedy bitch that stumbled onto our plan, and then decided to treat herself to a hefty portion of our money. Blackmail," he whispered.

"Blackmail," Elle repeated. "My mother wouldn't…"

"She would and she did," Henry argued. "This may come as a surprise, Elle, but Sherry wasn't going to win any mother of the year awards."

Elle's legs felt like Jell-O; she was glad she was sitting. Otherwise, she knew that she would have fallen down onto the hard floor. This was too much to take in.

First, there was the fact that she was trapped in her own bedroom with a coldblooded killer, and now the revelation that her mother really had been involved in something illegal. Elle's entire body was trembling; she wasn't sure if she could take much more of this.

Henry had forced his way in through the front door, and then he'd pointed a gun directly at her forehead. He'd pushed her back up the stairs, warning her not to try any funny business. This was the ending to his perfect plan, and for reasons that Elle didn't yet know, it concluded in her bedroom.

"I see that brain of yours working a mile a minute," he taunted, pacing back and forth in front of her bed. "You still don't have it completely figured out, do you?"

Elle couldn't answer his question; she didn't think she had the strength to speak. She just stared at him, eyes wide, taking in his appearance.

Henry was dressed in black, starting with his long sleeved shirt, which segued into black pants, and then stopped at his laced-up boots. He also wore a navy blue hat on his head, supporting the New York Yankees, which was pulled down in an attempt to conceal part of his face.

Henry Wren didn't look like a killer. But then again, Elle decided, looks could often be deceiving. Not to mention, nothing in life was usually as it seemed.

"Would you like me to educate you, Elle?" Henry asked, stopping directly in front of her. He was gripping the gun with his right hand; her attention had shifted to the small weapon. "After all, you're the one that's going to take the blame for all of this, the one Sheriff Douglas will believe was behind this whole killing spree. I guess you do deserve to know the truth."

"Me?" she asked, feeling the puzzlement swiftly swim onto her face. "I didn't do anything. I'm not responsible for…"

"I know," Henry said softly; he quickly shrugged his shoulders. "But that's not how it's going to appear. I'm going to make it look like you were behind the whole thing. Well," he corrected, "you and your boyfriend, Brian."

The tears started again. First burning in the corners of her eyes, before gradually drifting down her face. Her hands clenched into fists. Never in her life had she felt so utterly helpless.

She'd solved the deadly mystery, the gruesome murders — sort of, anyway. She'd found the evidence, the evidence that she'd actually had the entire time, the evidence that proved who the killer really was.

But she'd ultimately been too late. And now, she couldn't help but believe that she was going to die and take the true identity of the killer to the grave.

Elle looked down at the ground. So, this was how it was going to end? She was going to die, shot or stabbed or however he had planned, and then be implicated for the crimes that Henry had committed, all the while he just walked away scot free.

"You're surprisingly quiet, Elle," he said with a grin. "Don't you want to know why all of this happened? Don't you want to know why I killed your mother?"

"I already know why," she said. "You're crazy!"

He started laughing. The high-pitched shriek filled the room and echoed around her, almost causing her to get sick. Only a truly disturbed person could be enjoying this moment, and finding humor in it.

"That's really cute," he said in a deep, heavy breath. "But your mom's not that innocent; she's the one that's responsible for everything that's happened."

"My mother…"

"Your mother was just as bad as me. That's right, Elle, Mommy Dearest had secrets, lots of them. She may have been a pain in my ass, but she was smart; I'll at least give her that much credit."

"What are you talking about?"

"Are you that dense?" Henry shook his head. "You must take after your father, then." She felt the bed dip lower as he took a seat beside her. "We hit your mother's bank, Brian and I. Only something happened, something different, something that had never happened before, and quite frankly, something we had never expected to happen." He paused, and then tilted the bill of his hat upwards.

"Your mother figured out who we were and what we were doing."

"What?" Elle really didn't want to hear the sound of his voice; it sent chills racing up and down her spine, as if someone were scratching their nails down a chalkboard. But she had to keep him talking. She knew that she had to keep Henry occupied until she came up with a plan to somehow escape.

But she couldn't look into his eyes; she refused to. They seemed to glow, much like a snake's. Elle didn't care where Henry was staring; she shifted her gaze back down to the floor and tried to think.

"That's right," Henry went on. "Your mother caught us, even tracked Brian and me down. I guess she should have joined the fucking FBI or something, because she did what the police couldn't: she solved the New York bank robberies."

"But…"

"I know, I know," he said. He abruptly stood up and rolled back his thick shoulders. "It doesn't make any sense to me, either. I don't know how she did it, but she did. Only she got stupid, and pretty fast."

"What do you mean?"

"Well, my dear Elle, like I already mentioned, she got greedy. Instead of actually going to the police, your mother took photos, got hard proof of what Brian and I had done. The same proof that I'm guessing you found this morning, and why you were in such a hurry to leave the house when I, how do I say this? Bumped into you?"

Elle didn't acknowledge his question, but suddenly became aware of the flash drive that was in her pocket.

"Doesn't matter," Henry said, and then wrinkled his nose. "I'll be getting to that shortly. So, your mother blackmailed us. In exchange for a certain percentage of our hard work, she promised to keep her mouth shut and not go to the police."

Elle was struggling to accept his confession. If what Henry was saying was actually true, then that meant her entire relationship with Brian had been staged, just a lie.

"We went along with her terms, for a while. But then your great and wonderful mother decided that she wanted more money. And Brian and I knew that we had to silence her, once and for all. Otherwise, the problem would just continue to grow."

"So, then what?" Elle asked with a shrug. "I became part of the plan? Brian would randomly meet me, pretend to like me, get close to me?"

"There's that smart, young lady I knew you had in you," Henry said, offering a wink. "He was supposed to get into your home while your mom was away and collect the evidence. No harm, no foul. But he ultimately failed, and then I had to take matters into my own hands."

"You butchered my mother!" Elle yelled. She covered her eyes with the palm of her hands. She'd never introduced her mother to Brian; her mother had never known that she'd been dating the bad guy.

"I didn't have a choice!" Henry shouted. "Your mother put up a fight, refused to give me what I wanted, what I *needed*. My only option was to kill her."

"To stab her to death?" Elle roared, matching the tone of his voice. She abruptly rose to her feet. "To litter her mutilated body with candy corn, and then leave her sprawled out on the kitchen floor like some kind of dead animal?"

He was laughing again, only this time the painful noise wasn't as loud and didn't last as long. "I never planned to use the candy corn; it came as a pure afterthought. I only did that to save my ass."

"Excuse me?" she asked, protectively crossing her arms over her chest.

"I searched the house, but I couldn't find where your mother had hidden the evidence. I didn't want the police to think that who-ever had killed your mom had had an ulterior motive. So, I scattered her body with candy corn to make it appear as if a serial killer had murdered her. The candy was just a false calling card, my attempt to steer the police in the wrong direction."

"You're sick!"

"I'm smart!" he argued. "And it worked, too. But I knew that my bank robbing days were officially over until I found the proof your mother had collected. I couldn't chance you stumbling onto the damning evidence that could put Brian and me away for life. "

"So, you followed me to Ohio? Started hacking up women here?"

He shrugged again. "I figured that you'd unknowingly brought the evidence with you somehow. I came up with the perfect plan, one that would get ride of all of my problems once and for all."

"And what was that? Kill me, but also have me take the fall for everything?"

"Something like that," he nodded. "But first, I needed more victims. I started with Kimberly Sullivan. And let me tell you, it was definitely in my favor when you befriended her daughter. Don't you get it?" he asked. "I was killing women that were close to you, women that you could easily be connected to. And I was using the candy corn signature, the signature from New York that only *you* knew about."

"My father was…"

"Almost arrested for the murders?" he finished for her. "I know. Surprisingly, working with Mary Evans has its perks. Kind of funny, if you think about it."

397

Elle shook her head. This couldn't be happening. How was she possibly going to fight off Henry and get away? He was smart, strong, and most importantly, he had a gun.

"So, back to my perfect plan," he said. "It was really like nailing multiple birds with one stone: I kill you, setting you up for your own mother's murder, and never have to worry about anyone finding the incriminating evidence of me." Henry stopped, smiling once again. "Except things worked out even better than I could have planned; you did find the proof, didn't you? I can finally destroy it, and really be in the clear once and for all."

"Was killing Brian just another part of the plan?"

"I liked Brian," he admitted. "He was my friend, my partner in crime, but he had to go. He wasn't supposed to come to Gray's Lane. He was getting cold feet, decided at the last minute that he didn't want to hurt you… again, that is."

"But he was ultimately just another victim, right?"

"Yes, shooting Brian was actually rather easy, and really just another nail in your coffin. You see, Elle, you shot Brian with this gun." He waved the weapon around with his glove-covered hand. "And then you killed Niki, before finally coming home to shoot yourself."

"No one will believe that," Elle argued.

"Sure they will," Henry nodded. "The evidence doesn't lie. Sheriff Douglas will find the knife you used to kill all five women in your possession, along with a half empty bag of candy corn. This gun will be in your hand, along with a bullet hole in the back of your head. Not to mention, I'm sure someone saw you fleeing the Sullivan's home this morning."

"And what's my motive?"

"Does it matter?" he asked. He waited a moment, and then shrugged his shoulders. "Fine, then. You and your boyfriend murdered your mother for money. Only when you came to Ohio, you discovered that you enjoyed killing; you couldn't stop. The candy proves that whoever murdered your mother, murdered the four women in Gray's Lane, too. That's you, my dear Elle."

"No," she said heatedly; her skin was on fire. "That doesn't…"

"Shhh," he ordered, "let me finish. Brian sporadically shows up in town, and that's when you suddenly start feeling guilty. For whatever reason, your conscience kicked in, and then you decided to kill him, followed by yourself. Sound good?"

"Go to hell!"

"No? Then how about this?" he offered. "I don't give a fuck what that dumbass, delusional Sheriff Douglas and his team of misfit deputies in this shithole town believe. Do you honestly think Henry Wren is my real name? Or that Brian

Gleason even exists? They're both aliases, sweetie. That's rule number one of committing the perfect crime. And since my partner's dead, not only am I now twice as rich, but there are officially no witnesses left to identify me."

Elle's attention quickly went to the small lump in her pocket.

"Except, of course, for the evidence you have, which I'm going to need. Now!"

"I don't have…"

"Stop! I don't have time for your lies or games or whatever it is that you're trying to pull. I want the evidence, whatever it is you have on me, and I want it now!" He lifted the gun, pointing it at her.

"Please…"

"Don't start begging," he whined. "You're getting off a lot easier than the other women. Just a single, pain-free bullet through your head. No biggie." He nodded again. "But we have to hurry, because I still need time to stage the crime scene."

"Fine," Elle caved. "There's a flash drive; it's in my nightstand drawer."

"Well, what are you waiting for? I hate to break it to you, Elle, but no one's coming to rescue you; everyone's at the church."

Elle turned and slowly started for her nightstand. She tried to remember all of the items that were in it. She desperately prayed that she'd find a weapon of some sort that could aid her.

Elle seemed to glide across the carpet; she was hardly aware that she was even walking. Her legs seemed to have a mind of their own.

"Chop, chop!" Henry ordered.

Elle reached the stand. A half smile promptly formed across her face. Sitting on the surface was the pairing knife from the day before, the same one she'd used to cut her apple. It was in full view; she'd forgotten it was there. Elle reached out and grabbed it.

But now came for the hard part, the ultimate test. Could she actually stab somebody?

She turned and faced Henry. Elle pointed the knife at him. "You lose."

"Are you kidding me?" he asked with a smirk. "I have a gun, you have a little fruit knife. You can't be serious."

"Your plan only works if it looks like I killed myself. If there are kinds any defense wounds on me at all, my death will be ruled a homicide. They'll come looking for you."

"Put the knife down, Elle," he said flatly. "Besides, you won't cut me."

"You're right."

"What?"

"It's pretty simple, Henry. Or are you not following along?" She lifted her left arm, finding it surprisingly steady as she brought the dull blade across her skin, creating a jagged line. Her flesh broke open; blood began seeping out.

"What the fuck are you doing?" Henry took a step toward her.

"Making it look like I was attacked." She started a new wound, this time using her open palm as her cutting board.

"Knock it off!" He said, charging for her.

"Screw you!" Elle screamed back.

Henry was finally in range. She brought the knife forward. With a tight fist, she gripped the handle, pointed the blade, and aimed for the center of his chest. Elle thrust the tool forward, but he swiftly lunged away from it.

Instead of his chest, the weapon tore into his left shoulder. Her hand quickly became covered with Henry's warm blood. He howled in pain. With the blade still lodged in him, she didn't waste another minute, planning her second move.

Elle planted her feet, and with every ounce of strength she had, she pushed him to the side. He collided with her bed. She dashed for the bedroom door, threw it open, and darted for the stairs.

But he was right behind her. She gripped the banister for support, but he had a firm hold on her waist. She struggled, tripped, and they both tumbled together and fell down the stiff steps.

"You're not getting away!" Henry shouted.

Elle landed first. Her back hit the tile landing with a *crack*. Henry was rapidly on top of her, straddling her with his strong, thick legs. She was stuck, trapped. Elle wasn't going anywhere, she couldn't.

"No!" she screamed. She tried to claw, poke, pinch; he was too strong. He used his left hand to pin both of her arms down, and his right to point the gun directly at her face.

"Let the sheriff think you were brutally attacked," he said, slowly licking his lips. "I already told you, Henry Wren doesn't exist. No one will come looking for me."

Elle tried to lift her body; she needed to get him off of her. But her attempt was useless; he was more than double her strength; he was easily overpowering her.

Suddenly, the front door flew open. She tried to turn her head, to see who had entered, but all she could make out were black boots. Was there *another* person involved?

"What the fuck are you doing here?"

Elle looked up at Henry's face; she stared into his eyes. This time, they were wide, even darker than usual, and seemed to be filled with anger, maybe a little bit of fear, too.

"Drop the gun, Henry!"

"You're not in control! I am!"

"Drop it! Now!"

Elle recognized the stranger's voice. Underneath the weight of Henry, she felt her heart begin to beat faster; she thought it might explode. Was this it? Was she really being saved?

Was she going to survive Henry Wren, the Gray's Lane killer? The same person who had murdered her mother?

"Henry, you're not going to make it out of this alive, not if you shoot her."

Elle watched as Henry's finger quivered over the trigger. He looked up. He smiled at the new guest.

"Go fuck yourself!" Henry shouted.

She quickly slammed her eyes shut. Elle bit down onto her lower lip, and instantly tasted the salty tang of her own blood.

A sharp crack rang out, deafening her; she didn't even hear herself scream. Her head rapidly became light. Her entire surroundings faded to black.

THIRTY-FIVE

"MICHELLE," HE SAID LOUDLY. "MICHELLE, are you alright?"

"Elle," she corrected him, barely hearing her own weak, distraught voice. "It's Elle, remember?"

"Of course," he answered; she was almost positive that he was laughing.

Elle opened her eyes, suddenly becoming aware of several different things: first, the sharp, painful pounding in her head. She knew it would be a while before that went away, along with the high-pitched ringing in her ears.

Second, she noticed her upper body and neck had been sprayed with blood and gore; she did her best to keep her nostrils as tightly closed as possible.

Next, she realized that she was gently being pulled up off the ground by both of her arms. Benjamin Andrews, the man who had saved her, was now helping her stand up, all the while doing his best to avoid her self-inflicted wounds.

But the most important thing, Elle decided, as she struggled to balance herself and lean on Ben for support, was that she was alive. She looked down at Henry's still, lifeless body. His eyes were open, and blankly stared up at her. He had a large hole in the center of his forehead.

Henry Wren, the person responsible for this last month of horror, the killer who had brutally murdered five women, including her mother, was dead.

And she was alive.

"Let me help you to the stairs," Ben offered. "You should probably sit."

"Not in here," she demanded. "I can't look at him anymore." Elle nodded with her chin to the corpse. A dark puddle of scarlet was gradually staining the tile.

"Okay," Ben agreed.

She let him wrap his arm around her trembling shoulders, and guided him to the kitchen. Elle was relieved to reach the barstool, and immediately fell onto the seat. She asked Ben for a glass of water, pointing to the far right cabinet.

"I have to ask," she started, "how did you know to come here? How did you know the killer was going to come after me?"

"Believe it or not," he said, "Mary Evans."

"You're kidding." She reached for the glass he handed her, brought it to her mouth, and took a long, greedy swallow.

"After you came to see me at the station, I knew you were somehow involved in all of this," Ben confessed. "I didn't know how or why, but I knew the candy corn signature was too big of a coincidence to ignore. I knew in my gut that whoever had murdered your mom was now in Gray's Lane, murdering women here, too."

Elle set the glass down onto the counter, and slowly dug into her pocket. She brought the flash drive to eyelevel, looked at it for a few moments, and then handed it over to Ben.

She jumped into the story, the cocky revelation that Henry had been so eagerly willing to share. Two cases had simultaneously been solved — the bank robberies and the stabbings. And both responsible parties were now dead.

"Mary was the one who confirmed Henry's involvement for me," Ben admitted.

"How?"

"He gave her a hundred dollar bill from one of the robberies, not knowing that it was actually counterfeit. She used it, and it was flagged." Ben sighed. "It's too bad she can't be blamed for it, though; I would love to see her behind bars."

Elle felt herself smile. However, the gesture seemed awkward, and she quickly brushed it away.

"As soon as she told me that her cameraman gave her that bill, I rushed over here. I figured he'd make his move while everyone was preoccupied with the funeral."

She nodded. "You were right."

"But I should have pegged Henry as the killer much sooner. You could have died, almost did, and it would have been my fault."

"What do you mean?" Elle asked, aware that a slight frown had now replaced her smile.

"The Yankees hat," Ben said. "Henry was always wearing that hat. He was a New Yorker; his team should have given him away."

Elle shook her head, but immediately stopped when the pounding from before increased. "You figured it out in time. That's all that matters."

"Well, I knew Brian was involved," Ben stated. "I may not have known how or why, but I knew that he played a part, nonetheless."

"You were right," she said smoothly. Elle rested both of her elbows on the surface of the counter, and placed her chin on her bridged fingertips.

Whether Henry had been telling the complete truth or not, whether Brian really had had feelings for her, none of it mattered anymore. Brian had known about her mother's murder, and he'd been responsible for the bank robberies. He hadn't been a good guy, and in reality, Elle figured, had probably wanted her dead just as much as Henry had. She couldn't help but believe that both he and Henry had gotten what they'd deserved.

"Are you okay?" Ben asked, bringing her out of her thoughts.

She nodded. "I will be."

Sirens faintly sounded in the distance. Ben must have made the phone call while she'd still been knocked out.

"You saved my life, you know?" She reached for both of his hands, and firmly squeezed them. "Thank you."

"It was nothing," he said. But Elle didn't believe him. His disheveled hair and the ghost-white look that was still etched across his face told her that he, too, had been scared.

"So, what now?" she asked. She scanned the Gray's Lane police uniform that he was currently wearing. "Stay here?"

Ben gently shook his head. "Even if the sheriff asked me to rejoin the department, I wouldn't. I've been running from my past for so long, too afraid to just face it, accept it." He paused for a short moment; a heavy silence filled the room. "I'm going home where I belong, where I never should have left. I'm going home to deal."

Elle let his words sink in. She completely understood what he'd said, how he felt. She found herself nodding, and finally, after he'd finished, even smiling a little. But she didn't bother forcing this one away.

Though she and her father had had their differences, she still loved him, and appreciated everything that he'd done for her. But Gray's Lane was not where she needed to be.

Her mother may not have been a saint; she may have had dark and dangerous flaws, but Elle still loved her, and the relationship they'd shared. She'd known who her mother was after all, and despite the mistakes the woman had made, she would continue to love her mother.

Elle couldn't help but believe that her life somewhat mirrored Ben's. She'd run away from her past, too afraid to accept what had happened to her mother, too frightened to truly grieve.

She decided right then and there that she'd ultimately have to go back to New York. Elle, too, would need to go home to deal.

Acknowledgements

THIS NOVEL HAS BEEN A LONG TIME IN THE making. And while I wrote *The Next Victim,* it wouldn't be in your hands without the help of many people.

First, I want to thank my parents who have each supported me in different ways, and who continue to make sure my happiness is a top priority. I love you both so much.

Steve, I'm very lucky to have you on my side. Your talent never ceases to amaze me. Thank you for not only designing an amazing cover, but for also encouraging me to keep fighting.

Amanda, there aren't enough wonderful things I can say about you. You've not only assisted me in my writing journey, but in life too. You've played a huge part in getting this book to print. Thank you for being my person. Thank you for being you.

To Kaycee, Chad, and the entire team at Doce Blant Publishing, thank you for this amazing opportunity. Finding a publisher that believes in my writing and me is a dream come true.

I have so many wonderful friends and family members who have cheered for me since the very first day I picked up a pencil and started writing. All of you make this process even more enjoyable. Thank you.

And finally, I want to thank whoever purchases and reads my book—you're helping me pursue what I love to do, so thank you. I couldn't and wouldn't want to do this without you.

C.S.

OTHER BOOKS FROM

Doce Blant Publishing

www.DoceBlantPublishing.com

CPSIA information can be obtained
at www.ICGtesting.com
Printed in the USA
BVOW11s1147100316
439662BV00009B/139/P